"Kirk Douglas has packed every emotional element on record into his new book, a passionate treatise on life of the rich and famous . . . fast-moving . . . sweeping . . . intriguing . . . a wonderful, entertaining fantasy."
—Baton Rouge Magazine

"Vivid and passionate . . . quite a page-turner. . . . Kirk Douglas has mastered the art of authorship."
—Salisbury Post (N.C.)

"Fascinating . . . Kirk Douglas has proved to be an excellent writer . . . Longfellow once wrote that we are given various gifts, to charm, to strengthen and to teach. Douglas has been given all three."
—Asheville Citizen-Times (N.C.)

ALSO BY KIRK DOUGLAS

DANCE WITH THE DEVIL

Published by
WARNER BOOKS

KIRK DOUGLAS

The Gift

WARNER BOOKS

A Time Warner Company

WARNER BOOKS EDITION

Cover design and illustration by Andrew Newman

Warner Books, Inc.
1271 Avenue of the Americas
New York, NY 10020

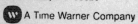 A Time Warner Company

Printed in the United States of America

Originally published in hardcover by Warner Books.
First Printed in Paperback: August, 1993

10 9 8 7 6 5 4 3 2 1

To my wife, Anne, as always

I wish to thank the following individuals for giving so generously of their time in guiding my research for this novel:

Reed and Jan Finfrock of the Sespe Creek Insectary, and Monte Carpenter and Billie Inman of the Fillmore Protective District; Dr. Ernest Burgess, the inventor of the Seattle Foot, and the staff of M + ND, its manufacturers; amputees Albert Rappoport and Jim MacLaren, who so frankly shared their experiences; Jerry Kammer and Sandy Tolan, whose investigative reporting led me to Nogales, Mexico; Luis Filipe Duarte Valença Rodrigues of the Centro Equestre da Lezíria, where I was first awed by the beauty of Portuguese dressage; Bartabas Zingaro, the horse magician of Paris; António Soares Franco, the proprietor of the José Maria da Fonseca vineyards; and Tom and Martha de la Cal, my guides to Portugal.

In addition, I owe a debt of gratitude to Gayland Hansen, whose painting *Hanging the Stars* inspired *The Starhanger*, and to the following writers whose insightful words and observations raised my consciousness: Elizabeth Arthur, author of *Island Sojourn*; Tom Brown, whose story is told in *The Tracker*; Viktor E. Frankl, psychotherapist and author of *Man's Search for Meaning*; and Nuno Oliveira, the renowned *écuyer* whose horse-training philosophies are outlined in *Reflections on Equestrian Art*.

God answers sharp and sudden on some prayers,
And thrusts the thing we have prayed for in our face,
A gauntlet with a gift in't.

ELIZABETH BARRETT BROWNING

Prologue

Lisbon, Portugal

A SLENDER HAND armed with blood-red fingernails reached out from a narrow niche in the dimly lit corridor and dug into Miguel Cardiga's muscular thigh.

"Isabel! What are you doing here?"

She glanced furtively down the corridor, where early spectators were beginning to stream into the arena, eager to get good seats for the final bullfight of the season, and pulled him into her hiding place.

"I want you," she gasped, her mouth hungrily seeking his, while her hand reached down, trying to coax an erection.

"For God's sake, control yourself! Your husband is here."

'Don't worry, Luis is too busy picking out a bull for you.'' Her hand held on to his shirtsleeve. "Tonight?''

"Yes.'' He freed his arm. "I'm late—I have to get ready now.''

"The usual place!'' She blew him an indiscreet kiss.

For a moment Miguel's eyes followed her silhouette—she was seductive even now as she hurried down the corridor. But it bothered him that she was getting so reckless. She took more risks than a bullfighter—if her husband found out, he'd kill them both. Maybe he shouldn't meet her tonight . . . but he knew he would.

Taking a shortcut to his dressing room to avoid eager fans, Miguel climbed a scaffold spanning the open space above the bullpens. Carefully, he navigated the rickety boards.

Beneath him, the bulls were turning and twisting in the close confines of their pens, the relentless sound of their scuffling hooves punctuated by loud thuds as they furiously rammed their horns into the cement enclosures. He could feel the pent-up fury of these huge beasts, their one aim to batter down the walls confining them, to kill everything in their path.

In less than an hour, one of them would thunder into the arena and focus his rage on him in a contest that pitted the brute force of the bull against the grace and skill of horse and rider. Miguel's actions would be strictly governed by ancient rules of chivalry; this was how his Portuguese countrymen—who revered tradition above all else and scorned the Spaniards' preference for gore—would judge his performance. If he accidentally killed the bull, he would be heavily fined.

In the corner, near the pens, Miguel spotted the stout

figure of Isabel's husband, one of Iberia's leading bull breeders, gesturing animatedly to his assistant. It was Luis Veloso's bull that Miguel would fight this afternoon. The assistant took up a long stick and, together with several keepers, separated one of the mammoth beasts from the others. The bull bellowed angrily as the men prodded him into a narrow chute.

All was ready.

A half hour later, Miguel gave himself one last look in the mirror. The gold filigree embroidery glittered against the midnight blue of his satin coat; tailored at the waist and flaring out above his knees, it fit his lean muscular body perfectly. His white britches were spotless, his black leather riding boots polished to a shine.

He narrowed his brown eyes. The olive-skinned face that stared back at him from under an unruly shock of black curly hair had the haughty expression of a man in charge of his destiny.

"You obviously like what you see," mocked his friend Emilio Fonseca as he sprawled in an overstuffed armchair, his long legs lazily draped over the side, a cigarette dangling from his fingers.

"I do," Miguel said softly, mocking back.

Emilio yawned, stretching his arms over his slicked-back hair, which hugged his head like a skullcap.

They could hear the rumble of the herd of oxen that always escorted the bull from the ring at the conclusion of a bullfight. Miguel felt his nerves tightening into coils of steel. He was up next.

Emilio sat up. "Ahh, I hear the patter of little feet."

Miguel laughed. He appreciated the effort his friend made to relax him before he entered the arena.

He opened the dressing room door and, with Emilio following, walked slowly down the darkened hallway into an Arabian Nights setting—pointed archways, crescent moons, wrought-iron scrolls and arabesques, Moorish touches that made this red brick structure the most unusual bullring in the world.

Nothing betrayed the apprehension that knotted itself inside of him—the fear that he might fail this time, bring disgrace to the famous Cardiga name. Of course, his father, who hated bullfighting, thought he had disgraced it already. Do sons of great men ever measure up?

In the alcove at the end of the hall, the groom was holding his horse, its mane braided with satin ribbons to match his coat.

Miguel donned his three-cornered plumed hat and eased into the elaborately tooled antique saddle. Today, he was using the Palomino, named Talar—"a slice of gold"—for good luck. Talar pranced nervously on the brick floor, his hooves ominously keeping time with Miguel's heartbeat. The horse was ready to explode, the tension vibrating within him like a live electrical current.

"*Fortuna*, my friend," Emilio said, slapping the horse's rump.

Miguel turned Talar toward the slivers of bright light filtering through the cracks in the heavy gates of the arena. He could hear the rustling murmurs of anticipation on the other side. Accounts of his success in the provinces had spread to Lisbon: he was billed as a rising star. Now, he was ready to enter the ranks of the best. He knew it. Today, he would make his mark at last. Today, he would become more famous than Paulo Cardiga—and as a bullfighter, not a riding master. He was twenty-five, and he refused to spend any more of his life in his father's shadow.

Trumpets blared and the gates parted slowly. Suddenly, all fear left him. Now instinct took over.

Miguel put the horse into a graceful *passage*—a prance in slow motion, the horse levitating above the ground after each step before descending like a ballerina to repeat the pattern. The epitome of haute école. It was just like Miguel to make his entry with the most difficult movement. The crowd rose to its feet, some nine thousand people shouting their appreciation—*"Miguelinho! Miguelinho!"* Clearly, they had filled the arena to capacity today, not just for his bullfight, but for his horsemanship. As the son of the greatest riding master of all time, he expected comparison to his father. He knew he didn't disappoint.

Mount and rider melded into one as they danced to the music, the horse delicately crossing his ankles, floating diagonally across the arena. Bravos reverberated in the bleachers as Talar cantered backward, a movement his father had made famous.

Miguel's only reaction to the repeated ovations was a slight bow in the direction of the VIP box below one of the four minarets that jutted out against the blue sky. From the box, Isabel's hungry eyes followed his every move. But her husband wore a grimace on his face. "I hope he gets it in the balls,'' Veloso muttered through clenched teeth to his assistant.

The trumpets stopped and a hush fell over the arena.

Miguel and Talar stood as motionless as a statue, waiting for the bull pen to open.

For a moment, all that could be seen was a tunnel into blackness. Then a roar erupted, and the bull thundered into the ring. His hind legs sent up a spume of dust as he slid to a stop in the sand. His huge black head, horns wrapped in leather to protect the horse somewhat, moved from side to side, sizing up the situation. Finally, his eyes focused on Miguel.

Now the horse and rider came to life. They approached the bull slowly, leisurely, contemptuously. *"Ehe! Ehe!"* Miguel shouted, taunting the bull, waving a small flag that ended in a steel dart. The *farpa* had to pierce the bull's hump in exactly the right place, and in accordance with the most stringent rules, to numb the nerve endings of the neck.

The animal charged—a half ton of fury barreling across the arena. Miguel pushed Talar forward, letting the bull come alongside; then, just when it looked like the horns might connect, he planted the *farpa* with flawless precision, the horse swerving easily out of harm's way.

The crowd erupted. It was a close call, and they liked the exciting opening to this bout. It usually took a while to draw out the full power of a bull, but this one was ready.

The horse and rider seemed perfectly at ease as they spun in a graceful pirouette, ready to flirt with the bull for a second pass. This time, the bull attacked head-on. Miguel swerved Talar to the right, aiming his dart, but the bull, undeterred, swerved in the same direction. Miguel pulled Talar so violently to the left, he had to struggle to recover his balance.

Fortunately, momentum carried the bull past them. But, as the bull slid to a stop in a cloud of dust, Miguel suddenly felt a knot of fear in his gut. This animal had a strategy of his own. He had figured out how to cut off the horse and rider. It was as if he had played this game before.

The *inteligente* officiating at the bullfight gave a signal and two men rushed in on foot to draw the bull away with capes. But Miguel waved them off.

His sweaty palms gripped the reins as he sent the horse into a flat-out gallop, getting ready for another pass. Momentarily confused, the bull hunched up in rage, eyes on his adversary, hooves pawing the ground. He lowered his head, horns poised. Then he charged, sending dirt flying in all directions, again stampeding straight on.

Miguel tried to veer to the left, repeating the earlier maneuver. But it was too late. The bull anticipated his move and was faster. The horns made contact, momentarily lifting the horse and rider up in the air before all three crashed to the ground.

The stunned crowd rose to its feet, screaming.

Miguel lay still, the yellow sand soaking up the blood streaming from his shattered left leg. But he felt no pain. In his mind, he saw that Talar, like Pegasus, had sprouted wings and was rising high above the arena.

The screams of the crowd became fainter and fainter as they flew higher and higher, past the towering minarets toward the bright blue sky.

Lausanne, Switzerland

PATRICIA DENNISON smoothed the pale blue coverlet for the tenth time, and sat down on the neatly made bed beside her suitcases. She folded her hands in her lap and forced herself to keep still.

She felt like a child left behind on the last day of camp, waiting for her daddy to come and take her home. But she was nineteen, an adult; she wasn't supposed to feel so insecure and vulnerable anymore. Well, at least her attitude to this place had changed—when she first came here after her mother's suicide, she thought of the sanitorium as a prison; now she thought of it as a camp.

The waiting was excruciating, but she had herself to blame—why had she packed, not knowing exactly when her father would arrive? Now there was nothing to do but wait. Maybe she should unpack her books and read—that would take up some time. Instead, she got up to look out the window again.

In all her uncertainty about life, she clung to one absolute truth—her daddy loved her and he wanted to be with her as much as she wanted to be with him. They would have a home again, like they did when she was little, when Mommy and Daddy were still together. It all went to pieces when Mommy took her to New York to live with her grandfather in the Stoneham mansion. J. L.—he never let her call him Grandpa—would get so angry every time she said she wanted to visit her father in California. After a while she stopped asking; it did no good anyway.

But they would make up for lost time now.

She stared out the window in a trance, trying to conjure up a figure coming down the walk. But there was no one. The grounds were devoid of people; no one was strolling even. Only the thin branches of the willow trees moved restlessly in the breeze, the dance of their wispy arms reflected in the water of the pond.

With her long fingers she traced the window bars which were bolted to the inside of the frame. This was the suicidal ward, after all. The glass had a yellowish tint, a special coating as precaution against breakage, and for good reason. When she first came here she would have crashed through the glass and carved herself up. She would have done anything to end the despair, the relentless pain of grief.

She remembered when Dr. Solomon said her therapy had progressed far enough that she could have a mirror. He brought it to her room and hung it himself. She looked into it and a face that was not her own stared back. It was a pale face, framed by short blond hair, as fragile looking as bone china, with the bottomless gray eyes of a hunted animal. It was her mother's face.

"Smile," Dr. Solomon had said. She watched the lips, barely pink, quiver a little and then curl up to reveal a row of white teeth.

"So, you have an overbite, huh?" he teased her.

She laughed and suddenly the happy face in the mirror belonged to her again.

Poor Mommy—she had been sad for so long. Only

in death did she seem at peace. Patricia remembered standing over the casket, pumped up full of tranquilizers, looking at her mother lying there—beautiful and serene, surrounded by white roses, her favorite flowers. Then the sweet scent was crushed by the smell of a man's cologne—overpowering, heavy, insidious. Her grandfather placed his arm around her shoulder and the odor almost made her gag.

Her next recollection was waking up in this room, in the Lausanne sanitorium, and looking up into large, compassionate eyes magnified by thick glasses. Then she made out a thicket of ruffled strawberry blond hair and a scraggly beard of the same color.

"I'm Dr. Solomon," a soft voice said. "Don't be afraid . . . You're safe here."

During the next six months, Patricia came to identify that voice with warmth and wisdom. He didn't grill her about her childhood or her dreams; instead, he brought her inspirational books to read about heroic people who found special meaning to their lives. Then they discussed what she had read.

She decided she would read something now—reading always made her feel better; it was a good way to pass the time. She unzipped her suitcase and found the little book she was looking for tucked next to her riding boots—*The Mystical Nature of a Horse*, by Paulo Cardiga.

Tomorrow, she would be meeting the famed Portuguese riding master. She loved horses and riding, and so her father was taking her on a vacation to Portugal where he had arranged lessons at the Cardiga riding school. Actually, he had wanted her to come to Portugal last year, when he was directing a movie in Lisbon and Tróia, but J. L. objected.

It wasn't too late, Daddy had said, when he called her from Italy yesterday. His last words to her before he hung up kept ringing in her mind: "Patricia—it's never too late. I just learned that myself. There is so much we have to talk about. I must tell you something very important." There was a tremor in his voice when he said that. What did he mean?

She sighed. She would find out soon enough.

She opened the little book and started reading. Absorbed, she forgot her anxiety. When she next checked her watch, she realized that an hour had passed. She calculated the time. It was more than twenty-four hours ago that her father had called from Trieste, saying he was on his way to Zurich. The airline connections were poor and there were always delays in Italy, she knew that, but this long? Shouldn't he be here already?

She stood up again and looked out the window. And now she saw him. He was coming up the walk, next to the rumpled figure of Dr. Solomon.

As he came closer, Patricia felt a scream rising in her chest, moving into her throat, but she couldn't open her lips to let it out. The old feeling of uncontrollable panic Dr. Solomon had taught her to banish was choking her again. It wasn't her father coming up the walk—it was J. L.

He had spoiled too many of their vacations. But not this time. Daddy wouldn't let it happen. He had promised.

J. L., tall and stiff, with steel gray hair and piercing blue eyes—a granite statue, Mommy had called him—entered the room without knocking, followed by a clearly agitated Dr. Solomon. "Patricia . . . you're coming with me," J. L. commanded, approaching her. The smell of his cologne was instantly overpowering.

She backed away and sat down on the bed, clutching the handle of her suitcase.

"Mr. Stoneham," Dr. Solomon was saying, "this is not the way to handle this crisis. Now more than ever Patricia needs to stay here and—"

"I'm sure *you* think so." J. L. snorted. "Judging by your fees, you'd like to keep her here forever."

The odor of his cologne was making Patricia dizzy. She took a deep breath and clenched her teeth. "I'm not going anywhere with you." Her voice quavered as she spoke the words. "I'm waiting for Daddy."

"Your father is not coming," J. L. said sharply.

"Mr. Stoneham—please—" Dr. Solomon's soft voice was now full of indignation.

Patricia couldn't stop her body from trembling as she looked directly into J. L.'s piercing eyes. "I don't believe you. You'll never separate us again."

J. L. leaned over her. "Now you listen to me—"

His face was inches away. She was gagging from the stench. She turned her head and pushed against him with both hands. "Leave me alone."

"You'll obey me—remember, I pay the bills."

"I don't want your filthy money . . ." Her quavering voice grew firm and clear. "I hate it. I hate *you*!"

He slapped her.

She stared at him in horror as Dr. Solomon grabbed

his arm. "Mr. Stoneham—I must insist on handling this. You are making a serious mistake."

"No!" Stoneham shot back. "She has to hear this, and she might as well hear it from me." Then he lowered his voice. "Patricia—your father is dead."

She sprang from the bed, staring wild-eyed. "It isn't true!" She was yelling now. "You lie! Get out!"

Stoneham stood watching her impassively. "Make yourself useful, Doctor—tell the girl."

Dr. Solomon sat down on the bed and tried to pull her down beside him. But she continued to stand mutely. "Listen to me, Patricia," he said gently. "It is true . . ."

Patricia's eyes were wide with uncomprehending terror. "Daddy . . . dead?" she whispered.

Then she turned back to J. L. and in a hollow voice that seemed to be coming from the deepest recesses of her body said, "So now everybody is dead . . . why are you still alive?"

She didn't know what happened next. She was suddenly transported very far away, too far to hear. Dr. Solomon, J. L., and all the things in the room became tiny and colorless—like a fuzzy newspaper photograph. Then, all went black and her feet gave way under her. She felt she was falling into a huge dark chamber—a small broken doll twisting and turning in the horrifying darkness.

When she came to, she was alone, lying in bed, under the pale blue coverlet. The suitcases had been put away and the mirror was gone from the wall.

Much later she found out that J. L. had flown back

TWO YEARS LATER

J. L. Stoneham—whose sole reason for living was the accumulation of money—would never have approved of Tom, a young surgeon who lived in stark poverty in war-torn Lebanon, caring for people the world had forsaken. But there were so many things she had done after his death of which he wouldn't approve. For one thing, his will specified that she continue to live in this Park Avenue mansion; even in death, he was trying to run her life. Only a loophole allowed her to turn the house into a museum, where anyone with an hour to spare could come to view the priceless works of art displayed on the walls of a billionaire's dwelling.

But today, the main dining room, often used for important social and diplomatic events, was closed off to the public. A large staff was working feverishly in the kitchen preparing for the fund-raising dinner Patricia was hosting. She had never done it before, and was anxious to make it a success—for Tom.

The young doctor had first captured her heart six months ago when she read a *Newsweek* article about him. Although she rarely left her farm in upstate New York, she decided to attend one of his lectures. Tall, blond, and boyishly sincere, he reminded her of a modern-day Albert Schweitzer, whose inspirational books she had read in the sanitorium. Tom spoke with an almost feverish intensity, at times looking straight at her: "In the mere act of caring for another human being lies wisdom and inner peace. If you do not care about others, you know only a life of conflict and torment. But once you start to care, you have found the road to peace and your life will become a victory over conflict."

Those words touched something deep within her. And

that day she became Tom's champion, channeling all the money she could pry from the trustees to his hospital in Beirut. In return, he became her source of strength, showing her that she was not necessarily chained to the curse of her grandfather's money.

She had completely alienated herself from people, living like a recluse on her farm, leaving the trustees to run the Stoneham empire. Now, with Tom's help, she could give away to the poor and disadvantaged more of the money her grandfather had heaped on her.

A loud cough startled her. She had been so absorbed in her thoughts she hadn't heard the caterer come in. "What is it, Francis?"

"I said, Miss D.—do these meet with your approval?" He held up two crystal pitchers brimming with white roses.

"Oh yes—you've done a beautiful job of arranging them."

Francis beamed. "These roses are exquisite. I've never seen white roses with just a hint of pink blush at the center."

"They're called 'Sheer Bliss'—I grow them myself on my farm."

"Do you really, Miss D.? How wonderful!"

The caterer returned to the kitchen, and she finished with the place cards, putting herself directly opposite Tom at the other end of the table with her back to the portrait of her mother. On this happy occasion it would be too haunting a reminder of the past. It hurt her to look at it.

Mother had never wanted to pose for that portrait, but J. L. had insisted—and he always got his way. The artist had done an incredible job—on both likenesses. He had painted J. L. like a stone statue, completely without expression—except for the eyes, which seemed to bore through Patricia like two steel drills. But her mother's portrait shimmered with life. Whenever she looked at it, her mother's hands seemed to be trembling as they plucked the petals from a single white rose. Patricia had stood before that painting a thousand times—studying the exquisitely beautiful face, the fragile, frightened expression of the gray eyes, so full of the unbearable sadness that finally made her mother take her own life.

Patricia, too, would get overwhelmed by helplessness—often, she felt like a little piece of driftwood, lost at sea. She would cry herself to sleep many a night. But not lately. Now she would lose herself in the fantasy that someday Tom would be there with her, lying next to her, his arms wrapped around her, making her feel anchored, secure, loved.

Did her mother give up on life because, after the divorce, she had no one to love?

People had always told Patricia that she looked exactly like her mother; she thought so herself. They had the same long fingers, the same blond hair, but Patricia's was cut short, and it curled like her father's had—except his had been jet black with just a little gray around the temples. Why had she lost both of them? How could death follow death in such quick succession?

All she knew of her father's murder came from newspaper articles. Danny Dennison was on his way from Trieste to Zurich when his Alitalia Airlines flight was hijacked by Palestinian terrorists. They had segregated the Jews and managed to execute three people before being overpowered by the pilot and crew. Her father was one of those killed—mistaken for a Jew.

Oh Daddy, Daddy—how I miss you, she thought, her eyes involuntarily filling up. I'll never know what you wanted to tell me that day.

She had done her best to find out. She tracked down one of the stewardesses on the flight whose name was listed in the newspaper article.

"It was a horrible mistake," the stewardess told her. "Horrible. That filthy man with the sweaty face kept yelling, 'All Jews up front!' He forced me to collect everyone's passports. Your father handed me his and started walking up the aisle with the others. I said, 'Not you, Mr. Dennison—they just want the Jews' . . . but he didn't hear me." Patricia waited patiently while the stewardess took a sip of coffee as if to wash away the bitter taste of her memories. "Then the shooting started . . . the crew was wrestling with the terrorists . . . I don't know how we survived."

Patricia kept thinking: This was happening in the sky while I was waiting for him in Lausanne.

The stewardess sighed. "I wish I could tell you more—I understand how you must feel."

"Well, it's just that—" Patricia found it hard to talk without her voice cracking. "He called me, you see, and said there was something very important he had to tell me . . . and I never found out what it was . . . and it haunts me . . ."

The stewardess seemed lost in thought for a moment. "You could try the Alitalia office in Trieste," she finally volunteered. "Usually, when there is an important passenger they provide an escort to the gate. The special services person there is Sophia—maybe he said something to her, maybe she knows.''

But Sophia didn't know. When Patricia tracked her down, Sophia was very kind. She remembered Danny Dennison well. ''What a handsome man—he had such presence. He looked more like a movie star than a director. He was upset that the plane was late.''

''Did you talk to him?''

''Yes, but not much. He was preoccupied writing a love letter.''

''A love letter?''

Sophia giggled. ''That's what he said it was. He asked me to mail it to London.''

''To whom?''

''A woman . . . a foreign name . . . maybe Russian . . . Sasha? . . . No, no, it started with an *L*. Lara? No. Oh, now I remember—it was Luba!''

''Luba? What was the last name?''

''I don't know. I remember Luba because it was so unusual.''

That's where the trail ended. After a while, Patricia accepted that she would never know what her father wanted to tell her.

She pulled a tissue from her pocket and wiped her eyes. It wouldn't do to start falling apart now when there was so much to be done. The trustees' meeting . . . Oh God, she was late.

She hurried upstairs to the library to face the trio. Their job was to head up her grandfather's multifaceted corporation until she reached age twenty-five or got married, assuming, of course, the suitor met certain criteria. Even from his grave, J. L. reached out to thwart any fortune hunters.

All the specifications of his will could have made her life a nightmare, but thank God for Horace Coleman—she called him Uncle Horace—who ran the board. Her grandfather's chief investment advisor for many years, Coleman took all the corporate responsibilities from her shoulders and—except for these monthly meetings when she was needed to sign certain documents—ran everything and let her live her own eccentric life.

Ordinarily, the trustees preferred to hold the meetings in the conference room of the Stoneham Group headquarters on Wall Street, where they felt more at home, but this time they made an exception. This meeting was especially important to her—she needed their approval for a large contribution to Tom Keegan's hospital, and she sensed that Coleman was getting a little suspicious about the amount of money going out to this single cause. She had dressed carefully for the occasion—in a navy blue suit with white buttons and white collar—very businesslike. She could not appear like a weak little child begging them to satisfy her whims. She must assert herself, present her case in a convincing way. But as soon as she saw them seated around the small Queen Anne table, she felt intimidated, a supplicant facing a tribunal.

"I'm sorry to be late," she said meekly, despite her resolution to be strong.

"Not at all," said Horace Coleman, shifting his substantial proportions in the delicate antique chair. It creaked, and Patricia threw a glance at the fragile legs;

she was sure they would cave in at any moment. At Stoneham headquarters, his throne was easily three times this size.

"You look lovely, my dear," said Margaret Sperber, the spindly British barrister. The childless widow of one of J. L.'s early partners, Mrs. Sperber had been her grandfather's longtime assistant on international investments. As if trying to obliterate her female gender, she always wore her gray hair mannishly short and dressed in severe gray flannel suits, never a hint of color. Today, she also wore a gray high-necked blouse. The effect made Patricia recall the story of Lot's wife, who was turned into a pillar of salt for having glimpsed Sodom and Gomorrah. What corporate secrets had Mrs. Sperber glimpsed?

Mrs. Sperber usually took Patricia's side when charitable contributions were debated—sometimes to the annoyance of Horace Coleman, who hated to be contradicted on anything.

Robert Ash, a small energetic man in a loud plaid sports jacket, bounced up to pull out a chair for her. Patricia wondered if Ash knew that, behind his back, Stoneham staffers called him "the ash-kisser."

Ash was content to let Coleman run the show; he had only one interest—how to lower his golf handicap. She suspected he got his seat on the board because he always let J. L. win at golf.

Patricia took a deep breath—a five-inch stack of papers was awaiting her signature. She hastily started signing without even bothering to read the headings. These were mergers, acquisitions, proxy statements; she wanted no part of any of them—these matters so far removed from her life on the farm—but J. L.'s will forbade her granting a power of attorney to anyone. What had his diabolically constructed will meant to accomplish—to turn her into a tycoon consumed only with his money, busy multiplying his fortune, a female replica of J. L. himself?

She finished and looked up. "Have you read my proposal to transfer funds to the Keegan Foundation?"

"Yes," said Coleman. "And I must admit, my dear, with some degree of incredulity." She could read his displeasure in his quivering multiple chins—the more she could count, the less happy he was; today he was holding at three. "Please tell me you're not serious, my dear."

Patricia could feel butterflies starting to dance in her stomach—she abhorred challenging him, but there was no other way of getting the money she had promised Tom.

"I'm very serious, Uncle Horace." She hoped her voice communicated her determination. "I can't think of a more fitting tribute to grandfather's memory than a children's hospital in his name."

"In Lebanon?" Ash interjected.

"The Israelis will bomb it before it's completed. A colossal waste of money," Coleman said.

"I have to agree with Horace," Ash piped up.

Mrs. Sperber, always the pacifier, cleared her throat. "Gentlemen, don't you feel that the Stoneham Charitable Foundation is of sufficient magnitude to contribute to hospitals—"

"In *this* country," Ash interrupted.

"But can't we also be concerned with the welfare of people in other countries?" Patricia asked.

"She does have a point," said Mrs. Sperber.

Ignoring her, Coleman addressed Patricia, his tone kinder this time. "There are worthwhile causes all over the world, but where do we stop?" She tried to answer, but he went on. "My dear girl, understand that we are not fighting you—"

"We're here to help you," Ash finished his sentence. "This is why your grandfather appointed us—to guide you, to give you sound advice."

"Patricia"—Coleman cleared his throat—"you're twenty-one. You are a very bright girl, but your education—such as you've received in those fancy foreign schools—seems to have been limited to philosophy, psychology, and ah . . . animal husbandry . . ." Coleman lingered on the last two words. "Hardly the best preparation for running a hundred-million-dollar charitable foundation, not to mention a world corporation with assets approaching ten billion dollars! You are a target. We must protect you."

"But I'm only asking for a million dollars—to save children's lives."

"It's the principle, my dear." Coleman was trying to be conciliatory.

"But why is it that I can indulge *myself*"—she sounded desperate—". . . buy dresses, jewelry, cars . . ."

Coleman reached over and took her hand. "You know that your grandfather wanted you to have the best of everything, and we wouldn't dream of trying to put controls on your personal purchases.''

"But I want to share what I have with others—"

"Let's be fair!'' Coleman's patience was reaching its limit. "You already *share* more than enough—you've turned your farm into an old-age home for broken-down horses—"

"The farm is also *my* home."

Ash perked up again. "Your grandfather wished for you to live *here*, but you—"

"Are you denying my request?" she broke in.

Ash leaned back, waiting for Coleman to speak. Mrs. Sperber fidgeted with her pen.

"It hurts me to say no to you, my dear, but in this case, I must." Then Coleman's voice rose: "All in favor of Miss Dennison's request for a million-dollar contribution to the Keegan hospital in Lebanon signify by saying aye." He made it sound like a Senate roll call.

Mrs. Sperber tried, "Frankly, gentlemen, I think we can grant it . . .''

Coleman regarded her with his three chins imperiously thrust forward; Ash kept a frozen smile on his face. There was dead silence in the room.

"All opposed?"

And in unison, Coleman and Ash chorused, "Nay."

Patricia wanted to burst into tears, but she mustered all her strength to rise with dignity. "Thank you," she said softly and left the room.

She had promised Tom that money, and she would get it for him—somehow.

*   *   *

The guest list had been made up solely of those who were rich and contributed generously to philanthropic causes. Patricia could hear the early arrivals chattering animatedly below as she hurried to get dressed. It had been a long time since she wore a formal gown—she rarely got out of blue jeans—but tonight was very important. Appearances mattered to these people, and she wanted to look just right. She had selected one of her mother's dresses—she hated buying clothes and her mother had left such a lavish wardrobe. It was a simple emerald green satin gown that flowed over her slender shape and created a dramatic showcase for the diamond necklace she had bought for the occasion.

She was late as usual. She took a deep breath—*Are you with me, Daddy?* In moments of great stress or happiness she found herself talking to her father and somehow always her eyes involuntarily sought a patch of sky as if trying to make contact. Once he had given her a painting called *The Starhanger* and told her he was the man in the picture, climbing the ladder with a star in his hand. When he was gone, he would always hang the first star for her in heaven, he promised. She knew it was a child's illusion—that Daddy was up there somewhere looking out for her—but she clung to it nevertheless. Dusk was gathering outside and the blue had faded to gray, but there were no stars yet. She turned away from the window and hurried downstairs.

Tom Keegan was waiting below, leaning on the balustrade, smiling up at her, handsome in his tuxedo, exuding charm and vitality.

"You look ravishing." He brought her hand to his

lips. "I've never seen you wear jewelry before . . ." His eyes took in the extravagant array of gold and diamonds around her neck. "That's a stunning necklace."

"Thank you, Tom. I bought it this afternoon—especially for you."

"Patricia! Darling!" It was the unmistakable throaty voice of Joanna Benson—once a Hollywood sexpot, she'd had the good fortune of marrying an aged tycoon on his deathbed, and now she gloried in seeing how much tabloid space his money could buy her. Her beehive hairdo, which was held together with so much hair spray Joanna herself joked she was personally responsible for the hole in the ozone layer, sported an oversized ruby tiara. Patricia thought she was good for at least fifty thousand dollars tonight.

Tom squeezed her hand as Joanna swooped down on both of them.

The dinner was going well. Francis had done a superb job with the food, but Patricia hardly ate. She had the urge to chew on her nails more than once, but kept her hands in her lap clutching her napkin. She wished now she had gotten a manicure, but such things had gone out of her life; on the farm long nails only got in the way.

Finally, the waiters cleared the last course. Tom caught her eye across the table and winked. Then he stood up, raising his wineglass.

"Please join me in a special toast to a very special person." His eyes were holding hers and Patricia couldn't prevent the rush of blood from flooding her cheeks. "She made this evening possible," he continued, "and it is through her efforts we have been able to double the size of our infirmary in Beirut. But most important of all, our dream of constructing a badly needed children's wing is almost within reach because of the unfailing help and support of our young hostess—Patricia Dennison.''

He waited for the applause to subside. ''She reminds us that we are all in this together, helping these frail, frightened people . . . these children maimed by bombs . . . They all want nothing more than to be left alone, but to leave them alone is to leave them to die.''

Patricia was riveted. He went on: ''All of us here tonight share one thing in common: a concern for others.'' He stopped and looked around the table with a slight smile, his eyes connecting with each person seated there. ''I thank you for your support. God bless you all.''

As the applause died down, Patricia stood up shyly. A hush fell across the room. ''Tom,'' she said softly, ''you owe us no thanks. We owe you. We stay behind in comfort while you risk your life each day in a war-torn country.'' She raised her glass. ''To Dr. Thomas Keegan, and to the wonderful work that he's doing.''

''Hear! Hear!'' resounded through the room.

She set the crystal glass down and continued, ''The men gathered here have been very generous in their corporate and individual support. Now, we women must do no less.''

Her hands went up and unlatched her necklace. Holding it draped over her fingers, the diamonds glittering in the candlelight, she said, ''This is my offering. I ask you to join me.'' And she laid it on the table.

The silence in the room erupted in tumultuous applause. Then a stately dowager got up and removed her emerald bracelet and placed it beside the necklace. Others followed. And soon, the table was glistening with jewels of every description.

Patricia looked up and caught Tom's eyes—they were brimming with tears.

It had been a long evening, and Patricia bade her guests good-bye with great relief.

Tom was still at the piano, where he had been since coffee was served. Joanna had persuaded him to play some Cole Porter. "*I've got you under my skin . . .*," he sang, his eyes repeatedly seeking out Patricia, who was trying not to blush.

People were reluctant to leave—a sign that the evening had been a spectacular success. Having made sacrifices to help the less fortunate, they were engulfed by a pervasive feeling of self-satisfaction. Patricia smiled—a few had made their offerings more reluctantly than others, but Tom was guaranteed his children's wing. That was what counted.

Joanna, who had plunked down her ruby tiara, was the last one out the door. "Darling, I was tempted to give you this bracelet"—she touched a thick band of gold and diamonds encircling her wrist—"but I worked too hard to get it." Then she planted a wet kiss on Patricia's cheek and whispered loudly into her ear, eyeing Tom. "What a hunk you landed—I approve!"

Patricia walked back into the living room. "Everyone gone I hope?" Tom asked.

"Yes, at last. How about a brandy?"

"No, no, I'm still jet-lagged."

"Maybe you'd like some more coffee?"

"What I would like is some sleep."

"Of course, you must be exhausted."

But he didn't move from the piano. Instead, he started playing again, singing softly, *"Night and day, you are the one . . ."* He lifted his fingers from the keys and turned to her. "That was my mother's favorite song. She was a music teacher . . . taught me to play the piano."

"I didn't know you played so well . . . like a professional."

"I was—I worked my way through medical school playing in bars."

He got up and arched his back. "Time to go. I overstayed my welcome I'm sure."

"Never," she said, walking beside him through the foyer, wishing she could find some excuse to keep him longer. She had already offered him brandy and coffee . . .

At the door, he took her hand. "How can I thank you for all that you've done?"

"Oh no . . . I thank you for giving meaning to my life . . . my grandfather's money has been such a burden. I want to do more."

"There is so much more to be done."

"Let me help you."

They stood there looking at each other.

"You're very precious to me," he said, gently stroking her cheek.

Her heartbeat quickened, but the words she had practiced wouldn't come out.

Then his arms enveloped her. His lips felt soft and gentle as they pressed against hers.

The excitement was building up within her, but he suddenly pulled away.

"What is it?" she asked, slightly bewildered.

"I have no right," he said, cupping her face in his hands, "no right to involve you in my life now."

"Oh please, Tom . . ."

He laid his finger gently on her lips. "When my job is done . . . in a year . . ."

She waited for him to say more, but he only kissed her again, a featherlight kiss, and closed the door behind him.

She brought her hand to her lips—she still felt his touch—and took a deep breath. She went up the stairs floating on air.

How wonderful to find someone you could talk to, listen to; someone who wasn't interested in accumulating money, so unlike J. L., so unlike any man she'd ever known.

She loved him. She was sure this was the real thing. She wanted him in every way. Maybe it would happen next time. Yes. When he came back from Lebanon in the fall, she would invite him to the farm—that was the right place for the magic of making love.

Chapter 2

Lisbon

THE SLEEK SILVER FERRARI wove in and out of traffic on the crowded Estrada 249, which led north of Lisbon into the Valley of the Almond Tree. Emilio Fonseca's gloved hand expertly guided the car, his eyes aimed straight ahead. Miguel Cardiga sat beside him.

"Don't be too hard on the old man, Miguelinho— he's not as bad as you make him out to be."

"But he's done this behind my back."

"Be fair. You gave up the horse, so he sold it."

"It was the best horse I ever trained!"

"So ask him to void the sale."

"Beg him? So he can get me under his thumb again— running his fucking school for fat rich girls?"

The car turned into the tree-lined gravel roadway lead-

ing to the Centro Equestre da Cardiga. "Miguelinho—
you want to get out from under his thumb? Go back to
the bullring."

Miguel's face seemed to blanch, and his jaw tightened
as he faced his best friend. "I've told you a hundred
times Emilio—I can't. *I can't.*"

"All right, all right." Emilio put a comforting hand
on Miguel's arm. "I'm going to miss you, my friend—
good luck."

"Won't you be coming to visit me?"

"Of course, when you get into another fight with your
father—call me." He revved up the motor and peeled
out of the driveway.

Miguel's boots made a strange arrhythmic sound, one
heel hitting harder than the other, as he crossed the
cobblestoned courtyard. Filipe, one of his father's
teaching assistants, greeted him effusively. "How nice
to see you again, Senhor Cardiga—back here where
you belong."

Miguel was painfully aware how hard the young
man's eyes strained to stay on his face, to avoid looking
down at his left leg. But Filipe couldn't help himself;
he lowered his gaze for an instant and then raised his
eyes so fast his head jerked up.

Miguel smiled bitterly. He would never get used to
those furtive glances. He endured them because the
worst was behind him.

The most painful moment came the day after the accident when he opened his eyes in the hospital and saw
the archbishop standing next to the doctor, pity on both
their faces. The archbishop reached over and made the

sign of the cross on his forehead, muttering a prayer in Latin. Miguel winced.

It seemed an eternity before the doctor spoke. "Senhor Cardiga, I tried . . . but there was no alternative . . . we had to amputate part of your left leg . . ."

A cold shiver coursed up Miguel's spine, anesthetizing his nerve endings, freezing his mind on the word *amputate*.

The doctor's voice seemed far off. ". . . but we were fortunate enough to preserve some bone and muscle below the knee joint . . ."

Miguel didn't listen—"amputate" was reverberating through every chamber of his brain, obliterating all other words.

The archbishop made the sign of the cross again, mumbled a blessing, and the two men quietly left the room.

It wasn't true. It *couldn't* be true. His leg was not gone—he could feel the toes itching. But he didn't dare scratch them. For a long time he lay there with his eyes closed. Then, ever so slowly, he pushed himself up into a sitting position, and still keeping his eyes shut, he reached out over his left leg and slowly forced his hand to move downward. It seemed as if his hand kept moving endlessly. Finally it rested on the mattress. But the itching in the toes was still there. He forced his eyes to open and stared at his hand lying on the flat sheet. Then he knew his leg was gone.

For weeks he lay in a deep depression, ignoring all calls, refusing to see anyone, even Emilio. But no army of nurses or doctors could prevent Paulo Cardiga from seeing his son.

He barged in—his facial muscles twitching with re-strained tension. Miguel had never seen his father's face so ashen, almost the color of his gray hair, his ice blue eyes frozen with anger.

"The doctors tell me that my son's injuries have healed, but he refuses to move. They tell me my son lies in a stupor, without the will to live."

Miguel stared at his father mutely.

"I told them that they were sadly mistaken. My son is a Cardiga. He has steel inside him. He is preparing himself for the battle ahead—"

"I'm preparing myself for death."

"Don't you dare say that." Paulo was on the verge of losing control.

"I have nothing to live for."

"Put those thoughts out of your mind. You've rested long enough—it's time to work."

"You are cruel," Miguel said softly.

"I don't mince words with my son—you will get on a horse again."

"You're mad! I'm a cripple!"

"You *must*."

"Are you deaf?!" Miguel yelled. "I am a cripple!" He yanked the sheet off and stuck out his dismembered leg at his father. "Look!"

Paulo gently touched the outstretched stump, saying nothing.

Miguel threw the covers over his leg again. "All my life I hated being second rate, always behind you—now what is left for me?"

"To be the best," Paulo said softly; his anger had completely vanished.

"Ahh, to become the best one-legged rider in the world." Miguel snorted.

"Miguelinho, I need you at the Centro—"

"To run my life again?"

Paulo sighed and placed a slim volume on the nightstand. "Read Baucher—"

Miguel ignored the little book.

"—he was the most respected rider of the eighteenth century."

"He has advice on how to ride with one leg?" Miguel mocked.

"Perhaps—he lost the use of both." Paulo walked toward the door with heavy steps. He turned. "Goodbye, my son."

And then Miguel saw it. His father wore the same expression that he had seen on the face of the archbishop and the doctor. All his life he'd yearned to see admiration and respect on his father's face—not pity. The door closed.

Miguel threw his head back against the pillow, closing his eyes to hold back the tears that were welling up under his eyelids. He squeezed them tightly. He hated the pity of others; he hated self-pity more. But he couldn't stop himself. The tears seeped out against his will.

Then his rage boiled over—rage against his father, against himself. He grabbed the water pitcher off the side table and hurled it against the elevated television set. The screen shattered, and shards of glass sprayed across the room. A nurse rushed in and gasped to see him flinging a chair against the window. Three men had to hold him down, while the nurse injected a strong tranquilizer into his arm. His last memory was the look of pity on her face.

What he remembered next was Emilio sauntering into the room. He carried a large brown paper bag from which he extracted, with great ceremony, two bottles of wine. *Periquita 1938!* Miguel knew that the famed Fonseca cellars held only three cases of this, the finest of wines. Emilio's family had agreed to open one bottle every five years—on the most special occasions—and here, Emilio had brought two.

A silly grin on his face, Emilio opened both bottles without a word, handing one to Miguel as he took a long swig from the other. "Ahh!" He wiped his mouth with the back of his hand, leaned over, and whispered in Miguel's ear, "Fuck 'em all."

For the first time since the accident, Miguel laughed, and then he raised the bottle to his lips.

They drank and talked, and when both bottles were empty, Miguel promised to go live with Emilio amid the Fonseca family's vineyards on the Arrábida Peninsula.

A few days later, the doctors were relieved to see their most difficult patient depart the hospital. Emilio pushed Miguel out in a wheelchair, stuffed him into his Ferrari, and whisked him off with the prosthesis—that mass of straps and metal and wood that Miguel hated so much and refused to touch—locked out of sight in the car's trunk.

Emilio's home—what he grandly called "Castelo da Arrábida"—had been built as a king's hunting lodge in the fifteenth century. Emilio had bought it some years back in a fit of romantic impulse. Miguel had joked that he could take pride in the antique originals of the place, especially the plumbing, but little by little, Emilio had reclaimed the roof from the pigeons, reglued the exquisite tile murals back onto the cracked walls, and turned the ruin into a comfortable dwelling. Miguel was glad to see the gray melon-shaped domes atop the castle's three towers come into view.

No sooner had Emilio, with the help of his gardener, managed to get Miguel up the castle's stone staircase, than the revelry began.

Emilio broke into another case of rare wine and did his best to bring his friend out of his depression, exhausting every means possible to make him laugh. Sometimes he succeeded. But most of the time, Miguel just drank himself into oblivion. He'd sit, morosely staring down from the second-floor loggia onto the riding ring where his bullfighting career had begun, where he had first dodged the horns of a young heifer on a dare from Emilio. During the days he'd sleep till lunch, nursing his hangover through the afternoon, waiting for Emilio to return from the vineyards.

One drunken evening, Emilio convinced him to strap on the hated prosthesis, and from then on Miguel would occasionally stumble out of the house—struggling laboriously with his new limb across the castle's plaza—to the long, red-roofed building, fronted by an arched arcade, that served as Emilio's stable. Even though he had sworn he would never ride again, Miguel couldn't stay away from the horses. He felt more comfortable with them than with people.

He limped past the stalls. The horses were beginning to recognize him, and they poked their heads out over the tops of the chest-high doors to greet him. He did not fail to give each of them an affectionate scratch or caress. His soft voice, almost a whisper, communicated a tenderness and affection that he had never expressed to the many women in his life.

Emilio tried several times to coax him into the saddle, but Miguel was adamant—he would never ride again. He would not even give Emilio advice on training. Yet one day he appeared, leaning against the rail of the riding ring with a glass of wine in his hand. Emilio was on a horse trying to execute a pirouette, which somehow looked more like a lopsided oval.

"Sit back," Miguel yelled. "You're confusing him with your weight forward."

"Fuck you!" Emilio yelled back as he continued to spin, topsy-turvy. Miguel had never seen him ride so clumsily.

"Sit on your ass, for God's sake!" Miguel was losing his patience.

Emilio reined in the horse and jumped off. "I know perfectly well how to sit on my ass."

"Well, do it then," Miguel snapped, draining his wineglass.

"I was."

"No, you weren't."

"Show me."

"Don't be ridiculous."

"You can sit on a horse at least—even if you won't ride," Emilio taunted. "Here—I'll help you get on." And he cupped his hands to give Miguel a leg up.

"I don't need your help," Miguel retorted drunkenly.

He shoved his prosthesis into the stirrup and sprung up on his good leg, clearing the horse's back without trouble.

Once in the saddle, he sat straight up and looked around. *He was sitting on a horse!* A tingle of excitement coursed through his body. The power of the animal vibrated beneath him. He was no longer a cripple. He was the equal of any man.

He looked down at Emilio, who was wearing his usual silly grin.

Slowly, Miguel put the horse into a trot. Emilio ran ahead of him and flung wide the gate leading out into the vineyards. Miguel looked at the verdant countryside before him, and with a yell of triumph sent the horse racing across the fields.

The next morning, when he awoke, he didn't feel the usual depression strangling his chest, that pain that only drinking seemed to dull. He felt whole again, eager to run out to the stables and play with the horses. He threw back the covers and jumped out of bed—and crashed to the floor. He had not yet attached his prosthesis. He had forgotten that he was a cripple. But he had no time for self-pity—he could ride.

The course of events was dramatically changed some months later, when a horse van with the crest of the Centro Equestre da Cardiga pulled into the castle's plaza. The driver presented Miguel with a short note from his father:

I am happy to hear from Emilio that you are riding again. Perhaps you might see what can be done

with this stallion. Ultimato has fantastic poten-
tial—in the right hands. He is five years old and
has all the necessary basic training, but a clumsy
student has been riding him without my knowledge
with disastrous results. The horse has become a
rebel. Perhaps a change of scene—a different
stimulant for his talents—might bring him around.

Miguel threw the note to the ground with disgust. "God damn it, Emilio—I wish for once you'd stay out of it."

"What do you mean?"

"Why the hell are you talking to my father behind my back?"

"Oh, knock it off Miguel. He called, he asked about you, and he was happy to hear you got on a horse. At least you have a father to care about you; I don't."

Miguel stalked off, and Emilio, shrugging his shoulders, quietly motioned to the groom to unload the horse and get him in the stable.

Miguel felt bad—why the hell had he blown up like that? Emilio had tried so hard to get him out of his slump, helped him ride again, and he had repaid the kindness by acting like a sulky child. It was just that he hated being manipulated by his father. Yet he couldn't help being curious about this rebel called Ultimato.

When Miguel walked into the stable, the horses whinnied as usual, craning their necks over the doors in his direction—all except the horse in the last stall.

There was no head peeking out. The stallion, a beautiful gray animal, was wedged into the farthest corner of the stall, eyeing him suspiciously from under a wild shock of matted mane.

"You don't like people, do you, Ultimato?"

He waited as if for an answer.

"I don't either. I'm like you."

Softly, he talked to the horse, staring into the liquid eye, the iris like a blue flame flickering with understanding. He stood there quietly for a very long time until slowly Ultimato moved toward him.

With great tenderness, he caressed the horse's nose and scratched his neck.

When he started riding Ultimato, he found himself not drinking as much. Now he needed to be alert to work with this difficult horse. But at night the melancholy bitterness still overtook him, and he could not fall asleep without several drinks. He felt worse when Emilio took off for Lisbon to carouse with women. But in spite of his friend's urgings, he would not go along.

"I saw Isabel in Lisbon—she wants to see you," Emilio reported after one of his trips.

"I don't need her pity."

"No, you're wrong—she's as hot for you as ever." Emilio winked suggestively. "She said her husband is taking a load of bulls to Spain, and she could come out to visit next weekend."

"She needs a man with three legs—not me."

"Miguel, come on—you can't hide out here forever."

"I don't want to see her, I said."

"What's with you? You planning on becoming a priest?"

Miguel didn't answer.

"I remember when you couldn't get enough of her. You sure?"

"I'm sure."

"All right, become a priest—but you're not going to find me in your church."

For more than a year Miguel stayed with Emilio, working with Ultimato in solitude, away from pitying eyes. This rebel stallion had more energy and elegance than any horse he'd ever trained.

One day while he was guiding Ultimato through a complicated dressage step, Emilio appeared, pushing a wheelbarrow with the horns of a bull mounted on the front. *"Ehe!"* he yelled, and rushed at the two of them. Laughing, Miguel guided the horse away from the horns with ease. Again and again Emilio pursued them until he was exhausted.

Puffing as he collapsed into the wheelbarrow, Emilio gasped, "That horse is a natural!"

Miguel knew it was true. How he would love to fight a bull on Ultimato! He imagined the horned head coming at them, Ultimato swerving gracefully, a hair's breadth away from collision, the crowds cheering. With this horse, he could make it to the top again. They would throw flowers as he took his walk of triumph—

And there the fantasy ended. *Some walk of triumph!* It would be a pitiful hobble—a cripple begging sympathy from the crowd. He would never do it.

The next day he returned Ultimato to his father's school.

A long letter came from Paulo complimenting him on retraining the horse, and again asking him to come home to the Centro Equestre da Cardiga. Miguel sent a curt note back declining the invitation. Then he received a message that Ultimato had been sold.

And now, despite his vow never to return here, Miguel found himself approaching this place he hated. He hesitated by the fountain, watching Filipe hurry off across the courtyard, bracing himself for the encounter with his father. The glass door to the study stood ajar; Paulo was intently peering through thick spectacles at papers on his desk and didn't hear him enter. It was a warm summer day, but there was a fire in the stone hearth near which his father sat.

Miguel studied the old man. He seemed more hunched over than usual. His skin was stretched like parchment across his gaunt face, the aristocratic cheekbones sticking out sharply.

Suddenly, Paulo raised his head and noticed his son. He got up from the desk with a look of happy surprise. "Miguelinho! It's so good to see you!"

Miguel did not move forward though his father had stretched out his arms. "I came to talk about Ultimato," he said stiffly.

"You've done magnificent work with that animal. I rode him myself the other day—what a difference! Complete control with complete ease should be your trademark as a trainer—"

"But you've sold him!"

"Yes. Actually, I sold two horses—Ultimato and Harpalo—to an American—"

"How could you do that behind my back?"

"How could I? This is what I do—I train horses and sell them. I don't understand you, Miguel. The horses brought a magnificent price—three hundred thousand in American dollars."

"You can't sell Ultimato."

"Miguel—be reasonable. You returned him."

"I changed my mind."

"The deal has been made. *I gave my word.*"

Miguel looked at the pained expression on the old man's face. Yes, he thought, he gave his word—that means honor to him. He'd never go back on it. Not even for his own son. "Who is the American?"

"A woman." Paulo glanced down at the paper in front of him. "Patricia Dennison."

"You mean some middle-aged woman with a fat rump is going to bounce around on that magnificent stallion?"

"She is neither middle-aged nor does she have a fat rump—in fact, she has an unusual sensitivity with horses."

"But can she ride?"

"She has a lot to learn. But I do have a special clause in the contract. If the rider can't handle the horses properly, we can rescind the deal."

"How can you enforce such a contract across the ocean in America?"

"A trainer will accompany the horses and work with the rider for six months."

"Six months?!"

"That's the deal."

"She wanted that?"

"No, Miguel—I wanted that. I would never permit any horse to leave here unless the rider was properly schooled."

"Who is going with the horses?"

"Filipe."

"Filipe?"

"Yes, he's good and he's trustworthy."

"You need him here at the Centro. I'll go."

"You?"

"I trained Ultimato—I'll decide if his new owner is fit to ride him."

Without making a sound, Miguel stood in the doorway of the dining room, watching Isabel arranging the table centerpiece of yellow orchids, which matched her dress perfectly. She certainly was beautiful. She didn't look in his direction, but he knew she felt his presence— he could see the blush rising from the nape of her long, graceful neck and flooding her cheeks.

The last time they had made love was on the night before the fatal bullfight. How often had he thrashed in bed frustrated, imagining himself with her again. In his fantasies he was whole, in his fantasies he did not risk rejection. Yet what was the real reason he ignored Isabel's phone calls and love letters? After all, Isabel knew of his injury and still she was reaching out to him. *He* was rejecting *her*.

Then, two days after his return from the wine country, he received an invitation from Luis Veloso to join him and his wife for dinner; he accepted. This time, he couldn't resist seeing her again.

"Oh," she said, finally turning around, "I didn't hear you come in."

"Thank you for your gracious invitation to dinner."

"I was so happy to hear you've come home. Why didn't you return my calls?"

"I haven't been seeing anyone for some time."

"Yes. Emilio told me."

"But I'm back from seclusion now."

"And your rest has done wonders for you." She smiled seductively. "I've never seen you look better." She came closer and took hold of his hand.

"Where is your husband?" he asked abruptly.

Just then, as if on cue, the footsteps of Luis Veloso could be heard down the hall. Isabel moved quickly to the other side of the table.

Luis entered, arms outstretched. "My dear Miguelinho, you honor us with your presence."

Miguel allowed himself to be embraced—too warmly, he thought—and to be led to the seat of honor at the head of the table. He wondered why—in a gesture of uncommon hospitality—he had been given the host's seat. Or was there something symbolic in Veloso having placed himself between his wife and her lover?

Isabel, sitting directly opposite Miguel, under the searing eyes of her husband, fidgeted with the catch of the thick band of gold that encircled her slender wrist.

Veloso filled the crystal goblets with champagne—clearly the best had been brought out for the occasion—and offered a toast: "To my lovely wife." But he did not raise his glass in her direction. Instead, he bowed to a new portrait of Isabel hanging above the serving table. She was depicted reclining on a chaise longue in a black velvet gown, her hand—its nails coated blood red—reaching out, beckoning; her long raven hair was wound demurely in a braid, but her dark eyes were slightly hooded and her full lips parted sensuously. "The artist caught her mesmerizing qualities very well, don't you think, my friend?"

Miguel nodded and drained the champagne. How often had he kissed that insatiable mouth—how often had he seen that hair tumbling down across a pillow—how often had those nails raked across his skin in the heat of passion.

"And now to your health, Miguelinho." Veloso refilled his glass.

"And to yours, Luis," Miguel responded.

After the second course, and the second bottle of champagne, Miguel had his fill of this extravagant show of feigned warmth and hospitality. Of course, Veloso knew that he had been sleeping with his wife. The proof was in the bull that he had sent into the ring, a bull who already knew the game—a killer bull, no fair match for any *toureiro*. He studied his host's smiling face. This man had tried to kill him. And in a way he had succeeded. So what was the reason for this celebration? To gloat over a cripple? To make his wife squirm?

Isabel ate very little, said almost nothing, keeping her eyes on her plate. Finally, she addressed Miguel. "I am pleased that your injury has not stopped you from continuing in your father's tradition. It must be very difficult for you . . . with . . . ah . . ."

"One leg?" he finished, looking squarely into her eyes. "You ride a horse with your ass, not your legs."

There was a stunned silence at his bluntness. He didn't care; the champagne was taking over. He drained his glass and Veloso immediately refilled it.

"So—what are your plans now that you're back in Lisbon?"

"I'm not back for long. Next week, I leave for America to bring two of my father's horses to a rich heiress."

"Ahh, rich—she must also be beautiful, no?" Veloso eyed his wife's face. "Perhaps you will stay in America."

"Six months only, just long enough to train the rider in the fundamentals of horsemanship." He looked squarely at Veloso. "I could never stay away from Portugal longer than that."

Momentarily, the smile disappeared from Veloso's face. Then it returned. "Of course not. It is only in Portugal that we have the most beautiful women." He reached over and squeezed his wife's hand.

"And the best horses."

"And don't forget our bulls."

"How could I," Miguel said with a sardonic grin.

"Yes, I am very sorry it was one of mine that caused your unfortunate accident."

The son of a bitch, thought Miguel, he can't keep the glee out of his voice.

"Oh!" Veloso raised both his arms. "I must show you my new prize bull."

Miguel looked at him through an alcoholic haze. "I'd like that."

"Fine, then let's go." Veloso dabbed his thick lips with a napkin as he rose from the table.

Miguel got up awkwardly, knocking over his empty glass. He knew he was drunk, but some self-destructive impulse was driving him to obliterate all rational thought. On the way out of the door, he grabbed a full bottle of champagne the maid had just opened and placed in the ice bucket.

"Come join us, my dear," Veloso smirked, taking Isabel's arm and leading the way to the bullring in the farmyard. "This one will be the foundation of a new line of great bulls for Portugal," he continued. "This one I will never send to fight."

Miguel looked around. The place was deserted. "Where are your ranch hands?" he asked.

"Off in the fields rounding up the bulls . . . we need all the men for that. Wait here a moment," he said over his shoulder, "I'll let him out."

Miguel took a sip from the bottle as he watched Veloso pull the cord that released the gate. A huge black beast charged out into the dimly lit arena.

"One half ton of muscle and courage," said Veloso with pride. "Miguelinho, would you like to be the only one to make a few passes with a cape—" He stopped abruptly, pointedly glancing at Miguel's leg. "I'm sorry, how stupid of me."

"No, no, I'd like that."

Isabel turned to him sharply. "Miguel—perhaps you've had too much to drink."

"Of course not," Miguel retorted, wiping his lips with the back of his hand and handing the bottle to Isabel.

"Isabel may be right. Are you *sure*?" Veloso said, his excessive solicitude taunting Miguel.

"I'm sure," he said, stepping behind the wooden barrier. It was in this protected spot that the *toureiro* watched the movements of the bull—did he hook to the right or left? What he saw could save his life.

The lamps cast eerie shadows over the arena, and the farmyard, absent of people, held a sepulchral stillness.

"Here it is." Veloso handed Miguel a red cape. "But please, don't go too far into the ring—in case you need to retreat."

"Don't worry, Luis—ah, but first I'd like to watch one of his charges."

"Certainly." Veloso cautiously took a step into the ring and waved the cape. The bull tensed, then charged, and Veloso ducked behind the barrier next to Miguel. The horns crashed into the wood, digging deep, sending splinters flying. As the bull jerked free and swerved away, Miguel noticed a cut on the animal's hump that could only have been made by a badly placed dart. A wave of sobriety washed over him. This bull had played the game before.

Adrenaline started pumping through Miguel's body. "A good one," he said quietly, his mind racing. This bull was another killer; Veloso obviously meant to finish the job.

"The best I've had in a long time," Veloso was saying. "I hope he gives me many sons."

"Let me see him charge once more."

"Ahh, you've become cautious, my friend."

Miguel looked directly into Veloso's eyes. "I don't move as quickly as I used to."

"Of course, of course." Veloso again stepped out in

front of the barrier and waved his cape at the bull pawing the ground in the center of the ring. *"Ehe! Ehe!"* he yelled. The bull thundered toward him.

Before Veloso could duck to safety, Miguel's strong arm was around his neck, bending his head back, holding him firmly against the barrier, throttling the yell in his throat.

The bull smashed into Veloso. The horns pierced his body, the barrier reverberating with the impact.

Isabel screamed.

The bull jerked his head free, but Miguel did not let go. He whispered in Veloso's ear, "I would like to help you, but I only have one leg—you son of a bitch." The horns ripped through flesh a second time. Miguel released his hold and Veloso crumpled into a heap.

Isabel stared at the body of her husband. "Is he dead?" she whispered.

Miguel leaned over the barrier, breathing heavily. He didn't answer. Slowly, he backed away and started to walk toward the house, but Isabel ran up behind him. "Oh Miguel . . . please hold me. I'm afraid." Her arms encircled his waist, and she clung to him desperately.

"Isabel, don't—" He freed himself from her grasp. "I need a drink." She handed him the champagne bottle.

He drank from it greedily, as if trying to quench a terrible thirst; then, feeling suddenly weary, he slumped to the grass.

She knelt beside him. "I love you so much . . . I'm glad he's gone." She started to kiss his face frantically, licking the beads of perspiration from his forehead. "I'm all yours now," she burst out.

"Pull yourself together. We must notify the authorities."

"But what will we say?"

He spoke softly, his voice full of sarcasm. "Your husband was a brave man. When I stumbled, he rushed in to save me."

"Yes, yes, you're right—that's exactly what we must say."

"I drink to his courage . . ." And he took another long gulp, and closed his eyes. His head was spinning.

Then he felt Isabel's fingers unbuttoning his pants. He opened his eyelids and, through an alcoholic haze, he could make out in the dim light the black mass of the bull lumbering around the arena. Against the barrier lay Veloso's mangled body.

He looked at Isabel. Didn't she see it? But her eyes, burning as if with fever, were focused only on him. He took a swig of champagne as she reached out hungrily to kiss him. He spat the champagne into her open mouth.

"I know you did it for me, Miguel," she whispered hoarsely. Her lipstick was smeared in a twisted grin.

A feeling of revulsion at what he had done was overwhelming him. He loathed himself. He loathed her. But he could not move away. He just lay there in a stupor.

He felt her take him into her mouth, wet with champagne.

Chapter 3

Stone Ridge, New York

PATRICIA WIPED THE SWEAT off her brow with the back
of her arm as she rode Sport to the stable, her rounds of
the farm completed. It was an unusually muggy August
evening, with mosquitoes swarming in cloudy halos,
the air hanging thick and heavy. Against the dusky sky,
she could see silhouettes of bats taking off from the loft
of the hay barn. So early for bats to be out, she thought,
they too must want to escape the oppressive heat. Her
faithful dalmatian—named Taxi because his black-and-
white spotted coat made her think of a Checker cab—
was not his perky self either; he usually covered the
distance three times over, running circles around Sport,
but today he seemed content to lope lazily behind the
horse.

She tied up outside the stable and turned on the water to hose Sport down. She was tempted to hose herself too, clothes and all.

Despite the many grooms, she liked washing Sport herself after a ride—it was her way of saying thank you to this awkward Appaloosa, her favorite. He turned his head and stared at her. It tickled her the way the whites showed around his eyes and his bottom lip hung loose, giving him the look of a forlorn little boy. As she scraped the water off his back, she watched the farmhands milling around making preparations to receive the two highly trained Lusitano horses that were due to arrive from Portugal tomorrow.

She'd bought the horses several months ago, when, on the second anniversary of her father's tragic death, she decided to make the trip they had once planned together. Dr. Solomon had warned her against fantasizing about what might have been, but she had to do it.

She traveled all over Portugal pretending she was with Daddy, trying to imagine where he would have taken her, what he would have told her. His last words still echoed in her mind—"I have to tell you something very important." Somehow she came to believe that the key to the secret lay in Portugal. What was so important? she asked over and over, pacing the beach at Tróia, touring the cathedrals and palaces of Lisbon. But the answer never came.

Back then, Daddy had planned a visit to Paulo Cardiga's famous Centro Equestre, where horses and riders were still trained in the Renaissance tradition. And, of course, she went there, observing in fascination the master at his art. Impulsively, she asked to learn his method, but he demanded at least a six-month commitment. Since she could not take that much time from the responsibilities of her farm and her fund-raising activities on behalf of Tom Keegan, she begged for a compromise. Money was no object. He finally agreed to sell her two horses and, along with them, provide the services of an instructor who would come to America to work with her. And now, the horses and the instructor were on the way.

A long list of the horses' needs had come two weeks ago—demands for special hay, grain, bedding. These animals were royalty. A wave of excitement went through her as she remembered how beautiful they were, how exquisitely trained.

Edgar, the foreman, was out front double-checking the arrangements with Dennis, the exercise groom. Edgar, a robust Appalachian redneck, towered over the diminutive Dennis. "So you checked everything, huh?!" he bellowed. "Well—how come them ropes is lying on the ground in that there stall?"

Patricia sighed. Edgar was known for his hot temper, but he was loyal and worked as hard as a mule from daybreak to dusk. He didn't exactly approve of Dennis, who had come to work on the farm a couple of months ago. Behind Dennis's back, he called him "that snooty city boy." But Patricia felt sorry for the shy young man; he seemed considerate, conscientious, and was a good rider.

Now, noticing she had returned, Dennis called out, "Miss D.—I'm glad you're back. Mr. Cardiga just telephoned—"

"From Lisbon?"

"No—from the van."

"Mr. Cardiga himself? I thought he was sending an instructor."

"Well, the man said he was Mr. Cardiga and he said the horses are a half hour away."

"They are? Oh my God—they weren't supposed to be here until tomorrow."

She was flabbergasted that Paulo Cardiga would come himself. What should she do? Where should she put him? She had fixed up the bluestone cottage adjoining the grooms' quarters for the instructor, but surely that would not be good enough for this aristocratic man.

But it was too late to make new arrangements because the van was already rolling down the long driveway framed by two rows of elm trees. Taxi, sensing the excitement, came to life again and ran down to greet it with loud barks.

The van came to a stop. The door on the passenger side opened and a handsome young man stepped out of the cab. He took off his black flat-topped, wide-brimmed hat, which set off his dark eyes and olive features, and wiped the sweat from his face with the back of his hand.

"I am Miguel Cardiga," he said, addressing Dennis and Edgar. "I spoke to one of you on the phone earlier, yes?"

"You spoke with me—I'm Dennis, the exercise groom."

"*Miguel* Cardiga?" Patricia exclaimed. Now she could see the resemblance—obviously, he was Paulo's son. But he ignored her and walked stiffly, with a noticeable limp, to the side door and pulled it open.

"I want my horses unloaded immediately," he commanded.

What does he mean by "my" horses? thought Patricia.

"Stalls lined with fresh straw, yes?"

"We got the letter of instructions," Dennis answered.

"No sawdust or shavings—dries out their hooves."

"That's right," said Dennis, helping Edgar lower the ramp.

Patricia felt that she ought to resent his haughty manner, but there was something amusing in the contrast of the imperious gestures and the sweat-soaked shirt that clung to his body, outlining his well-muscled shoulders and arms.

"Mr. Cardiga," she tried again. "I'm Patricia Dennison—I own this farm. First I'd like to—"

"Mademoiselle," he interrupted with a slight nod. "Right now, I take care of the horses, then I take care of you."

"But I would like—" She stopped at the sight of the first animal, a dappled gray with a white mane cascading over his head and down his proudly held neck. As the horse, led by Edgar, delicately stepped down the ramp, Miguel moved slowly toward him. "Ultimato," he whispered, gently stroking the animal's neck and murmuring softly in Portuguese. His gruff manner disappeared completely. Patricia was sure that the horse understood him.

Miguel handed the lead line to Dennis. "Walk him around"—he made a circular gesture with his fingers—"*slowly*—for five minutes, then put him in his stall and give him water—lukewarm water. This animal is overheated. It's hot today," he announced as if he were the only one who noticed.

Erect, he stood by the van, like a host waiting to receive the next honored guest. "Easy, easy," he admonished Edgar. His eyes did not leave the horse descending the ramp for an instant. "Ah, Harpalo." The shiny chestnut nuzzled his neck. Again he spoke in Portuguese, and again Patricia watched the horse respond to the soothing touch of his hand.

"You!" he called to Dennis, who was still busy with the gray horse. "Remember what I just told you, yes?"

"Yes sir."

"Same with this one."

Patricia, annoyed at being ignored for so long, now approached him more assertively. "Mr. Cardiga!"

He turned toward her, took off his hat, and bowed. His attention was now totally focused on her. Patricia felt as if stage lights had been turned on in her direction. Suddenly, she didn't know how to put him in his place. Instead, she stammered, "If there's anything . . . I can do for you—"

"Yes," he cut her off. "Where do I sleep?"

She turned to Edgar, who was watching the whole show with an impassive air, chewing a blade of grass. "Edgar . . . please take Mr. Cardiga—and his baggage—to the bluestone cottage."

"Thank you." Miguel's insolent tone communicated no gratitude.

"Would you like something to eat?"

"No, I want to sleep."

Patricia watched him walking stiffly after Edgar; something was obviously wrong with his left leg. He better be the greatest trainer in the world to make up for this rudeness, she thought. But what a way he had with horses. And he spoke English quite well, with a charming lilt. This was going to be interesting.

A sound woke Miguel from a deep sleep. He yawned and stretched, not wanting to open his eyes. What was that? Oh—a rooster crowing. He sat up abruptly.

He was on a strange bed fully clothed. He looked about the room—the roughhewn walls were newly whitewashed, the oaken floors strewn with soft cotton rugs. On the opposite side, a stone hearth was set with kindling and logs just waiting for a match. It was a cozy room, he had to admit. His hostess had good taste.

How long had he been sleeping? Quite a while if roosters still crowed at dawn. Last night he had flung himself on the bed, too tired to undress after the trip in the plane's cargo hold—he had insisted on watching the two horses himself.

Now, he ached all over and had a painful cramp in his left foot. He reached down to rub it, but of course the leg wasn't there. Luis Veloso had seen to that—son of a bitch. *But it wasn't enough for him to have me crippled—he wanted me dead*. He wanted his wife to look at her lover hanging on the horns of a bull—dying in a dark arena.

Miguel's jaw tightened as he tried to push aside the thought that had plagued him for the past week. *I've killed a man. But didn't Veloso deserve to die? He tried to kill me—twice*.

The statement he and Isabel made to the police was

accepted without question; the captain in charge of the investigation could not have been more sympathetic.

The unbearable experience was the funeral mass at the Lisbon *Sé* Cathedral. He sat next to Emilio, in whom he had not confided the real story, listening to the archbishop recount the "virtues of this great man." From his pew he had a clear view of Isabel dressed in mourning. A heavy black veil hid her features, but the vision of her face grotesquely smeared with lipstick would not leave his mind.

He could not bring himself to attend the reception after the service; to avoid any contact with Isabel, he arranged to leave for America a day early.

He pushed aside those disturbing thoughts, got up, took off his clothes, and hopped into the shower. The cold water refreshed him, breaking through the haze of jet lag. He wrapped himself in one of the thick Turkish towels stacked on the counter, picked up his prosthesis from a chair, and sat down on the bed. He stared at this piece of steel, wood, and leather, a vague replica of a limb. He jammed his knee into the cup and tightened the leather straps around his thigh.

He stomped the leg against the floor to test its security. Then, quickly, he put on his black riding outfit, grabbed his hat, and walked out of the cottage.

A thin cool mist was rising from the wet grass, giving the entire landscape a ghostly aura. He could distinguish silhouettes of horses moving slowly behind a white fence. He headed toward them. The mist was dissipating quickly now. High above, the lonely moon still remained, deserted by all the stars, like the last guest at a dinner party who had overstayed his welcome. The new light revealed miles of white rail fences. More and more horses came into view. There must be at least a hundred of them, he thought. He came closer. These horses were so strange. They moved so slowly. Several plodded toward him.

Miguel was aghast—these were cripples, bowlegged, knocked-kneed, old. All of them! What was a beautiful young girl doing with so many old horses near death?

One chestnut leaned his head over the fence and nudged Miguel. This one is used to treats, he thought as he scratched the horse's head. A brass plaque attached to the leather halter read "Misty." He turned back the upper lip of the horse to check the teeth—more than twenty years old. On the inside of the pink flesh a number was tattooed: U65-82551. Yes, an old race-horse, foaled 1965—ancient, for his breed.

He walked along the corral. They were not all race-horses. He saw Quarterhorses, Arabians, Palominos, ponies. What a strange person, this Patricia Dennison.

The sun, a crescent of fiery red, peeked over a knoll in the distance and spread a thin blanket of golden light over the ranch. Miguel headed for the stable.

Patricia jumped out of the shower and scrubbed her-self dry. It was early—two hours more before the mail-man arrived. She quickly put on her blue jeans, boots, and checked flannel shirt. Outside her bedroom, she paused before a large painting on the wall—*The Star-hanger*. This was the picture her father had given her, joking that he was the man on the ladder. It always reassured her to look at it.

She bounded down the staircase of wooden planks that led into a large living room dominated by a huge stone hearth. She loved her home. It had been nothing more than a shell of a burned-out farmstead with half a dozen outbuildings and barns in various states of disrepair when she found it. The trustees were aghast when she announced her plan to move out of the Park Avenue mansion and buy it—she overheard Horace Coleman telling Ash that the restoration job amounted to "flushing money down the nonexistent toilet"—but she stuck to her decision.

Now, she walked into the big old country kitchen, where Concha, her Mexican housekeeper, was already pouring coffee into a mug with the picture of Sport on it. "Thanks, Concha," said Patricia as she reached for the mug and stopped. Lying on the table was a small brown envelope covered with colorful Lebanese stamps.

"Mailman come early," said Concha, grinning.

Patricia's heart started beating rapidly as she tore it open.

> *My dearest—I haven't written to you for a couple of days because our hospital was nearly demolished in an Israeli bombing raid. The guerrillas had established their headquarters in a building adjoining us, so that they would be free from attack. But they were wrong, and we got caught in the middle.*

Her hands were trembling. He is safe, he's alive, she reassured herself, trying to calm down.

She sat down at the kitchen table to read the rest.

*It will take a fortune to make our facilities func-
tional again—I will have to come begging to the
States. But that's not so bad—because I will be
able to spend Thanksgiving with you—I'm count-
ing the days.*

Those words brought a flush to her cheeks. She took
a sip of coffee and watched the peripatetic ants going
back and forth across the windowsill. She had given
Concha strict instructions never to destroy these tiny
creatures who did no harm. At first, Concha argued
fiercely, "Ants get in cupboards . . . in food . . . every-
where." That's when Patricia came up with the inge-
nious idea of feeding them at the point of entry, so they
didn't have to look elsewhere. Now a plate of sugar sat
on the windowsill and the little ants hurried back and
forth, each one lugging a grain to their anthill in the
yard. Concha, of course, thought her a little crazy and
would secretly scoop up the ants and send them down
the drain with a strong stream of water.

Patricia stared at the insects—one line zigzagging up,
the other down. As they passed each other in opposite
directions, they never failed to touch antennas briefly.
This morning, Patricia felt, they were giving each other
a high five as they said, "Tom's coming back!"

She folded the letter neatly, stuffed it in the pocket
of her jeans, and checked the little dish in the pantry
where she had put out food for Phoebe, the scrawny
stray cat she recently found hiding among the hay bales
in the barn. Phoebe stuck out her timid face from behind
the canned peaches, then ducked back.

"She'll come around," Patricia said to Concha, who

rolled her eyes. She drained her coffee cup and headed for the stable.

There, she found Dennis standing before the two adjoining stalls of the Portuguese horses.

"They are beautiful, aren't they?" Patricia said, rubbing the quivering nose of Ultimato.

"They sure are, Miss D."

"I can't wait to ride them."

"I wouldn't touch them if I were you."

"What? What do you mean?"

"He was here this morning—six o'clock, checked their food, walked each horse around for a half hour, and gave very strict instructions." Dennis imitated Miguel's speech: " 'Don't touch horses, yes?' "

"Where is he now?"

"Sleeping."

"Sleeping?"

"Yeah."

"Did he tell you when he plans to get up?" she said, unable to hide her annoyance.

"I was afraid to ask."

"When he gets up, you tell him I want to see him," she said sternly, and walked away.

"I'll try."

She turned to catch the expression on Dennis's face, but he had already disappeared inside the indoor riding arena, which adjoined the stable.

One of the grooms handed her the reins—Sport was all saddled and ready for the morning rounds. Farm chores always gave her great pleasure. This was her reason for being. These animals were her family—she had no one else. Except now there was Tom.

As she rode out past the bluestone cottage, she noticed that the shades were tightly drawn. What an arrogant man. Maybe she ought to throw a rock through the window and wake him up. They had not even discussed the training program.

She rode around, her eyes scanning the water troughs to make sure that they were clean and full, that the fence rails were secure, the gates closed, and none of the old cripples were down. Suddenly, she heard loud voices coming out of the barn where hay and grain were stored. "You dumb son of a bitch!" She recognized Edgar's gravelly voice. "Get them bags of chicken feed away from that there horse feed."

As she approached, she saw that he was yelling at one of the hired hands. The chastised man was muttering as he lugged the heavy sacks away.

"Is that so important, Edgar?" Patricia said placatingly.

"Sure is, Miss D. They's too close together—God forbid they get mixed up. Accident like that happen back in Jersey—seventeen horses killed."

"Chicken feed?"

"Yes ma'am. Them bags of chicken feed got a kind of medicine—antibiotic—that's poison to a horse."

"Well, you keep that chicken feed away from my Misty," a female voice said from behind.

Laura Simpson, a chubby woman with stringy gray hair, was approaching, pulling Misty by a lead line.

"Are you trying to steal that horse?" Patricia called out playfully.

"Caught again," Laura responded in her throaty chuckle.

Patricia dismounted to walk along with her friend and immediately smelled a familiar odor. "Laura! You promised you wouldn't start drinking this early."

"Kiddo, when you hit fifty-five, you'll need a shot to get your old bones oiled too."

"But Laura, you're ruining your health."

Laura snorted. "My health! I couldn't care less. What have I got to live for? When Joe and Bobby died in that car crash I lost everything."

"Oh, I know—that was a terrible tragedy."

"To tell you the truth, the only thing that keeps me going is Misty. If you hadn't taken him in and I had lost him too, I would have done myself in."

"You mustn't talk like that, Laura."

"But it's true. You know this year Misty is twenty-five, Bobby's age exactly. But when I walk around here, I pretend that Misty is still a young colt and Bobby is a little kid dreaming about becoming a cowboy. We walk around this beautiful place together and have long talks. It's the only thing I have in life. I know I'm just another charity case—you got hundreds of them here—but giving Misty a little piece of heaven . . ." Laura's voice cracked, and she loudly wiped her nose with her sleeve.

Impulsively, Patricia put her arms around Laura and hugged her tightly. "I'll always look after Misty and I'll look after you too. You're my best friend. Do you know what it means to me to have somebody I can talk to and tell my secrets to?"

"Okay, okay, kiddo—look at the two of us getting sappy. Thank God I didn't put my mascara on this morning."

Patricia laughed. "Laura—you always have a wise-crack in your back pocket."

"Talking of back pockets . . ." Laura reached behind her and extracted a carrot. "Misty is worse than a rabbit." And she popped it into his mouth. "How about those foreign horses, are they allowed carrots?"

"I guess I better ask Miguel Cardiga."

"Who's he?"

"He came with the horses."

"And what'll he do here?"

"Teach me to ride."

Laura snorted, "One thing you don't need is more riding lessons."

"You don't understand," said Patricia. "This is *classical* riding—Portuguese style. These horses *dance* and you hardly use your reins."

"I'll believe it when I see it."

"Oh Laura—they are incredibly beautiful."

"And expensive, I bet."

"Very . . . I feel a little guilty about that."

"Guilty? What, with your dough?"

"I just feel guilty about spending so much money on myself, but when I get married, that will change."

"You're getting married?"

Patricia giggled. "Tom hasn't asked me yet, but I can't help fantasizing that when he comes here next time . . ."

"Well, you sure could use a man in your life."

"You know . . . when I get married, I intend to give all of J. L.'s money away."

"What!? Are you nuts?!"

"Tom feels exactly like I do."

Laura shook her head. "You're not for real."

"Nothing could make me happier than to get rid of that burden . . . and to do something good with that money."

The look on Laura's face was one of stupefied astonishment. "Well . . . good luck . . . ," she stammered out, "that's all I can say."

Chapter 4

Stone Ridge

PATRICIA TURNED OUT THE LIGHT, rolled over on her side, and bumped into Taxi. Ahhh, Taxi, she thought, one day Tom will be lying here, and you might have to move to the foot of the bed. Would you mind that, huh? And she scratched the top of his head. Taxi didn't move but his tail thumped against the blanket.

She lay there quietly, drifting slowly across the border of sleep. In her dreamy state she had the sensation of something scratching her face—she opened her eyes. The moonlight made a path through the window to her bed, illuminating Phoebe, the stray cat, sitting on the pillow licking her cheek with her sandpaper tongue. Patricia didn't dare push her away—this was the first time the scared half-wild kitten had shown her any kind of affection. The cat kept on licking. *I won't have any skin left soon.* She giggled, and the startled cat jumped off the bed.

Now Patricia was wide awake. She looked at the clock—it was only four-thirty. She got up to fetch herself a glass of water. Sipping it, she walked over to the window. What? She pushed the curtain aside to see more clearly and caught her breath.

Miguel Cardiga was riding the gray horse, Ultimato, in the silver light of the three-quarter moon. They moved gracefully across the ring, as if in slow motion, the horse suspending each leg in the air before floating into the next step. The rider's cues were imperceptible as he sat erect and in control, dressed in a form-fitting jacket and wide-brimmed hat.

My God, to be able to ride like that, she thought as the horse went into a complicated maneuver, his hind-legs and forelegs crossing each other, gliding sideways across the ring—a magical sight in the soft moonlight. She quickly threw a woolen shawl around her thin night-gown and hurried down the stairs. The moist grass felt good under her bare feet as she made for the riding ring. But when she got there, Miguel was gone.

He had a knack for disappearing. For the past week she had not seen him at all. Dennis had told her that he was up very early tending to the horses and seemed to sleep all day. Obviously, he was also drinking—the day he arrived three cases of wine were unloaded along with his saddles and other baggage, and Concha had found several empty bottles when cleaning his cottage.

He was an irritating fellow. He had given strict orders to Dennis that no one was to ride the horses for at least a week, and never without his supervision. But here, at last, was a sample of his riding ability—he was clearly his father's son.

As she approached the ring, he suddenly entered in a collected canter on Harpalo. He passed her but kept his eyes straight ahead. She was sure he had seen her. She marveled at his finesse as he effortlessly put Harpalo through his paces. With the last pirouette, he left the ring and headed for the stable.

Hypnotized by what she had seen, she followed. When she came in, he had already unsaddled and was rubbing the horse down with a wet cloth. She walked toward him, ignoring the wisps of hay prickling her bare feet.

"You are magnificent!" she blurted out.

He gave her a quick glance, nodded, and went back to rubbing.

"Do you always train your horses at night?"

"My father taught me that in the stillness of the night it is easier to make an animal listen."

Patricia felt awkward—uncertain whether to say something more or leave. While she was debating her dilemma, he put Harpalo back in the stall, murmuring in Portuguese. She wished she could understand the language. The words sounded gentle and affectionate, a man talking to his beloved.

She had just decided to leave, when she heard his voice: "Mademoiselle—you will ride like that someday."

"I don't think so, but I'll try if—"

He interrupted her, "I will teach you."

He advanced toward her, a long, tapered dressage

whip in his hand. He stopped an arm's length away and lifted the whip. The pointed tip almost touched her lips.

"When you sit in the saddle, you and the horse will meld into one," he said softly.

She was mesmerized.

The whip began a slow descent along her neck, lingering on the curve of her breast.

"You will experience a sensation you have never known before."

Intoxicated by his words, she stood rooted to the ground, unable to move.

He dropped the whip, put his arms around her, and kissed her hard on the lips.

An electrical current shot through her body—it was at once exciting and terrifying.

She broke away and jumped back. "How dare you!"

He didn't move. He just looked at her without a change in expression, his eyes hooded. "I'm sorry, mademoiselle. I misunderstood your visit—in a nightdress—at four-thirty in the morning." He seemed to be looking deep into her. Then he turned abruptly and walked out.

Patricia practically bolted out of the barn, racing for home, for the safety of her bedroom. She slammed the door shut behind her as if a posse were in pursuit. Out of breath, she sat down on the bed next to Taxi, who merely looked up and yawned.

Her head was a jumble of thoughts. She was crazy—running out in the middle of the night half-dressed like that. But she was so carried away by the magic of his riding, she didn't think. How could she work with him now? She must ask him to leave—but then he'd take the horses with him. It really was more her fault than his. Of course, he misunderstood. *Oh, why do I always make a mess of everything?*

She went back to bed, trying to pretend that it never happened, refusing even to consider the thought that she had found the kiss stimulating.

"Oh Tom, hurry home," she whispered into her pillow.

Miguel sat on the bed. He reached for the bottle, refilled his glass, and took a large swallow, but the wine wasn't having its usual effect. His whole body was vibrating with agitation.

What the hell could he have been thinking? But she was almost naked . . . her breasts pushing against that thin flimsy material. But what would he have done if she had responded? Taken her there—right in the stable? Let her help him unstrap the prosthesis? Watch her stare at his stump with pity . . . or disgust? *God, I was stupid!*

Eventually, the wine started to work. In his alcoholic stupor, he heard an insistent ringing. It took some time for him to realize it was the telephone.

"Emilio!"

"When are you coming home, Miguelinho?"

"Next week I think. After a few lessons, Ultimato's new owner won't ever get on a horse again."

"You don't like the old heiress—is she that ugly?"

"Oh no—she's not old and she's not ugly. She's beautiful."

"So? Are you sick?"

"Yes, Emilio—homesick."

"I'll send another case of wine."

"Bring it over yourself."

"I'll send Isabel."

"What the hell are you talking about?"

"I ran into her last night at the Bairro Alto Club. She kept asking about you."

"Just don't give her any answers."

"I had to."

"What do you mean?"

"She was upset that you didn't come to the reception after the funeral . . . you left so suddenly without saying good-bye . . ."

"So what did you say?"

"I gave her your phone number."

"Oh shit! I've been trying to get her off my back."

"Why?"

"She's a fucking bore."

"Ahhh . . . but is she a boring fuck?"

Emilio succeeded again—Miguel couldn't hold back the laughter. "You can have her."

Suddenly, there was a crackle on the wire. "Emilio . . . Emilio . . . ?"

The Portuguese operator broke in. "What number are you calling?"

"Oh forget it," Miguel said. "He'll call back."

Patricia curled up under the willow tree in the horse graveyard, hugging her bare knees and crying. The letter from Tom was on the ground beside her—he was postponing his visit for another month. He had very good reasons—terribly sick people needed him—and he promised to spend New Year's with her. Still, she couldn't stop crying. She didn't feel sorry for herself; she was just incredibly sad. Some part of her was empty . . . a part she was always yearning to fill. Tom would fill it, she was sure, but right now she felt so alone. Of course, she could call a friend—Joanna Benson, Laura—but she hated to show people what a mess she really was. Sometimes she felt she was strong, and then sadness would engulf her, and she couldn't stop crying. At those moments, she would come here and think how peaceful it would be to lie buried among her old friends, unafraid, just quietly sleeping.

Right now, overwhelmed by this wave of melancholy, she didn't have the strength for any kind of confrontation with Miguel Cardiga. She decided to say nothing about the incident in the stable and see how things went.

For her first lesson, Miguel led Harpalo, the chestnut, into the ring on a twenty-foot lunge line. The horse wore a saddle and bridle, but the stirrups had been removed and the reins were missing. Before she could question it, Miguel imperiously motioned to Dennis to hoist her up on the horse. She sat there, her hands helpless without the reins, her legs dangling.

"What do I do now?" she asked with a nervous laugh.

"Nothing," he replied flatly. "Just feel the rhythm of the horse."

He clucked his tongue and Harpalo started to walk slowly. But almost immediately he whistled. The horse stopped. He took a few steps forward. "Have you ever been on a horse before, Miss Dennison?"

"Mr. Cardiga, I've been riding all my life. I have won many trophies in hunter shows."

"But you have no feeling for the horse. You sit stiff like a board, legs gripping the horse's belly. How is it possible for you to communicate with the animal when you are so tense?"

"I am not tense!" she objected, growing angry at the humiliation.

"You are not tense? Oh, excuse me, mademoiselle." He dropped the lunge line, leaving her there feeling silly, wondering if she should get off. But he returned momentarily carrying two eggs.

She tried to cover her apprehension. "No bacon?"

He ignored the joke. "These are raw eggs . . . I will place one between your thigh and the saddle. Hold your leg firmly so that the egg will not fall, but without tension so it will not break." He handed her the other egg. "Place this one at your other thigh."

Now she felt more ridiculous than before, sitting there without reins or stirrups, gently hugging two eggs with her thighs.

He extended the lunge line and signaled with his whip. Harpalo moved into a slow canter. Within seconds, yellow yolks were oozing down her britches and into her boots.

He stopped the horse and handed the lunge line to Dennis. "That will be all for today."

She jumped off the horse and stared down at the omelette on her pants. When she looked up, he was already walking away. She yelled after him, "You are right, Mr. Cardiga—I am tense! I am tense! But so are you!"

He turned around and flashed her a grin. She had not noticed before how white and even his teeth were.

Come to think of it, this was the first time she saw him smile.

Miguel came into his cottage, the smile still on his face.

Chalk one up for Patricia Dennison, he thought.

He was sure she was going to cry. He had to admit that maliciously he looked forward to the moment when, in tears, she called him all kinds of names and demanded he get off the farm and take his lousy horses with him.

But she had surprised him.

He saw the redness rising to her cheeks, the anger in her eyes, but then, instead of breaking down, or losing her temper, she made him laugh.

She has spunk, he thought, as he tossed his hat on a chair and plopped himself on the bed. She's not going to be easy to break.

He reached over to uncork a bottle of wine and found another message that Isabel had called. He drained his glass. When the hell would she give up?

A fire was crackling in the living room hearth, warding off the chill of early autumn. From the stereo came the soft voice of Billy Joel. Concha walked in with coffee and flan.

Laura took a sip. "You know I love this old house of yours—but with all your money, couldn't you replace that wormy wood on the walls?"

Patricia laughed. "Oh Laura—I *put* that wood there. It comes from an eighteenth-century barn that couldn't be restored. I love how cozy it makes the room—like a hay loft."

"Well, good thing you stopped before you put hay on the floor and Sport in the kitchen."

Patricia laughed so hard she almost spilled her coffee. Laura was such a wiseass at times.

"Laura—I know you think I'm nuts, but if I didn't have this farm—these animals—I really would be insane. You, of all people, ought to understand what a horse can mean to a person's life."

"I know, I know, kiddo," Laura said, looking off into space. Then the sad look disappeared as soon as it came, and she turned to Patricia. "Talking about horses—how are the dancing lessons coming?"

Patricia sighed. "Please—I'd rather forget this whole month. He's a terrible man. I've got egg yolk all over my best britches."

"What do eggs have to do with riding?"

"It's too long a story. I'd rather talk about something pleasant."

"Like Tom Keegan?"

Patricia sighed, reached into her pocket, and pulled out a letter.

"From him?"

Patricia nodded. "He writes me twice a week."

"Don't bother reading me everything—just the sexy stuff."

"Oh Laura—it's wonderful to be in love." She pointed to a calendar on the wall marked with large X's. "One hundred and fourteen days left."

"You sound like a prisoner."

"I am—and I'm waiting for Tom to release me."

"Wow—that's gonna be one hot night on the old farm!"

Patricia blushed, not knowing how to answer, and walked toward the window. Miguel had Harpalo on the lunge line and was working him at a trot in a wide circle. His limp seemed more pronounced today. She had never asked him, but she wondered about it. Was it the result of an accident . . . or maybe polio . . . or a birth defect? It certainly didn't interfere with his riding. She kept watching him—his rapport with the horses always mesmerized her.

"You know, Laura—today, men look at you, grab you, and expect sex."

"They do?" Laura chortled. "I wish somebody would grab me once in a while."

Patricia didn't laugh. She hadn't told Laura about the incident in the stable, and didn't want to bring it up now. "But Tom isn't like that—he really loves me. He has respect for me as a person."

"You sound like a virgin," said Laura with a mouthful of flan.

"I wish I were . . ." Patricia sat down at her desk, took a sip of coffee, and looked pensively across at Laura. "You know, at school, I'd go out on a date, maybe see a movie, and then have sex."

"What's wrong with that?"

"It was for the wrong reason . . . I almost threw myself at every man I met. I was starved for affection; I never seemed to get enough. Later, Dr. Solomon explained to me that I was just using sex to get a hug. But I always ended up feeling used afterward."

"Why?"

"When someone looks at me—what do they see? The real me? Or my grandfather's money?" And then she brightened. "When Tom looks at me, I know that he sees the real me. Money means nothing to him."

"Does sex mean anything to him?"

"Oh Laura—why do you always go back to sex?"

"Can't think of a better subject."

Patricia sighed dreamily. "Sex will be wonderful for both of us, because it starts with real love. I fantasize about lying next to him . . ."

"Instead of Taxi."

"Laura! I'm being serious."

"You sound like one of those romance novels."

"But I want romance—it's important to me."

"Well, kiddo, maybe you found it."

Chapter 5

Stone Ridge

AFTER SEVERAL MORE embarrassing lessons, and six pairs of stained britches, she was able to sit to Harpalo's walk, trot, and canter without crushing a single egg. Of course, Miguel never let her try Ultimato.

She ached for a word of praise, but all she ever got was "Yes" when she fulfilled his request well. That "Yes" became a word that she craved more than any other in the English language. And lately when he said it, he sometimes smiled. And that always made her blush.

Then the day came when he brought out Harpalo saddled and with the stirrups in place. But still no reins.

He entered the ring carrying two glasses filled halfway with what looked like red wine.

"Ahh, a party?"

"No, mademoiselle, a test. If you do not have perfectly steady hands at all times, you will injure the delicate nerve endings in the horse's mouth. This is Periquita, one of Portugal's finest wines—don't waste it." And he placed a glass in each of her hands. "Now pretend you are holding the reins—gently, like a flower, not like a stone."

He had a poetic way of saying things that did not fit his severe demeanor.

Carefully, Patricia rode Harpalo through his routine. Not a drop was spilled. When Miguel brought the horse to a stop, she was grinning.

"You must be very proud of yourself, mademoiselle."

"I am."

"The test is not over." He uncorked the bottle and filled the glasses almost to the brim.

Before Harpalo could break into a canter, the red liquid was sloshing over her white britches.

As she looked down at the mess in dismay, she heard him say, "That will be all for today, mademoiselle."

"Mr. Cardiga!" she called out, as he started walking away. He turned and she raised a half-empty glass in a toast. "I congratulate you—you succeeded again."

Miguel's fingers drummed on the telephone as he waited for the international operator to connect him with Lisbon. Through the window of his cottage, he could see Patricia setting out on her Appaloosa, the spotted dog following the spotted horse.

He had to hand it to her—she never missed her

rounds, morning or evening. He was almost sorry about all the ruined britches, and despite himself was very pleased with the progress that she was making. It would not be easy to get Ultimato back. Of course, he never complimented her, but lately he had begun to soften his criticisms.

"Hallo!" Emilio's voice answered.

"Guess who?"

"Oh, it's you, Miguel. Are you back in Lisbon?"

"Not yet."

"You told me one week. It's been almost two months. What's wrong?"

"It's not what's wrong—too much is right. She's too good a rider."

"So she doesn't hate horses yet?"

"No, but I need another case of Periquita."

"She loves wine?"

While Emilio went on teasing him, Miguel's eyes involuntarily followed Patricia. She had dismounted now and was inspecting the hoof of a horse in the first paddock. As he watched, a gold maple leaf drifted down and gently nestled in her hair. The reflection of the sun transformed it into a sparkling topaz. He was sorry to see it fall to the ground when she stood up.

By the time he finished his conversation, she was gone.

Miguel had Ultimato at a flat-out gallop the entire length of the hayfield, but he slowed the horse down to a nonchalant trot when he caught up to Patricia coming out of a small glass house labeled INSECTARY.

She looked up, puzzled. "What can I do for you, Mr. Cardiga?"

"Mademoiselle—I am curious about this building—the grooms call it bug house. What does it mean, 'bug house'?"

She laughed as she tucked two glass vials full of small red beetles into Sport's saddlebag and remounted.

"Yes, the grooms laugh, too," he said.

"But it's really not funny. I grow good bugs here, so that I don't have to spray insecticides on my roses."

"How do you grow good bugs?"

"I feed them bad bugs that I also grow—on the blades of alfafa you can see through the greenhouse windows. But I keep the bad bugs prisoner here."

His face wore an intense expression. "Ahh—but how do you tell them apart?"

"The aphids—they're the bad guys—are black, and the good ones"—she held up the vial—"the ladybugs, are red. When I have enough red ones I take them to the rose garden to eat the bad bugs there."

"Oh, I see."

His furrowed brow told her that he probably didn't see—but then maybe he was the first person who did.

She urged Sport forward and was surprised that Miguel followed, though he kept enough distance between them so that conversation was not possible without a strain.

She pulled up to the picket fence framing an acre of rose bushes and opened the vials and released the insects; they buzzed about in a zigzag course among the last of the season's roses.

"Why so many white roses?" he asked abruptly.

"White roses were my mother's favorites. I guess I got carried away when I first moved here. I wanted to re-create the best times of my childhood—before a lot of bad things happened . . ." She broke off. Without another word, she continued on to the duck pond, and the chicken house.

There was something peculiar and touching in the way she communicated with her creatures, Miguel thought. She was no farmer minding her stock, nor was she a sentimental girl playing with her toys. He didn't know exactly how to describe her—a mother with her children perhaps.

The horses' hooves swished through the thick carpet of leaves as they rode silently for a long time. She stopped on a small rise. He pulled up beside her.

"Isn't this beautiful?" she said softly.

He followed her gaze to the yellowish green sea before them dotted with slowly moving silhouettes of horses. The white rails of the fences sparkled in the sun. The soft contours of the Catskill Mountains looked like a woman stretched out under a dappled sky.

"It's like a painting," he said.

"It's better—it's a living painting. It changes every day. Let the old masterpieces stay on the walls of my grandfather's mansion . . . I have this . . ." She took a deep breath. "*This* is my kind of painting."

Suddenly, she became aware that Miguel was no longer looking over the landscape but studying her intently. She felt uncomfortable. "Why don't you take the low road home, Mr. Cardiga. I'm going to take a shortcut and jump some fences."

He tipped his hat in agreement. He stood still for a moment, watching her fly over the meadow, then decided to follow.

Hearing the hoofbeats behind her, she turned around and broke out into an impish grin.

Taxi barked excitedly behind Sport as the horse cleared a fallen tree. Ultimato hesitated slightly, then also jumped over the obstacle.

They raced over the countryside—a trail she clearly knew well, jumping a narrow creek, a stone wall, a pile of logs. Finally they rounded a bend, and Miguel saw that they had made a full circle and were coming up on the white rail fence of the last paddock. She reined in her horse, and started to say something, but Miguel did not slow down. He urged Ultimato on. Horse and rider sailed smoothly into the air, clearing the five-foot fence by a good six inches, and made for the stable.

Miguel was rubbing down Ultimato's legs with liniment, when Patricia came in.

"Well, you showed me up—I didn't know he was trained to jump," she said.

"He wasn't—but, mademoiselle"—Miguel's lips curved up slightly—"a horse who can perform a flawless *capriole*, leaping three feet in the air from a standstill, can clear any obstacle from a full gallop."

From then on, Miguel materialized every evening and, without a word, always keeping a fair distance between them, accompanied her on her rounds. At first, Patricia enjoyed having his company. But after a while, she began to feel guilty. It was as if somehow she was cheating on Tom—spending so much time alone with another man. She decided she would tell Miguel she preferred making the rounds alone.

She rehearsed the speech she would make until she felt confident of delivering it, and marched to the stable.

But Miguel wasn't waiting there as usual.

"Dennis—have you seen Mr. Cardiga?"

"No, Miss D. Shall I tell him you went on without him?"

She hesitated, patting Sport absentmindedly. "Yes." She rode out of the barn, turning around trying to catch sight of him, but he did not appear. Slowly, very slowly, she went on alone.

By the time he caught up with her near the chicken house, her well-rehearsed speech had been forgotten. She said nothing, concentrating on her chores.

Miguel felt no need to speak either; he just liked watching her. She seemed to be negotiating with the rooster who eyed her suspiciously as she removed an egg from the laying box. "You have too many children now, Caruso," she was saying.

"Mademoiselle—do all your chickens have names?"

"Yes," she said with an embarrassed smile.

"But how do you tell them apart—they all look alike to me."

"Oh, it's easy—their combs have different ridges—and of course, they all have different personalities."

"Mademoiselle," he said with a chuckle, "you remind me of a shepherd I met while riding in the Arrábida countryside."

"A shepherd?"

"He asked me to take an injured sheep to the town

veterinarian. Of course I agreed. And then the most amazing thing happened.''

"Nothing surprises me when it comes to animals.''

"The shepherd gave a command and his dog leapt up on the mass of white sheep and traveled over their backs to a particular one.'' Miguel shook his head, as if still amazed at the recollection. "He separated it from the others. I was astounded. 'How did the dog know which sheep you wanted?' I asked the shepherd. He looked at me like I was stupid, and do you know what he said? 'Have you ever seen two sheep that look alike?' ''

Patricia burst out laughing.

"You are like that shepherd.''

She looked at him in surprise. "I'll take that as a compliment, Mr. Cardiga.''

They continued riding until they came on a path leading into a thickly wooded area. They traveled some distance into the wood and then she reined Sport in and put her finger to her lips not to make a sound.

After a few moments she whispered, "Thousands of eyes are watching us.''

He looked at her questioningly.

"Oh yes, we can't see them, but they see us—they're all around us.''

"Who?''

"Chipmunks . . . foxes . . . rabbits, deer, snakes, birds, little insects—''

"I believe you, I believe you,'' he cut her off with a smile.

"And we must never hurt them, because they have more right to be here than we do.''

Miguel looked around as if he were seeing his surroundings for the first time in his life, feeling animal eyes staring at him from every direction. Yes, people were the intruders. He had never thought of it before.

They rode on silently in a large loop, eventually coming to her favorite spot—the weeping willow in the graveyard. She dismounted and tied Sport to the trunk of the tree. Miguel did the same with Ultimato.

The horses immediately started nibbling on some wild oat grass, and Taxi sprawled out on the moss.

"Look there," she said, motioning.

His eyes followed her hand to where several flat stone markers dotted a gentle slope. Each marker bore a simple inscription: BLACK VELVET, KNIGHT, SIR LANCELOT—the names of horses.

"So this is where you bury the old horses?"

She nodded and sat down in the grass, looking wistfully ahead. He remained standing.

"Why do people think graveyards are dreary places? I think it's peaceful here. Don't you?"

He didn't answer, surveying the scene.

Patricia pointed. "That spot right there—between Velvet and Dancer—is for me."

Miguel was jolted—was she joking?

"When I bought this farm, I decided to become friends with death. That's why I brought these old horses here. I want them to have a peaceful end. The horses lying under those mounds seem to be saying to me, 'It's all right, nothing to be scared of.' It helps me—but I'm still afraid."

He was totally taken aback by this conversation. What

eerie dark thoughts went through her head. "Mademoiselle, you are too young to fear death."

"No. I am not afraid for myself, Mr. Cardiga. I'm scared that death will take others near me and leave me completely alone. There is someone special to me who works in a dangerous part of the world, and the thought of losing him paralyzes me with fear."

Miguel took off his hat and ran his hand through his thick black hair. "Mademoiselle," he said with a wry smile, "as a bullfighter I faced death many times. And you know what I learned?" He paused. "I was less afraid of the bull than of the public . . ."

She looked up at him with childlike eyes.

"Yes. I was not afraid of dying but of failure. I was afraid of dishonoring my father's name. Then I realized—death was not my enemy; my enemy was *fear*."

Patricia didn't know what to say.

He untied Ultimato and remounted. "I think I'll go back," he said.

She wanted to stop him—she wanted to hear more.

Back at his cottage, Miguel poured himself a glass of wine and put it on his nightstand. He stretched out on the bed thinking of that evening's ride. What a strange girl—surrounded by death, she had a unique appreciation of life. She drew out of him feelings that he rarely acknowledged to himself. He had never spoken to any woman like this before.

He couldn't sleep. He strapped on his prosthesis, tossed a robe around his shoulders, and limped out into the night.

He looked off at the farmhouse and saw a light in the upper window. She wasn't sleeping either. He leaned against the oak tree, listening to the wind rustling the barren branches above. Yes, Patricia—we seldom pay attention to what's around us. And often we don't listen to the voices within us.

He looked up at the farmhouse again—the light was out. Good night, Patricia.

In the morning the glass of wine was still full on his nightstand, and yet he had slept soundly. His first thought when he woke up was of Patricia. He liked the strange emotions she aroused in him. She was so fragile, so vulnerable, incapable of hurting anything. How would she react if she knew he killed a man?

Chapter 6

Stone Ridge

THE NOVEMBER RAIN was beating down hard on the glass skylights of the indoor riding arena, and the dark clouds gave the filtered light an ominous cast. Patricia stood transfixed in the center of the sand floor. Miguel was approaching, but he was not leading Harpalo, he was leading Ultimato—for the first time.

She tried not to show her nervousness as she sprang lightly into the saddle. Her long, sinewy legs hung loosely in the stirrups.

Miguel's voice was barely audible over the pulsation of the downpour. "This horse is named Ultimato—the Ultimate One. You will soon see why." He came closer. "Remember, tense no muscle," he said, putting his hand on her thigh. "Let him carry you. He wants to carry you. He wants to take you without force."

He placed the reins in her hands and draped them loosely through her fingers. "You will barely need them," he said. "Let us begin."

The horse moved forward. The motion was fluid, purposeful.

"Imagine that you are floating on a river," Miguel was saying from the center of the ring.

She smiled, giving herself over to the feeling.

"Now, turn your shoulders to me."

She did.

"Look at me."

His eyes held hers, and the horse turned to him too. She felt as if the current of water had changed under her, and all was flowing to Miguel.

"Yes," he said.

She followed his instructions—merely turning her shoulders, shifting her weight ever so slightly left or right to have the horse respond and change the current of the flow. She was under a spell. She no longer knew what had hypnotized her—the rain, the horse, or the man. It was an experience she would never forget, and she knew that riding this horse or any horse would never be the same.

New York City

WALKING THROUGH THE LOBBY of the Stoneham Group headquarters, Patricia shivered slightly. She hated coming here to this building, so cold, so devoid of ornamentation—a cavernous space paved with hard gray slate, the walls covered with plates of stainless steel—a fitting monument to J. L.

Two guards flanked the elevators, and even though they greeted her effusively as they motioned her around the metal detector, she still felt as though she were passing a security check at the Pentagon.

She hoped this meeting with the trustees wouldn't be too long—afterward she would be meeting Miguel for lunch. She wanted to treat him to something special and had made a reservation at Le Cirque. He had come into town with her to renew his passport at the Portuguese consulate. He told her, somewhat cryptically, that he had expected to be back in Lisbon before it expired.

As she opened the door to the boardroom she braced herself. This was certainly not a cozy spot for a meeting, with tall narrow slits pretending to be windows and a twenty-five-foot-long glass table with two dozen over-stuffed chairs around it. The three trustees huddled at one end.

Mercifully, the pile of papers was not too high. In a half hour her duties were taken care of, and she got up to leave, but Horace Coleman's question stopped her dead.

"My dear—some disturbing rumors are going around. Is it true that you are planning to marry Dr. Keegan?" Coleman's white starched collar bit into the flesh of his chins, which hung so low they obliterated the knot of his tie.

Patricia, her face reddening, glanced at the three of them. Mrs. Sperber sat very erect, her hands in her lap; Ash seemed to be twitching nervously. "Uncle Horace—I've never known you to pay any attention to rumors."

"Ordinarily not, but you have shown an unusually strong interest in this young man."

"Well—if there is a wedding in my future you'll be the first to get an invitation." She tried to cover her embarrassment with a laugh.

Coleman looked up sharply, but then his features softened into a forced smile. "I'm afraid we'd need more notice than that—there are procedures to be followed."

"What procedures?"

Ash cleared his throat and came in on cue. "Your grandfather was very concerned that you not fall into the hands of an unscrupulous fortune hunter."

Patricia felt herself stiffen. "Dr. Keegan is not a fortune hunter, Mr. Ash."

"Bob!" Coleman shot a stern glance at Ash. "You're out of line." Then he turned to Patricia. "I'm sorry, my dear. We hate to interfere in your private life, but we have a mandate to uphold. Paragraph eight, subsection e of J. L.'s will requires us to assess the qualities and intentions of your future spouse."

"Are you saying that you object to Tom?"

Mrs. Sperber gave Patricia a benign smile. "I personally find Dr. Keegan beyond reproach." She opened a folder. "Graduate of the Harvard Medical School, the youngest recipient of the American Medal of Freedom, and—"

"And the largest recipient of funds from the Stoneham Charitable Foundation," interjected Coleman.

"Uncle Horace! A hospital is a very worthy cause."

"Of course, of course . . . calm down, Patricia." Coleman tried to placate her. "We just want you to think very carefully and not do something stupid."

Patricia stood up, bristling with emotion. "I am not stupid! I know the provisions of J. L.'s will as well as you do. Take a look at paragraph eight, subsection *f*."

After Patricia left, there was a dead silence in the boardroom.

"What did she mean—paragraph eight, subsection f?" asked Ash.

"That's the part that lets her tell us to go to hell when she gets married," Coleman sputtered, his face red with anger.

"Well," Mrs. Sperber said cheerily, closing her folder and getting up. "At last we will be free of this awesome responsibility. I must say—I find it difficult to place restrictions on such a lovely and well-meaning young lady. All's well that ends well."

"We need more than Shakespeare to help us now," Coleman snapped.

"But what can we do?" Ash asked, taking out a rubber ball, which he squeezed to strengthen his golf grip.

Coleman wheeled around and hit his pudgy hand against the table. "I helped build this empire. And she thanks me by throwing paragraph eight, subsection f in my face? This is what I get for my loyalty?!"

"We have all been quite adequately paid for our services," Mrs. Sperber said. "After Patricia marries, there is nothing more we can do." She smoothed out her skirt primly and picked up her briefcase. "Good day, gentlemen."

Coleman stared at the closed door.

"Well, Horace, she's right. We do get five million apiece at the dissolution of the board."

"Peanuts!" Coleman roared into Ash's face. He threw a manila folder across the table and rasped, "Look at that! Remember how hard I fought to shift the insecticide division to Mexico? Go ahead, look at it."

Ash dropped the ball and obediently opened the folder as Coleman roared on. "I increased the revenue of that operation by over seventy percent." He leaned across the table and growled: "This company is worth more than ten billion, Bob. *Ten billion*—that's money. And I made it worth that."

"But what can we do?"

"Plenty. I'm not gonna be kicked out on my ass."

As Sirio, the owner of Le Cirque, escorted her to her table, Patricia was still quivering from her encounter with the trustees—she was glad Miguel was not there yet. She ordered a double vodka with orange juice. Sirio's eyebrows shot up, but he said nothing.

By the time Miguel arrived, the liquor had relaxed her and she was feeling almost festive.

"Mademoiselle." He bowed in greeting. "I'm sorry to be late."

"You're not late . . . *Miguel*." It was the first time she had called him that.

He looked up, startled.

"Don't you think 'Mr. Cardiga' has been here long enough?"

The beginning of a smile formed on his lips as he nodded. "Yes, mademoiselle," and sat down.

"And I am not Mademoiselle," she continued. "My name is Patricia."

His smile widened. "Yes, Patrizia." He gave the *c* a *z* sound. She liked it.

"That's better." She laughed. "You're so charming—I hardly recognize you."

"*Como?*"

"Usually you're so gruff—except with horses—you're *always* gentle and patient with horses."

"That I learned from my father—he hates people and loves horses."

"But when I met him, he was so pleasant."

"I am sure he was, but he can be a son of a bitch."

"I find that hard to believe."

Miguel leaned over the table. "Let me tell you a story: Once, I rode his favorite horse—Amante, the one he loved above all others—without his permission. I was just a kid, but I was furious that I could not make Amante do what he could. I brought the whip down sharply on her flank. Amante, accustomed to my father's gentle handling, reared and I had to yank on the reins to regain control. That is when my father walked in. 'Get off that horse!' he ordered. I dismounted, and at first he ignored me totally. He rubbed Amante's nose, whispering in her ear, and called for one of the grooms to take the horse away. Then he turned to me. He ripped the whip from my hand and snapped it across my face."

"He whipped you?"

"He was out of breath when he finished. Then he said: 'A man has a choice, a horse does not.' "

"And this taught you to be gentle to horses?"

"It taught me to hate my father. I felt like an animal who could not fight back. But I realized for the first time what a horse might feel. I have never been cruel to a horse since.''

Patricia watched him quietly as he looked off in space. Then, his dark brooding eyes met the gray innocence of hers. ''Patrizia—treat a horse with kindness and affection, and he will obey you, serve you, and let you be the master.''

Patricia took the skin of a grape from the tip of her tongue and put it on her plate. A little smile was growing on her face.

''You find that funny?''

''I find that touching. I wish you'd treat me like a horse.''

He broke out into a warm laugh. ''But Patrizia, I can never be the master; you own the farm.''

She concealed her blushing face behind her wineglass.

''Darling!'' a loud voice interrupted. ''You *promised* to *call me* next time you came into town!''

Joanna Benson, her beehive hairdo bouncing up and down, wagged a ring-laden finger into her face.

''Oh Joanna! Ah . . . I . . .''

But Joanna's eyes were already riveted on Miguel.

''Oh, let me introduce you . . . ,'' Patricia managed.

Miguel stood up and bowed formally.

Joanna's eyes swept over him as if evaluating a piece of merchandise on display. ''Please, don't let me hold up your lunch. By the way, the vichyssoise is delicious,'' she purred as she moved to the doorway to join two other women who, like her, were overdressed and overmade-up, although Joanna stood alone in the overcoiffured category.

''A close friend?'' asked Miguel.

"Oh, not really. But she is lots of fun—has a great sense of humor."

Over Miguel's shoulder, Patricia could see Joanna at the doorway urgently beckoning to her. She excused herself, and went over.

"*Darling*—do you grow these hunks on the farm?" Joanna cornered her by the coat closet. "This one is even better looking than the doctor."

"No, no . . . ," Patricia stuttered. "You misunderstand. It's not like that . . ."

"All I want to know is—does this mean the handsome doctor is now available?"

"Oh no. Miguel is just my riding instructor. Tom will be here in a couple of weeks . . ."

"Rich men, poor men—bankers, thieves—lawyers, *doctors* . . ." She giggled. "I think you're right—there is nothing better than a good doctor to keep you healthy." She nudged Patricia. "If you know what I mean." With a suggestive wink, Joanna went off to join her friends, adding in a loud whisper, "Maybe *I* should take up riding."

Patricia was left standing by the coat closet totally unraveled. Joanna had brought out into the open what she had been concealing from herself all this time—her growing attachment to Miguel. Joanna could see it. Suddenly, she was overcome by guilt and remorse. She was having a good time playing with horses, while poor Tom slaved in Lebanon. She wasn't worthy of his love—she was shallow and cheap.

Tom would be here in a week's time. She would cancel all her riding lessons until then and avoid Miguel completely.

Chapter 7

Stone Ridge

PATRICIA GALLOPED SPORT through the snow toward the open meadow, keeping her eye on the approaching helicopter. She had arranged for the Stoneham pilot to pick up Tom at JFK Airport and bring him directly to the farm; she didn't want to spend another minute without him.

As the helicopter started its descent, stirring up a whirlpool of snowflakes, Sport shied and made a quick dive to the right, ready to bolt for the stable. "Hoa! Sportie, hoa!" What a dumb thing it was to ride the horse here. But her soft, calm voice managed to reassure the skittish animal long enough for the helicopter blades to stop turning.

By the time Tom's tanned face emerged, Sport was

perfectly calm, but now Patricia was nervous. She jumped down from the saddle and ran toward his out-stretched arms.

"Oh Tom—Tom—you're finally here."

He hugged her fiercely. "I'm sorry I couldn't get away for the holidays."

"It doesn't matter—you're here now."

"Well, Merry Christmas—" He kissed her. "And Happy New Year—" He kissed her again.

The chopper started up again, and they turned around to see Sport trotting off on his way back to the stable. They both burst out laughing.

Patricia took Tom by the arm and shouted above the roar, "Come on, let's get you settled."

They walked through the deep snow to the guest-house, which she had fixed up that morning with bunches of holly, and freshly scented soap. Now Patricia wished that she had not converted the extra room on the second floor of the main house into a study—it had a connecting door to her bedroom.

At the guesthouse, they stomped their boots to dis-lodge the snow. "You can't imagine how much I've missed snow," Tom was saying. Then he stopped to look at her. "And how I missed you." He reached over to brush some snowflakes from her hair. His hand lingered on her cheek. "You're so much more beautiful than you were in my dreams in Lebanon." He kissed her lips gently.

Patricia couldn't hear Taxi barking, her heart was beating so loudly.

"Now Patricia, give me a few minutes to change my clothes and start looking like a farmhand."

Dressed in a red parka, Tom couldn't have looked less like a farmhand sitting next to Dennis on a bench in the indoor arena watching a very proud Patricia take Ultimato through his paces. She felt relaxed and confident as she executed a series of flawless pirouettes and figure eights. Out of the corner of her eye, she could see Miguel leaning against the wall with an enigmatic expression on his face.

"I'm so impressed," said Tom when she finished and rode over to him.

Patricia blushed. "Thank you."

"You make it look so easy—I think I might get up on a horse again—"

"Why don't you?"

"Well . . ."

"Please, Tom—the trails are so beautiful in the snow."

"You've sold me—but I can't ride on one of your postage stamp saddles. I need a horn to hang on to."

Dennis broke in with a laugh. "A cowboy saddle— that's my style, too."

"Dennis—quick! While Dr. Keegan's in the mood— saddle up a horse for him."

"Will do! And how about you, Miss D.? Will you ride Ultimato or shall I saddle up Sport for you?"

"No—you two cowboys check out the trails on your own. I'll check out dinner."

"Let's go," said Tom, jumping off the fence, "before I lose my nerve."

"Put Dr. Keegan on Petunia," Patricia directed Dennis.

"Petunia?" Tom exclaimed. "Sounds like the old gray mare that ain't what she used to be."

"After all the dangers of Lebanon, we want you to be safe on the farm."

Patricia watched the two of them walking off to the stable. She wanted every moment here to be memorable for Tom, and she was thrilled that he had decided to take up riding again—it would be another thing they could share together. "Don't be too long," she called out. "Concha is fixing something special. We eat in two hours."

She dismounted Ultimato and walked over to Miguel, who had not changed his position.

"Miguel, would you break a long-standing tradition of eating alone and join me—join us—for a meal?"

"No thank you," he said, turning away from her to take the reins.

"I'm sorry I haven't had time for lessons this week, but I had so many preparations—"

"I understand."

"Well, if you change your mind about dinner, please let me know."

He didn't respond.

Leaving the indoor arena, she caught sight of some of the farmhands building a snowman bearing an astonishing resemblance to Edgar. She giggled at the exaggerated pot belly. They sure were having fun. Everybody was happy.

Back in the stable, putting away Ultimato, Miguel watched Tom and Dennis as they rode off laughing toward the white-covered hills. So this is the famous doctor who devotes his life to helping underprivileged people in far-off countries. What a noble thing to do. Too fucking noble! Could he really be the male Mother Teresa?

Miguel decided he would change his mind—he would accept the invitation to dinner.

Carefully, Patricia arranged the tortilla chips and fresh vegetables around the guacamole. It sure looked good. She dipped her finger in the bowl and licked it. "Concha—*muy caliente!* Too spicy!"

"No, no, Miss D.—*perfecto*."

Seeing Tom and Dennis ride past the kitchen window, Patricia flung open the door. "How was it?" she called out.

Tom pulled up and dismounted, stretching his legs in mock agony. "Terrific!"

"He's not as rusty as he claims, Miss D.," Dennis said as he tied up Petunia behind his horse for the short ride back to the stable.

Tom came into the kitchen. "Dennis was very patient with me. He gave me some great tips for staying in the saddle."

"He's an excellent rider."

"I invited him to join us for dinner. I hope you don't mind, darling."

"Of course not. Miguel's coming too. And believe me, Concha's cooked enough for an army."

"Anything I can do to help?"

"Sure, taste this—" She pushed the bowl of guacamole toward him. "Too hot, don't you think?"

He dipped the spoon in and licked it off. "Nope—perfect."

Concha beamed smugly, and Patricia sighed. "You two are ganging up on me." She grabbed a pile of plates and playfully thrust them into Tom's hands. "Here—make yourself useful."

The dinner went smoothly and conversation was flowing.

The only one not saying much was Miguel; withdrawn like a turtle in a shell, he nursed his glass of wine.

Patricia groped for some topic that might bring him out. "Why did you become a bullfighter?" she finally asked.

"Because I could never be the rider that my father was."

"How can you say that?"

"Have you ever seen my father ride?"

"Yes, but—"

"Well, then you know—he is the best in the world."

Dennis and Tom were talking quietly at the other end of the table.

Miguel continued, "I remember, as a child, hearing thousands cheer as my father entered the ring on horseback. To me, he seemed like someone descending from heaven. A giant man on a giant steed. When I grew up, the dream never left me that one day the public would admire my skills the way they admired his. I almost succeeded."

"Almost? But—" Patricia felt Tom's hand on her shoulder and didn't finish.

"Darling! What is Mr. Cardiga saying that is so fascinating?"

"Oh—he was telling me about his father . . . he considers him the greatest rider in the world."

"I think Mr. Cardiga does extremely well himself . . . in spite of his handicap."

Patricia could see Miguel stiffen. "Let's all have coffee in the other room," she said cheerily.

"Last week, just before I left Beirut," Tom was saying as Patricia poured espresso into demitasse cups, "I saw a young boy, no more than nine"—and he addressed himself to Miguel—"who had *both* his legs amputated, and above the knee—"

"Oh, how awful," said Patricia, sitting down on the floor by his chair. Everyone was listening intently.

"It happens every day, darling." And he turned back to Miguel. "We had attached two artificial limbs to his thighs—primitive—but you should see that spunky little fellow . . . He was stumbling, falling as he tried to walk, and *laughing*. Would you believe it?"

Miguel just sat there, impassively listening.

"To him, it was a game. He had no awareness of what being a cripple would mean to the rest of his life."

Tom leaned back and stroked Patricia's hair. "But thanks to this young lady we will supply him with modern prostheses. In a short time, he will be able to walk, jump, run. You see . . . ," he said, getting up and approaching Miguel. "May I?" And without waiting for a reply, he lifted up the pant leg covering Miguel's artificial limb.

Patricia was stunned. She would have never guessed. How did Tom know?

"This prosthesis is old-fashioned . . ." Tom was pointing to the ugly mass of wood and rubber. "Too heavy." He felt the ankle joint. "No bounce, no flexibility. You ought to see Dr. Burgess in Seattle. He invented a new prosthesis for athletes."

"I manage quite well, thank you," said Miguel, pulling down his pant leg.

"But you could have much more mobility with less stress." He turned to Patricia. "Darling, where are those pamphlets I brought with me?"

Without a word, she pointed to the table in the corner. Tom went over and riffled through the papers. "Read this." And he handed Miguel a color brochure. "You'll be convinced. The Seattle Foot really works."

Miguel took the pamphlet, but Patricia saw that his jaw was clenched. She winced—why is Tom going on about this? Her thoughts scrambled, searching for a way to change the subject. "More coffee, Miguel?" she blurted out.

Miguel got up and smiled tightly. "I thank you for your medical opinion, Doctor—a most educational evening. And Patrizia, thank you for a wonderful meal. Dennis, I'll see you at the barn early." And he left the room.

Dennis jumped up. "Well, I better be going, too . . . and I certainly appreciate being invited."

Tom followed him to the door. "Thanks for your riding tips today."

Dennis mumbled something in return, but Patricia

didn't hear it; she was looking out the window at Miguel. He was shuffling more awkwardly than usual through the snow.

She turned to Tom. "How could you?"

"What do you mean, darling?"

"You humiliated him."

"Who?"

"Miguel."

"I did?"

"None of us knew that he didn't have a leg."

"But darling, it was obvious. I was trying to help him. That's why I gave him that brochure—an athlete like him could function normally—"

"But he's very proud."

Tom shook his head and sighed. "I guess you're right. But you see, darling, for so many years, in order to function as a doctor, I had to cut off my personal feelings. I think I must be losing my compassion for people." He moved toward the door. "I'll go over and apologize to him now."

"No, no—it's best to leave it alone."

He stopped. "Yeah, I suppose . . ." He poured himself another cup of coffee, deep in thought.

"I know you didn't mean it."

"But it's no excuse. That's what frightens me."

"What, Tom?"

"Too much horror, pain, and misery changes a man. It anesthetizes you to the suffering of others."

She watched him sympathetically as he slumped on the sofa.

"I'm burned out. It's time for me to leave."

"Leave Lebanon?"

"Yes, before it's too late."

He seemed dejected; she didn't know what to say.

He continued, "The children's wing will be rebuilt by next year. Thanks to you, the Keegan Foundation is on its feet. Others, fresher and stronger than I, should take over."

"Oh Tom, I'm glad—you've done more than your share. But what will you do?"

"Maybe I could become a country doctor around here." He smiled. "You could get me a little horse and buggy to make my rounds, huh?"

"I'll even drive the buggy." She giggled.

"But seriously, Patricia—I have been offered a very good job at the Lenox Hill Hospital on Park Avenue. I've decided to take it. I want to come back home—to you."

"Oh Tom." Patricia put her arms around his neck and kissed him.

He hugged her tightly and pulled her down beside him. "I want to talk to you."

Her heart beat rapidly in anticipation of what he was about to say. He reached in the pocket of his cardigan and took out a little ring. He held it up. She looked at it glistening in the lamplight. It was made of tiny silver beads joined together.

"This Moslem ring was given to me by a mother for saving her child's life. In the Arab world, a circle is perfection. It has no beginning—it has no end. It is continuous. That's what I want my life with you to be. Will you wear it?" And he took her hand and placed the ring on her finger. "Look, Patricia—it fits perfectly."

Tears were forming in her eyes. She put her head on

his shoulder. "Tom—how can I tell you how I feel . . . how much you . . ."

"Don't try. Together—we can make a great life."

"Oh yes, yes, Tom, I want that very much."

He kissed her tenderly on the forehead.

Miguel slammed the door behind him and tossed Tom's brochure in the wastepaper basket. *Who the hell is he to tell me how to be a better cripple!* He sat on the bed and unstrapped his prosthesis.

Tonight was the first time since he lost his leg that he had felt deliberately humiliated. Usually, people were too solicitous, but Tom Keegan intended to be cruel. That son of a bitch! He looked at the artificial limb in his hand and with disgust hurled it across the room.

Smoldering with rage, he threw himself down on the bed. The sight of Keegan's hand on Patricia's golden hair wouldn't leave his mind.

By morning the temperature had dropped considerably and everything was frozen solid. When Tom and Dennis set out for a ride again, Patricia cautioned them not to take any icy trails. Now she watched apprehensively as they disappeared into the trees; she wanted to make certain nothing would mar Tom's enjoyment of his visit.

The telephone interrupted her thoughts. Patricia picked it up. A highly accented woman's voice came on the line: "I would like very much to speak with Senhor Cardiga, please."

"Just one moment," Patricia said, and pressed Miguel's intercom button. She buzzed several times, but there was no reply. "I'm sorry—he doesn't answer. May I tell him who phoned?"

"Yes. Isabel Veloso. It is important."

Patricia wrote the name down on a slip of paper. This must be the woman Concha said had called Miguel numerous times. The woman sounded aristocratic—was she related to Miguel? She decided to walk over and leave the message under his door.

Miguel was sitting on the bench encircling the old apple tree in front of his cottage. Why was he out there—wasn't he cold? His shoulders slumped, his head resting on his chest, he looked very different from the haughty man riding Ultimato. He was so absorbed in his thoughts he didn't hear her approach.

"Miguel!"

He raised his head.

"Someone just called you from Portugal." She handed him the slip of paper.

He barely glanced at it as he rose to his feet. "Thank you, Patrizia."

"And I wanted to tell you . . . ah . . . that I'm very happy . . ."

"Oh?"

"Tom and I have just become engaged."

"Engaged?" he asked, not understanding.

"Yes, we're going to be married."

"Aah—*noivado*." But he didn't return her smile. "My congratulations . . . but then we should both be congratulated."

"Both?"

"Yes—I am . . . as you say . . . engaged too." And he held up the message.

"Well then, my congratulations to you and Miss Veloso."

"Thank you."

"When will you be getting married?" she asked.

"As soon as I return home."

Something about his steady gaze made Patricia uncomfortable, but just then she caught sight of Tom and Dennis coming back.

Miguel watched her graceful movements as she ran toward them. He crushed the slip of paper in his fist. *Marry Isabel? I'd rather die.*

Patricia wanted Tom's last night to be an extra-special one. She had Edgar drive Concha into town to see a movie so that she and Tom could have dinner alone at the farmhouse. She baked a loaf of bread, made a soufflé with eggs she collected that morning from the chicken coop, and picked fresh herbs from the greenhouse for a vegetable stew—her own recipe. Tom ate it with gusto, but Patricia found that she couldn't enjoy the dinner; a melancholy feeling had overtaken her. She toyed with her spoon, trying to push out of her mind the thought that he would be leaving tomorrow.

Tom stopped eating, put his spoon down, and reached over and took her hand. He touched the ring he had given her, then his eyes went up to her face with a smile. "Come on Patricia, cheer up—I'll be back in a little while—to stay."

"Take me with you to Beirut."

He squeezed her hand. "I can't expose you to such danger."

"I wouldn't be afraid," she said, her small voice childlike. "I'd be with you."

He cupped her face in his hands and said very softly, "When I get back, Patricia, we'll talk about spending the rest of our lives together."

The feeling of his good-night kiss still on her lips, Patricia stood at the bathroom sink washing her hands. She did not dare take off the ring he had given her, for fear it might fall down the drain. The ring reassured her—it joined them together even though he was going away.

She dried her hands and watched the tiny silver beads glisten in the light. The ring was beautiful. She twisted it around her finger, lost in thought. She felt sad and restless. Tomorrow he would be gone. But why didn't he spend the night with her?

She moved over to the full-length mirror and let her robe drop to the floor. She looked at the reflection of her sinewy body. She let her hands glide down her firm breasts and flat tummy and linger on the moistness between her legs.

Tom shouldn't sleep alone in the guesthouse tonight, his last night here. She wanted him. And he wanted her, she knew it. They had waited too long.

She picked up her robe and hurried down the stairs in her bare feet. She hesitated in the doorway as the frosty air hit her and then ran down the snowy path to the guesthouse. The crust of ice on the surface made the soles of her feet tingle, but her body was burning. She could feel her heart pounding as she reached his door.

She was about to turn the knob when she heard a voice from inside: "Come on Tom, I'm waiting."

Dennis? What was he doing here?

"I'll be right out." Tom's voice came from the bathroom.

Patricia stood bewildered at the door.

"What took you so long at the house?" It was Dennis again.

"Hey—I needed time to say good night to the girl I'm going to marry."

They both laughed.

Patricia retreated as if the doorknob were on fire.

Backing away, she could see through the window the silhouettes of the two of them. Tom was approaching Dennis. He reached out for him, their bodies interlocking in a tight embrace.

She was stunned, paralyzed, unable to move.

Then she saw Tom's mouth descend on Dennis's in a passionate kiss.

"Oh my God," she gasped. "No."

Her head was swimming; a surge of nausea rose up inside of her. She felt a sharp pain in her stomach and doubled over. Barely able to force her quivering legs to move, she staggered away to the shelter of a big fir tree. Holding on to the trunk, she vomited into the snow.

"At *four* in the morning?"

"Please!"

"What is it?"

"I need you, Laura."

"Of course, of course. I'll be right there."

Finally, the crying exhausted Patricia. She felt numb as she scribbled a note to Tom: *"I don't want to see you again. I saw enough last night."* She put it in an envelope together with the silver ring. Concha could give it to him after she was gone. She threw some clothes in a bag and wrote a letter of instruction to Edgar—she could count on him.

Drained, she looked out the window, waiting for Laura. Miguel was exercising Ultimato in the snow-covered ring. Even in the cold, he preferred the outdoors to the heated riding arena. She felt calmer watching his graceful controlled movements, and her finger involuntarily traced the same pattern on the windowpane that the horse's hooves were making in the snow. She had an urge to mount Harpalo and join him, and pretend that all that had happened was a bad dream.

Just then, she heard the wheels of a car crunching over the icy gravel. It was Laura's station wagon pulling up. Laura looked a sight—her hair was hanging in scraggly strands, and she was wearing a torn pair of overalls and a stained peacoat. She looked at Patricia's face and threw her plump arms around her. "Kiddo, whatever it is—it'll be all right . . . it'll be all right."

Patricia's body shook uncontrollably and she began sobbing again.

Laura tried to calm her down, but she was still inconsolable as they drove to Stewart Airport where the Stoneham 727 had arrived and was waiting.

"At least, tell me where you're running off to."

"Switzerland."

"Why?"

"I must see Dr. Solomon."

"Kiddo," Laura said with a sigh. "You do what's best for you."

"Oh God . . . I hope the farm . . ."

"Don't worry. I'll watch over everything."

Patricia looked at her gratefully through puffy eyes. "Oh, thank you, Laura . . ." She gave her friend a quick hug and scrambled up the plane's steps. At the door she called out above the whine of the engines, "Tell Miguel I'll phone and explain."

The plane roared down the runway and swooped up over the hills like a large hawk. Laura, with her hands over her ears, watched it disappear into the early morning sky. She got back into her battered station wagon, glanced into the rearview mirror, and grimaced. With one swift motion, she wound the dirty strands of hair into a sloppy bun. She opened the glove compartment, removed a pint of scotch, and took a big swig. "Ahh." She let out a contented sigh and put the car in gear.

At 4:00 A.M. Miguel was putting Ultimato through his paces, but it wasn't going well. The horse was not responding as smoothly as usual, and Miguel was irritated with himself. He knew it wasn't Ultimato's fault—it was his.

Then he saw the light come on in Patricia's bedroom

and for a moment he thought he saw her silhouette at the window—maybe she was watching . . . maybe she would come to talk with him.

His mind went back to the first night he rode in this ring when Patricia came down in her nightgown. He remembered her soft moist lips and the firmness of her breasts as he pressed against her. He couldn't stand the thought of that arrogant doctor holding her in his arms, lying close to her in bed after a night of lovemaking.

He jumped off Ultimato's back and hit the frozen ground with more force that he had intended—his knee-cap jamming against the prosthesis hurt like hell.

He was leading Ultimato to the stable when he was startled to see Laura Simpson's station wagon pull up the driveway. What the hell—at this hour? He rubbed the horse down and put him away, looking up at the house from time to time. Closing the stable door, he saw Patricia walk out with a suitcase and drive off with Laura. Where was the doctor? Something was very wrong. He had a sudden premonition that someone had died. Patricia was always haunted by the thought that those close to her would die.

He went back to his cottage and threw himself on the bed fully clothed. He tried to doze, but couldn't. Then, just as it was getting light, he heard a car drive past. He lifted himself on his elbows and looked out the window. A limousine was waiting in front of the guesthouse. Dr. Keegan hurried out with his bag and drove off. What was happening? Patricia leaves with Laura in the middle of the night—now the doctor takes off.

He strapped on his prosthesis and headed out to the feed barn in search of Edgar. He found the foreman

there, leaning against a stack of hay bales, reading
something. As Miguel came in, he quickly put the paper
in his pocket.

"Where is everybody?" Miguel asked, but Edgar
only mumbled something unintelligible and shuffled off.

That afternoon—another surprise. Dennis had packed
up his bags and left the farm. Perturbed, Miguel cornered Edgar again. "What the hell is going on?"

"Good riddance to bad rubbish, I say," Edgar
scoffed.

"Who'll take care of my horses?"

"I'm in charge of that, Mr. Cardiga. Nothing's gonna
change. Not to worry."

But Miguel was worried, very worried. Laura would
know what had happened, but she hadn't come back.
Even though it was late in the afternoon, Misty was still
waiting expectantly for his carrot, his head hanging over
the paddock fence.

Miguel had to find out. Quickly, he made his way to
the house and knocked at the kitchen door. Concha
opened it—her eyes red from crying.

"What happened, Concha?"

"Oh I don't know, I don't know."

"Where is Miss Patrizia?"

"Switzerland."

"What! Switzerland? Why?"

"I don't know. She cry all the time." Concha turned
away, trying to hide her own tears.

"So when is she coming back?"

"I don't know . . . I don't know."

Dumbfounded, Miguel limped away. His prothesis
was irritating his stump, weighing heavily from his

knee. He hobbled back to the stable. He stroked Ultimato's muzzle, and felt a sudden deep ache as he thought of the pleasure of riding with Patricia, side by side.

Each day he had looked forward more and more to the time he spent with her. She had an amazing talent—an unusual feeling for horses. He couldn't resist looking toward the house, expecting her any minute to come bouncing across the snow, dressed to ride. But she never came.

He saddled Ultimato and slowly rode past the old horses, past the graveyard, and came around the insectary, circling the farm from the other side. He traced the path that they had often taken together. It was lonely without her.

New York City

HORACE COLEMAN, his glasses perched on his bulbous nose, sat at his desk signing documents. Bob Ash was also working—practicing the forward movement of his left hip on the down swing of his golf club.

"God damn it, Bob—will you stop that."

"Sorry Horace, but I lost fifty bucks at the country club yesterday. I gotta practice."

"You'll lose a hell of a lot more if we don't find some way to stop this marriage."

"What did Ted find out?"

Coleman glanced at his watch. "He should be here any minute."

"I like Ted, but—," Ash started.

"But what?" Coleman barked. "He's a team player."

"Well . . . don't you think his background . . . ah . . ."

Coleman took off his glasses. "Go on."

"Geez—he did serve a couple years in a federal pen."

"Let's get this straight, Bob—"

Ash was already squirming.

"Ted Rosemont was a close friend of J. L. Stoneham."

"I know."

"And he's Patricia's godfather."

"I know."

"Those two factors qualify him to replace Sperber on this board."

"I'm all for it, Horace. It's just . . ."

"It's just nothing! Ted was trying to rescue his savings and loan. He was protecting his stockholders and depositors. It's not his fault the junk bond market fell apart."

"All right, all right, Horace."

"Would you rather have Sperber bucking us at every step, huh?"

"Heaven forbid." It always made Ash uneasy to see Coleman upset. "How'd you get rid of her so quickly?"

"She was delighted to get back to London to manage the British holdings."

Just then, Ted Rosemont came in. His artificially tanned face wore a grimace; his teeth, like blocks of chalk, were clenched together. He slumped into a chair opposite Coleman.

Ash shot an anxious glance at Coleman's face, who stared impassively at Rosemont. "Well, let's hear it."

"I got nothing. My friend at the CIA says he needs a couple of weeks to check him out . . . How much time do we have?"

"She might have eloped already," Coleman grumbled.

"Yeah Ted, you might be out of a job before you begin." Ash laughed feebly at his own joke.

"Knock it off, Bob," Coleman snapped. "We've got to figure out what to do."

Rosemont jumped up. "I know—garbage!"

"That's a good idea," Ash nodded.

Coleman wrinkled his nose. "Garbage? What the hell are you talking about?"

"Yeah, Ted—explain what you mean," Ash immediately corrected himself.

"Sift the garbage that comes out of her house."

"To find *what*?" Coleman's look cut him down.

Rosemont was saved from answering by a sudden commotion at the door. The secretary was attempting to block someone from coming in. "Please! Let me announce you."

"That's all right, Miss Kelly," said Coleman, and the secretary scurried out.

Rosemont's jaw dropped open at the sight of a disheveled woman in overalls who marched right in, a cigarette hanging out of her mouth. He shot a questioning glance at Ash, who mumbled under his breath, "Speaking of garbage . . ."

"So good to see you, Miss Simpson," Coleman was saying. "Come in."

"I am in," said Laura.

"Of course you know Mr. Ash, and this is our new board member, Mr. Rosemont." Coleman nodded at Ted, who was still taking her in. "Laura's our baby-sitter—she's done a great job looking after Patricia."

"Yes, she has, and she deserves a raise," Laura said.

"And is that why you're looking like a bag lady—pathos manipulation?" Coleman smirked.

"I didn't have time to get dressed." Laura was indignant. "I rushed here with good news."

"The wedding's postponed?" Ash asked hopefully.

"There will be no wedding." Laura looked around with satisfaction at their startled faces.

"Are you sure?" Coleman asked.

"Do you think she would marry a man she found naked embracing a farmhand?"

"What?!" they asked in unison.

"You heard me—she caught the two of them. He's gay."

"Oh my God," said Coleman, a slow smile creeping across his face.

"That must have been a blow to her," Ash said.

"No kidding," Laura said scornfully. "Right now, she's heading for Switzerland."

"Back to the sanitorium?"

"That's right, Mr. Ash."

"How sad. Her third nervous breakdown." All eyes turned to Coleman, who leaned back in his chair resting his head on his folded hands.

"Well, that psychiatrist will piece her back together again—he's done it before," Ash said.

"Yes. And she'll come back ready to get married to some other yo-yo," Coleman retorted.

"That's true," Ash nodded.

Coleman wagged his chubby finger. "Let's not forget, gentleman, that in four years, she can kick us out—husband or no husband."

"That would be a disaster," Ash piped up.

"That's an understatement," Rosemont chimed in. "What do you suggest, Horace?"

"We have to help that poor girl before it's too late. Laura, you must—"

"Just a minute—*I* need some help first."

"You'll get your raise," Coleman said patronizingly.

"And I need a vacation—now. I'm getting flat feet dragging that old nag around every day."

Coleman shook his head. "You can't leave now."

"Yes, I can!"

"How will it look when she comes back and finds you've ignored your beloved pet?"

Laura fixed her eyes on Coleman. "How big is that raise?"

"Name your price."

"Depends on what you want."

Coleman placed his hands together as if in prayer. "Laura—you're the closest person to a very troubled girl. When she comes back, she might think she's cured again—it will take a *special* friend to make her see she's not thinking straight, to make her realize how sick she still is."

"Just how sick do you want her to be?"

Coleman's narrowed eyes pierced Laura's. "Mentally incompetent," he said softly.

Chapter 9

Over the Atlantic

PATRICIA STARED OUT of the plane window at the ocean below. Her puffy eyes were dry. She had no more tears, but the thought of sleep was impossible. Sounds and images kept moving in and out of her mind . . . a piano playing . . . slender masculine fingers on the keyboard . . . *"night and day, you are the one"* . . . naked embracing forms . . . Moments before, he was holding her in his arms. How could he?

She was so blind, naive, seeing only a white knight charging over the moat into her castle of dreams. Waves of self-pity and anger swept over her. She felt like a piece of driftwood, lost again. She got up and paced the cabin, forcing herself to think of other things. Thank

God for Laura. She could count on her to take over while she was gone.

She glanced at the monitor—a red blip was now moving across the map of the Atlantic Ocean inching its way toward Europe, the digital clock ticking off the minutes—two more hours till landing.

This had been J. L.'s personal plane. More lavishly appointed than any of the fleet belonging to the corporation, it was kept, as per J. L.'s will, for her sole use, but she freely lent it to the trustees—in fact, Bob Ash had come to see it as his private ferry to the nation's golf games. She never used it herself—partly because she never went anywhere, but also because it reminded her all too poignantly of the trappings of wealth that J. L. had exploited to drive a wedge between her and her father. It wasn't until both her parents were dead that Patricia realized how J. L. had manipulated her, how much time and happiness with Daddy he had stolen from her. She had wished him dead—she told him so— and her wish came true—all too soon. Questions came tumbling in her mind, one after another. Was she responsible for his death? Was Tom her punishment for what she had done? How much more would she have to bear? Wasn't the burden of J. L.'s money punishment enough?

She winced at the irony.

"With money, life is awfully simple," Joanna Benson once told her. "Without it, it's simply awful." Well, she was proof that life could be simply awful with money. She had been so lonely, so lost with all her billions—until Tom. And now the dream of a life with him, doing something worthwhile, was crushed forever.

Patricia glanced at the monitor again—the blip was just passing over Ireland, arrival time in forty minutes. Better get ready.

She rang for the stewardess. "Where did you put my bag?"

"In the bedroom cabin, ma'am."

"Oh . . ." She took a deep breath and opened the door to what had been J. L.'s suite. In two years, she had never set foot in here. She looked at the bed where he had his fatal heart attack. Hesitantly, she walked into the dressing room.

From the marble shelf by the sink, it seemed to glare at her—a large crystal flask containing a yellowish liquid. J. L.'s cologne. She came closer. She couldn't help herself—carefully, she lifted the stopper. A pungent odor that she knew so well hit her. The smell of death. She corked the flask quickly and ran out.

Stone Ridge

EVERYBODY ON THE FARM went about their chores as if nothing had happened, but a general gloom pervaded. Miguel moved about in a trance. So many questions and no answers. Where was Patricia? Why had Laura not been back to check on her horse for two days? Misty looked so forlorn—he seemed to feel the gloom too. Miguel stroked the horse's forehead and fed him a carrot.

Then he heard Concha: "Señor Miguel . . . Señor Miguel . . . telephone," she was yelling from the kitchen.

It had to be Patricia.

"I'll take it in my cottage."

He was annoyed that he couldn't move faster, but a blister had developed on his stump and it hurt like hell to walk. He limped as quickly as he could, each jarring step excruciatingly painful.

"*Hallo?*"

A woman's voice said, "Mr. Cardiga?"

"Yes, who—"

"The doctor will be right with you . . ."

"The doctor?!" But she had already put him on hold. What the hell was Keegan calling him about?

"This is Dr. Burgess." A pleasant gravelly voice came on the line.

"Burgess?"

"Didn't Dr. Keegan tell you about me?"

"I am sorry, I do not recall . . ." And in that same instant his eyes spotted the brochure sticking out of the wastepaper basket. "Oh yes! Yes, he did!"

"I just wanted you to know, Mr. Cardiga, that your case interests me very much."

"It does?"

"Yes, I have outfitted the Seattle Foot for boxers, mountain climbers, basketball players . . . but I need a bullfighter to round out my collection." His throaty laugh reverberated in Miguel's ears.

Standing there with the phone in one hand, Miguel picked up the rumpled brochure. "NATURAL SPRING . . . DYNAMIC ACTION . . ." leapt out at him from the cover.

"Hello! Hello! Are you there, Mr. Cardiga?"

"Yes, yes . . . let me think about it."

"Well, if you ever decide, I'll be glad to see you. By what Dr. Keegan tells me, it shouldn't take long to put a bounce in your step."

Lausanne

THE WIND WAS WHIPPING down into the valley, and Dr. Solomon pulled his woolen cap tighter over his head, but tufts of strawberry blond hair still stuck out at the sides. "I'm not sure you should have made this trip, Patricia, but I must confess I missed you," he said, helping her out of the car.

"Thank you for seeing me on such short notice."

He squinted at her through his thick glasses. "I decided not to put you in the main hospital—you'll be more comfortable in one of our bungalows." He led the way to a small A-frame chalet with a tiny sitting room overlooking the snowcapped mountaintops glazed by the setting sun. A thermos of hot chocolate was on the table. "Sit down and tell me all about it," he invited.

She managed to tell the story without breaking down, though sometimes her voice quavered.

Doctor Solomon took off his glasses and wiped them with his tie. "Losing one's first love is always a crushing experience."

"You make it sound so commonplace."

He only smiled.

"But I've been destroyed!"

"Not at all, Patricia. You're far too strong for that—stronger than you realize."

"When I saw Tom with . . . oh God . . . I couldn't bear it."

"Patricia—" He paused and tugged on his scraggly beard. "Are you sure you loved him?"

"Of course I did."

"Isn't it possible that you were *using* Tom?"

"Using him? Of course not!"

"I mean . . . using him to remove the burden of your grandfather's wealth . . ."

"But that's why I loved him—we both wanted to do something good with that money."

"And you felt that he could give meaning and direction to your life?"

"Yes. I even wanted to go with him to Lebanon."

"And escape the responsibilities of the corporation?"

Patricia hesitated. "Well . . . that might have been part of it, I guess—subconsciously."

The doctor smiled. "Now you're beginning to sound like the psychiatrist."

She dropped her head.

"Patricia, suppose you had seen him in the arms of a woman?"

"What do you mean?"

"Did you feel worse because it was a man?"

"It was such a shock."

"Why?"

"To be attracted to a homosexual—it made me feel so foolish."

"Foolish? That's not so tragic." Dr. Solomon patted her hand. "Think about it, Patricia—ask yourself if your attraction for Tom wasn't self-manufactured."

"What do you mean?"

"You *wanted* to be in love with him—but were you really?"

"Oh, Doctor—I am so confused."

He stood up. "Get some rest. We'll talk about it some more tomorrow."

"But I need you *now*," Patricia said desperately. "Why are you leaving?"

"I have some patients with serious problems waiting for me."

"I expected you to help me . . . I'm sorry I came."

"You'll get over that, too—until tomorrow, okay?"

"Okay," she said meekly.

Through the window, she watched his galoshes trudging through the snow toward the main building. She felt more foolish than ever.

Seattle

"NOW HERE'S A MOUNTAIN CLIMBER, and see that— both of his legs have been amputated."

Miguel looked in awe at the slide projected on the screen in front of him: a smiling man ascending a sheer wall on two artificial limbs.

Dr. Burgess, a short, ruddy man, chuckled. "He asked me to make his legs two inches longer. Helps him in competition."

The next slide was a black athlete jumping high into the air with a basketball. "That's Bill Demby," the doctor said. "He was just here yesterday. Great guy— lost both his legs in Vietnam. Went through a hell of a period. Became an alcoholic because he thought he could never be an athlete again. Now look at him . . . look at the elevation. That's the dynamic action the Seattle Foot can give you—and it looks like a real foot with veins and nails." He clicked off the projector, and sat down next to Miguel. "But the miracle is not the cosmetic exterior, it's the space-age plastic in the heel, which—when compressed—stores energy and then releases it so you have spring in each step."

By the end of the afternoon with Dr. Burgess, Miguel was exhausted. He had undergone every examination imaginable—muscle tests, stress tests, measurements . . .

Dr. Burgess made a mold of the small stump jutting out from his left knee. "You're the easiest case I've ever had. This four-inch piece of muscle and bone will give you lateral movement as well." The mold set, he stepped back. "With your muscular structure you'll never need that tight harness around your thigh. I'll show you a prosthesis they made during the Civil War—not much different from the old-fashioned thing you've been wearing."

When Miguel got dressed, Dr. Burgess walked him out to the waiting taxi. "My lab will be working on your prosthesis tomorrow—you'll have it by the end of the week. Can't get faster service in a supermarket."

"I really appreciate this."

"Oh by the way," said the doctor through the taxi window, "you free tonight?"

"All I am doing is waiting for a leg."

"You like boxing?"

"I do."

"Meet me here at eight. We'll go to the Kingdome. A friend of mine is fighting in the main event."

The atmosphere of the boxing arena reminded Miguel of a bullring. The air was filled with smoke and raucous voices. Dr. Burgess nudged Miguel. "There he is now—Craig Bodzianowski."

Miguel watched a great lumbering giant bounce up into the ring, wrapped in a robe with a towel covering his head.

"Look at his right foot. The high-topped sock covers the attachment that I made for him."

Here was a one-legged man, facing an opponent— an equally muscular behemoth—without any physical handicap.

When the bell sounded and the fight began, Miguel's eyes were glued to the right leg of the doctor's friend. The leg moved around the ring, without stiffness or limping, as the boxer fought on, round after round, taking punches and giving out a hell of a lot more.

Suddenly, the roaring crowd went wild. Miguel had missed the punch with which Craig knocked the other boxer to the canvas. He only saw the right leg bounding in exhilaration.

When he returned to his hotel later that night, Miguel couldn't sleep. The images from the day were flashing through his mind—people with no legs achieving miracles . . . a man with one foot knocking out a man with two.

He looked at the clock. He didn't care what time it was in Portugal—he had to talk with his best friend.

"It's the crack of dawn," Emilio yawned. "I just got in and I'm ready for bed . . . alone, God damn it."

"I'm in Seattle . . . and . . ."

"Seattle? What are you doing there?"

"I'm getting a new leg."

"What? Are you drunk too?"

"Not at all. You'll see when I get back."

"Great! Come home and I'll line up a good-looking girl for you."

"Emilio—right now I'm through with women—just line me up a good-looking bull."

Lausanne

IT WAS A BRIGHT, sunny morning and, as had been her habit for the past three weeks, Patricia took a long walk through the carefully shoveled paths of the sanitorium. She looked at the patients strolling in the fenced-in yards of the various wards, many escorted by white-clad nurses, others walking alone. She passed close to a young woman kneeling in the snow, burrowing into it with her bare hands. What was this girl searching for? What had she lost?

Patricia thought of Tom—the feeling of loss was gone; the ache seemed dull now. But she missed her morning rounds on the farm, Sport's soft nicker, Taxi yapping at his hooves, all the animals turning their heads to watch her pass by. They needed her, and she needed them.

She missed riding through the thickly wooded forest, stopping to listen to nature sounds, sitting under the weeping willow in the graveyard, feeling the wind on her face as she raced Miguel back to the barn jumping logs and stone walls. She hadn't spoken with him since she left—she had been too upset for that. Of course, she could count on Laura to deliver her message, but now she was ready to apologize and explain.

It would be 10:00 A.M. at the farm now. She picked up the phone.

"Concha?"

"*¿Mi niña? ¿Cómo está?*"

"I'm fine—fine."

"When you come back?"

"Very soon, Concha."

"*Me gusta . . . me gusta.*"

"What's new on the farm?"

"Everything fine—Dr. Keegan call many time . . ."

"I don't want to talk with him."

"No?"

"But tell me, how's Taxi?"

"Fat."

"Phoebe?"

"Lazy."

Patricia chuckled. "Concha . . . buzz the bluestone cottage and get Mr. Cardiga on the phone."

"He no here."

"What?"

"He go away."

"Where?"

"He no say."

There was a knocking at the door, but Patricia ignored it. "When is he coming back?"

"One week . . . maybe two."

Where could he have gone? she thought as the knocking was repeated.

"I'll call you again . . . soon."

She opened the door to the rumpled figure of Dr. Solomon. "Would you care to join me for tea?"

"Sure thing, Doctor."

The dining room of the hospital, a very pleasant, airy place filled with hanging potted plants, was nearly empty in the afternoon. They had their usual—mint tea and strudel.

"How do you feel today, Patricia?"

"Numb."

"That's understandable. But now that you've had time to put things in perspective, does it still seem like such a tragedy?"

"Well, the hurt is still there. But you were right—I expected too much from Tom." She took a deep breath. "But this was the first serious relationship I ever had with a man. How can I ever trust my judgment again?"

"The only way I know is to examine how you relate to the men you meet. We know that the patterns set in childhood, we often repeat as adults. Your relationship with Tom was modeled after the one you had with your grandfather."

"That's impossible! Tom was the exact opposite."

"Was he?" Dr. Solomon took a big bite of his strudel and ignored the crumbs that lodged themselves in his beard. "Your grandfather directed your life, controlled it. Subconsciously, you looked to Tom to fill that role. Didn't you tell me that Tom gave direction to your life?"

"But I hated my grandfather."

"Yes, but you never questioned him. You leaned on him. You wanted to lean on Tom, too."

Patricia sat quietly, absorbing what the doctor was saying.

"The healthier male model in your life was your father—but that relationship continues to be unresolved in your mind."

"Yes, it torments me that I never found out what he wanted to tell me before he died."

The doctor slurped his tea. "Why is that so essential?"

But Patricia continued as if she hadn't heard him. "I can almost hear his voice on the phone—the way he emphasized 'must'—'I *must* tell you something important'—such urgency in his voice . . . If only I could track down this woman named Luba he wrote to before he died . . ."

"And then what?"

She looked at him, perplexed. "She might know what he wanted to tell me."

"But she might *not* know—or she might not *want* to tell you."

"But I feel I must try."

"Do you think that through this woman you can carry on a conversation with your father as if he were alive?"

Stung, she didn't answer.

"Patricia—the journey of life consists of going from room to room. But as we leave one room, we must close the door behind us—what we've learned there will always be with us, but we cannot be constantly looking back. Only when you close the door behind you, can you enter the next room.''

"But I can't."

"Why not?"

She paused, playing with the crumbs of strudel on her plate. Then she smiled ruefully. "Maybe I won't let myself . . .''

"Well, now we're getting somewhere," he chided her gently.

"I think I *did* try to close the door when I bought the farm . . . I gave up looking for that woman." She paused.

"Tell me—what made you give up?"

"Well, I guess I was busy, happy . . .''

"But now you're unhappy, and you think information about your father will fill the void."

"I just feel I need to try again."

"But suppose you don't find the answer you seek— suppose you find out things that will upset you?"

"I'm prepared for that. I think one of the reasons I stopped looking was—" She bit her lip.

Dr. Solomon wiped his glasses and waited.

"Well, I didn't like the idea of my father with a girlfriend.''

"That's not so bad. In fact I think it's healthy that you recognized a weakness.''

"In me?"

"Maybe both of you."

"But my father was not a weak man."

Dr. Solomon wrinkled his brow. "You know, listening to you I see a large pedestal, and all the men in your life are crowded on it—your grandfather, your father, Tom . . .''

Patricia managed a weak joke: "My grandfather and Tom fell off."

Dr. Solomon grinned. "Tell me—have you ever met a man that you didn't put on a pedestal, a man you could be angry with, admire, see his strength and yet see his vulnerability?"

Patricia looked off pensively, "Well, maybe . . .''

"Go on . . .''

"Miguel had some of those qualities."

"And were you attracted to him?"

"Oh God no! He was too arrogant, insulting. I only tolerated him because he was a great rider . . . He had a special feeling for horses . . . always treated them with an incredible tenderness. And he was a wonderful teacher, but . . . but—"

Doctor Solomon started to laugh, and Patricia stopped abruptly. "What's so funny?"

"When you talk about Tom, you describe a man on a pedestal. When you talk about Miguel, you speak like a woman in love."

"What?! You misunderstand completely."

"Do I? Has he ever shown any sexual interest in you?"

"Oh no—he's . . . he's engaged to be married."

Suddenly, the image of Miguel kissing her in the barn flashed through her mind. She felt hot and uncomfortable.

Chapter 10

Stone Ridge

HARPALO AND ULTIMATO were neighing and shaking their manes as Miguel headed toward them with a spring in his step. He found himself jumping over puddles that he used to limp around—just for the sheer fun of it. Two weeks in Seattle—a week to fit the new leg and a week of physical therapy—were all he needed. Dr. Burgess was proud of the result. The last thing he said was, "Go get those bulls!"

Miguel checked both horses quickly. They were in fine shape; Edgar had done a good job of keeping them groomed and fed. Then he hurried to the farmhouse, hoping, as he walked effortlessly across the yard, that she might be looking out the window.

He knocked at the kitchen door and heard a slurred voice yell, "Come on in!"

Sitting at the table, with a bottle of scotch in front of her, was Laura Simpson.

The kitchen was a mess—dirty dishes in the sink, empty cans and half-full coffee cups all over the counters.

Before he could say anything, she grunted, "Aah . . . the foreigner." And she raised the bottle to her lips.

"I'd like to see Miss Dennison."

"I would too," she snorted, "but she ain't here."

"When is she coming back?"

"God knows . . ."

The old crow was clearly out of it. He decided not to ask any more questions and started to leave.

"Oh Mr. Cardiga—"

He stopped at the door.

"Your services will no longer be required. You can go back to Spain or . . . Portugal or . . . wherever you come from."

Stunned, Miguel stared at Laura sitting there with a smug expression. "I beg your pardon?"

"Those are the orders."

"*Whose* orders?" Miguel snapped.

She looked up at him over the rim of her glass and smirked. "From the boss lady herself."

"Miss Dennison?"

"Yeah."

Bewildered, Miguel just stood there. Then he recovered. "And what is the explanation for this?"

Laura's head lolled on her shoulders and she spat out:

"She paid you plenty—explanations weren't part of the price."

"I see." He whipped around and walked out.

"Yo—wait a minute!" Laura called after him, holding up a piece of paper in her hand. "Your girlfriend called from Lisbon."

But Miguel ignored her.

"Well, fuck you too." Laura crumpled the paper in her fist and downed her drink.

Miguel had lost the spring in his step as he made his way to the barn. Why would Patricia dismiss him so abruptly? *What* had happened?

Lausanne

PATRICIA HAD A RESTLESS NIGHT. Strange images kept looming up in her dreams. She was riding Harpalo across an immense field of roses. She looked back and thought she saw Miguel on Ultimato, but the vision diffused into clouds of white. "Miguel!" she called out, but there was no answer.

She woke up with an uncontrollable need to talk with him. Before she even got out of bed, she called the farm.

"Concha?"

"My God—do I have a Mexican accent?"

"Laura! How good to hear your voice. I sure need a friend right now."

"Well, you got one if you come back."

"I'm on my way. How are things going?"

"Everyone's fine, but Concha had to go to Mexico."

"What for?"

"Her sister's sick."

"Oh no. Anything serious?"

"I don't think so. I slipped her a few extra bucks for the trip—was that all right?"

"Of course, Laura. I knew I could count on you. How is everybody else? How is—"

"Don't worry. I got my eye on everything. I moved into your study, the sofa bed is fine, and I even let Taxi sleep with me sometimes."

"You're such a good friend."

"Yeah, I must be," she rasped. "I'll even look after the bug house."

"Oh thank you, but there isn't much that has to be done there—the good bugs won't hatch till April. Then they have to be put out on the rose bushes right away."

"Ugh, do I have to touch them—"

Patricia laughed. "I'll be back long before then."

"Thank God!"

"You could do me one small favor—remind Edgar to check on the automatic water timer for the alfalfa."

"The alfalfa is what the bad bugs eat?"

"That's right—you remembered."

"Well it doesn't take a genius—you told me all about it so many times. The bad guys wear black—the good guys are the cute little red ones."

Patricia laughed again. "How are the horses?" she asked, trying to lead up to Miguel.

"Putting on weight."

"Well I'll take care of that soon enough." Patricia hoped she sounded nonchalant: "How is Miguel doing?"

"Gone back home."

"What?"

"Disappeared like a thief in the night with that gray horse."

Patricia almost dropped the phone.

"Hello—you there, kiddo?"

"Yes, yes . . . ah . . . did you say he took Ultimato?"

"That's right."

"And went back to Lisbon?"

"That's what Edgar said."

Patricia couldn't believe what she just heard. Laura babbled on—something about Misty—but she wasn't listening. She was hurt. Why would Miguel leave so abruptly?

Of course, she herself had left without an explanation. Could she blame him? What did she expect? He wanted to get on with his life—see his fiancée—get married—

She could understand all that, she tried to tell herself, but why take Ultimato? That was unfair! She was riding the horse well— he admitted it. She had lived up to her end of the contract, put up with his arrogance, his humiliating teaching methods. She had taken it all, and this was the way he said good-bye? He better take another look at that contract. She wouldn't let him get away with it.

Lisbon

EMILIO WATCHED MIGUEL leading Ultimato down the ramp of the cargo plane at the Lisbon airport. He was descending without a limp—what miracle happened in Seattle? But his friend seemed gloomy.

"Hey Miguelinho—what the hell is the matter with you? You're back here in Lisbon, you have Ultimato, and you move like a ballet dancer. Why do you look so miserable?"

"It's a long story."

"And I smell a woman." Emilio eye's twinkled with merriment as he nudged Miguel and whispered, "I guessed half the story when you told me the heiress wasn't fat and ugly. The other half I'll wait to hear over a glass of wine."

Miguel didn't answer. With a furrowed brow, he watched Ultimato being driven off in a van with the CENTRO EQUESTRE DA CARDIGA crest on its side. Then he got into the Ferrari.

Emilio sent the car squealing forward. "So, when are you coming to Castelo da Arrábida?"

"As soon as I can."

"Don't be too long, because waiting for you is the most beautiful"—and then he tasted each word—"small—round—shapely —sexy—" He paused; then, with his eyes on the road ahead, he leaned his lips toward Miguel's ear and whispered, "—little heifer."

Miguel chuckled. Emilio never failed to bring him out of a bad mood. "I'll be there as soon as Ultimato is over his jet lag. Right now I have to deal with the old man."

It proved tougher than even he expected. Paulo's hard blue eyes greeted him with icy anger. "Miguel, don't you realize—you can't take Ultimato back."

"Stop talking to me like I'm a child."

"Listen to yourself; you admitted she was an excellent rider—how can you justify it?"

"I have my reasons."

"I don't care about your reasons. I honor my contracts."

"She voided the contract. She ran off and dismissed me."

"Dismissed you? Why?"

"I don't know—I worked with her every day, she was making excellent progress until her fiancé arrived . . ." He stopped suddenly. "She's irresponsible."

"So why did you leave Harpalo?"

Miguel didn't have a ready answer. "Well—she has a good staff, but not good enough to handle Ultimato . . . he's *my* horse. I want him for the bullring."

"Oh really? Then write me a check for one hundred and fifty thousand dollars."

"God damn it! Haven't I paid my dues yet? You gave me a horse nobody could handle—*I* made him worth that money."

"So you could wreck him in the bullring?"

"I'm thirty years old. Let me do what I want for once."

"What you want is to be an exhibitionist."

"I'm the exhibitionist?! *You* are the one who always wants the center of attention. The great Paulo Cardiga. Nobody is as good as *you*. Not the Austrians—"

"Miguel!"

"—not the Germans . . ."

"Miguel, that's enough! My career was built on love for horses."

"Then why can't you understand that I love Ultimato the way you loved Amante?"

Paulo fell silent. Through the open window, they could hear Filipe calling out commands to the students.

Finally, Paulo said, "All right—I'll sell you Ultimato—for fifty thousand dollars."

"You know I don't have any money," Miguel said between clenched teeth.

"Then work for what you love," Paulo snapped.

"Doing what?"

"Come back to teach at the Centro. Help me prepare our next horse exhibition. Ride with me."

"Ride with you?"

"Yes. Once in my life, I would like to perform with my son—the only one who can match me in every movement."

Lausanne

SKILLFULLY NEGOTIATING the hairpin curves, Dr. Solomon drove Patricia down the long winding road to the airport. Absorbed in her thoughts, she barely noticed the crocuses beginning to peep through the snow.

"You certainly surprised me by your sudden decision to go home," Dr. Solomon interrupted her reverie.

"Doctor—I've been here two months, long enough. You should take care of people who really need you." She said it more sharply than she intended.

He shot her a quick glance through his thick glasses. "Are you angry?"

"Yes, but not with you."

"Well, I'm glad to hear that."

"Can you believe it—he left the farm and took one of my horses with him—"

"What are you talking about?"

"—and I paid his father one hundred and fifty thousand dollars for that horse."

"Miguel did that? There must be some misunderstanding."

"I always knew he didn't want me to have that horse."

"Sometimes we assign motives to people unfairly—"

"He's the one who was unfair."

"Shouldn't you talk with him before you jump to that conclusion?"

"No—I don't ever want to talk to him again. My lawyers will do the talking for me."

Dr. Solomon fell silent for a while; then he said, "Patricia—let me give you one last bit of advice."

"What's that?"

"Don't go back home right away."

"But I miss the farm."

"Don't use the farm as another way to escape."

"But where would I go?"

"Lisbon."

"Are you crazy?"

"Perhaps," he chuckled. "Most psychiatrists are a little nutty."

Patricia had to smile. "I didn't mean that. But what would I do in Lisbon?"

"Straighten this out. From what you've told me Miguel may be arrogant and insulting, but what rules his actions is love for horses. Perhaps the horse was ill—needed special treatment—"

"Doctor—we have excellent veterinarians in New York."

"Well, you may be right, but you'll only find out the real reason if you ask."

Patricia looked straight ahead. "To borrow your words, Doctor—that door is closed."

"Just what every psychiatrist hates—a wiseass patient." But he had a sad look on his face as he got out of the car.

The crew was waiting for her at the steps of the Stoneham plane. She threw her arms around the doctor and clung to him tightly. "I'll try never to bother you again," she said in a tremulous voice.

"If you don't call me from time to time, I'll be hurt."

He kissed her on both cheeks, and Patricia hurried up the steps to the cabin.

In flight, while the chef was preparing a light snack, Patricia let her eyes drift to the monitor where the tiny blip was inching across the map of Europe. She could see the spot marked "Lisbon."

One question kept rolling through her mind. Why did he leave so suddenly? And then Dr. Solomon's words: "You'll only find out the real reason if you ask." Her eyes shifted again to Lisbon. It seemed so close.

She pressed the intercom button to the pilot's cabin. "Captain . . . could we change our flight plan and head for Lisbon?"

"It's your plane, Miss D.," he said with a chuckle.

"Thank you." She quickly picked up the phone. "International operator? I'd like to place a call to Portugal."

"What is the number, please?"

"Just a minute . . ." She nervously flipped the pages of her address book and recited the number.

Beeping noises came over the international phone lines. And then she heard a steady ring. Suddenly, she panicked. What would she say? How would he react? She hung up.

She took a deep breath, and pressed the intercom button again. "Captain . . . could we please land?"

"Now?"

"Yes, please now . . . just land."

"Where?"

"Anywhere."

"Well . . . we're in the United Kingdom airspace. I'll request permission to land at Heathrow if you like."

"Yes, please."

"It's your plane, Miss D." This time he didn't chuckle.

Lisbon

THE GARDENS OF QUELUZ PALACE—the little Versailles in the Valley of the Almond Tree—were brilliantly lit. The terrace was overflowing with guests in elaborate evening dress—beaded gowns, silk and chiffon, the men in tuxedoes—all milling about President Soares, the host of the party. Suddenly, the buzz of the crowd was hushed by a blare of trumpets. Everyone's attention focused on the sand-covered area roped off with satin sashes just below the staircase of the stone lions.

The trumpets died down and now the symphony orchestra began—Chopin's Polonaise.

Paulo and Miguel Cardiga came riding in side by side. Their mounts wore no bridles. Only a fine silk string connected the riders' hands to the horses' mouths. Audible gasps could be heard from the gallery.

Out of the corner of his eye, Miguel watched his father's stooped shoulders straighten up as they came to the center. The crowd and the music always exhilarated the old man. The music paused briefly as both horses bowed in unison on bended knee; father and son doffed their plumed hats in a salute to the president.

Applause erupted from the crowd—for the first time, the great Paulo Cardiga together with his son, Miguel. Among the murmurs of approval were also whispers of "He has only one leg." The tragic accident in the bullfight arena was well known.

Then the music surged again. The two parted and the horses seemed to float diagonally across the arena. It was a pas de deux beyond compare—each rider mirroring the other's movements to perfection.

Miguel caught the expression of satisfaction on his father's face.

Now, ten additional riders entered the ring. Five lined up behind the father, the others behind the son. They were the most promising students of the Centro Equestre da Cardiga. They followed the two leaders, the horses weaving a graceful pattern in time to the music.

Tumultous applause broke out again and again. Finally, the students made their exit. Then, Paulo and

Miguel unsaddled their horses and let the animals race around the ring at liberty. In his exuberance, Ultimato dropped down to the ground and rolled on his back in the sand, kicking up his legs. Over the loudspeaker came the voice of Paulo: "This is the way animal and man should be—free—free."

The president stood up and the audience followed in a spontaneous ovation, cheering loudly. Only one member of the presidential party stood silent. Isabel Veloso just stared at the two horses happily racing out of the arena into the hands of father and son.

The reception, held in the richly gilded Hall of Mirrors, was a lavish affair. Everyone was in a festive mood, sipping champagne, munching on canapés. Miguel tried hard to avoid the penetrating gaze of Isabel, as he and Paulo graciously received compliments from the president.

At an opportune moment, Paulo drew his son out into the garden and sat down heavily on the ledge of a fountain. "Sit, Miguel, you're exhausted."

"But I'm not . . ." And then he caught the faint twinkle in his father's eye.

"Do you want me to admit that *I* am the one who is tired? Paulo Cardiga is never tired."

Miguel was surprised. He had never seen his father so weary—usually Paulo was animated, especially performing before a prestigious and appreciative audience.

"Miguel, I'm proud of you . . . you rode well today."

"Not too rough with the animal?" Miguel asked, unable to disguise his sarcasm.

Paulo smiled. "You have not been rough with a horse

from the day you were disciplined—do you remember?''

''How could I forget?'' Miguel responded softly, leaning over to dip his hand in the fountain's lagoon, trying to coax a pair of swans to come near.

Paulo placed his hand on his son's shoulder and stood up. ''Now I'm going home, but you stay. Someone must represent us,'' he said with a sharp intake of breath.

''Are you all right?'' Miguel rose quickly.

''Yes, yes,'' he said. ''You can tell me about the festivities in the morning.''

Miguel watched his father walk slowly away—for the first time he saw him as a tired old man.

Suddenly, the swans squawked in alarm as a woman, draped in a gold lamé shawl, appeared from behind the boxwood hedge. ''I've found you at last.'' Isabel hurried up to him. ''What a magnificent performance!''

''The credit belongs to my father.'' Miguel started to move away, anxious to avoid a conversation with her, but was held back by her restraining hand.

''I want to talk to you,'' she said softly.

''Of course . . . perhaps we can get together next week.''

''No, Miguel—now.''

He looked at her. She must have spent a long time in front of the mirror preparing for the occasion. Her black hair was pulled back tightly and encircled by a gold ribbon; diamond earrings hung below a perfectly symmetrical oval face that didn't need this much makeup. Reluctantly, he sat down beside her.

''Did you enjoy your visit to America?'' she asked pleasantly.

"Yes, I did."

"Obviously—since you had no time to answer my letters or phone calls."

"Forgive me."

"No, I don't forgive you. I am hurt, Miguel, very hurt."

"I'm sorry."

"That's not enough."

Miguel shifted his position. "What would be enough?" he asked with a cynical smile.

"Come to my house tonight," she said. "You know the way."

"I can't."

"You must."

"I *must*?"

"You owe me that."

"Isabel—we owe each other nothing. Our debts have been paid in full."

Isabel glanced toward the terrace, where the guests were talking and laughing. No one could see the two of them in the shadows of the fountain's statuary. Her head came close to him as she hissed, "You used me."

"No, Isabel." He shook his head. "We used each other."

"I love you, Miguel."

"No, you don't."

"It's the truth."

"I'll tell you the truth. We both wanted a good fuck. We got what we wanted. I paid a price for it." He tapped his artificial leg.

"You killed my husband . . . I watched you. What if I tell?"

He grabbed her arm tightly. "Why don't you? But wouldn't they be anxious to know why you kept your silence for so long?"

"Everyone knows I loved my husband."

Miguel released her and leaned back. "Everyone knows you married Luis Veloso for his money." And his hand touched her diamond earrings.

Isabel began to crumble as tears seeped down her cheeks.

"Please, I need you."

"You have everything you need." He stood up and walked away.

Chapter 11

London

PATRICIA FELT TINY and helpless, lost in the king-size bed that too seemed lost in the cavernous Stoneham suite at the Claridge's Hotel. When she arrived here, she was disappointed to learn that Mrs. Sperber was out of town—it made her feel all the more lonely that her only friend in this huge city was gone. What was she doing here, anyway? Why didn't she go right home as she had planned?

With all her might, she tried to bring to mind a comforting thought. She conjured up a dusky sky—the silhouette of Daddy atop his ladder, star in hand. She imagined herself curled up somewhere in the corner of that star—her father placing her high up, far above the problems below. She felt calmer and drifted off to sleep.

Then the beautiful dream somehow twisted into a nightmare. There was still the sky . . . the ladder . . . and the silhouette of the man . . . but when he turned his head, it wasn't Daddy, it was J. L. With a malicious grin, he started plucking the stars from the sky, one by one.

She woke up soaked in sweat.

She jumped out of bed, took a shower, and rang for coffee. She wanted her head clear enough to do what she had to do.

With a feeling of determination, she sat down at the desk and picked up a pen. She smoothed out a piece of hotel stationery. *"Dear Miguel,"* she began. She scratched it out. *"Dear Mr. Cardiga."* No. No "dear" for him. *"Mr. Cardiga!"*

And there the words sat, waiting for something to follow, but the next sentence eluded her. Instead, out came childish doodles of horses. With a sigh, she dropped the pen and got up.

She paced the floor, that helpless feeling overwhelming her again—why couldn't she write a simple letter? She sat down to try once more when the sharp ringing of the phone interrupted her.

"Mrs. Sperber! I thought you were away."

"Returned last night—found your message on my desk." A note of genuine delight seemed to be breaking through Mrs. Sperber's usually reserved British manner. "I am anxious to see you, my dear."

"You don't know how much I've missed you, Mrs. Sperber. They've replaced you with a terrible person. Now their decisions are unanimous—all against me."

"You poor child. I assumed your impending marriage would end the duties of the board."

"Oh . . . I broke my engagement—I . . . I have so much to tell you."

"Over lunch? One o'clock?"

"Love it. Where shall we meet?"

"My favorite restaurant—Harry's Bar."

"A pub?" Patricia giggled.

"No—a very elegant spot hiding behind a plebeian name."

Patricia hung up feeling better. Mrs. Sperber had always been in her corner. She looked forward to lunch.

Before getting dressed, she sat down at the desk again, took a deep breath, and this time the pen glided smoothly across the paper:

> *Mr. Cardiga—I am sorry that circumstances forced me to leave so hurriedly, but I am disappointed that you saw fit to invalidate our agreement in my absence and take my horse back with you. I expected more from you than that.*

She asked the concierge to mail the note as she went out.

Seated at the corner table in Harry's Bar, Patricia ignored her food and poured out her heart about Tom. With impeccable English manners, Mrs. Sperber didn't prod or pry, but only listened attentively.

"Mrs. Sperber, you don't know how much I wanted to do something positive with my life. I felt certain with his help I could accomplish it."

"You do not need a man to accomplish something

positive in life," Mrs. Sperber said wryly. "But I understand how you feel. When my husband passed away, I felt helpless too."

"So how did you cope?"

"I found that other people had worse problems than I. I became bored with self-pity and went to work."

"Yes, but you love business—I hate it."

"How do you know?"

"Oh . . . I'm uncomfortable in offices . . ." Patricia's eyes aimlessly drifted over the Arno cartoons on the walls; right behind her was one of a sad little boy in overalls gazing down at a spider on a bare cement sidewalk—the caption read *Spring in the City*. "I'm just a country girl at heart . . . but I did want to do something that makes a real difference in people's lives."

Mrs. Sperber shook her head slowly. "My dear, you make a difference in people's lives each time you write your name."

"What do you mean?"

"Occasionally, you might read those papers you sign so quickly—perhaps attend the shareholders' meetings. You might learn a thing or two the trustees do not care to tell you."

"Like what?"

"For example—your signature authorized moving the insecticide division to Nogales, Mexico."

"We have an insecticide division?"

"Indeed we do. One of the most profitable entities in the Stoneham Group—and the most shameful."

"Shameful?"

"Yes, Mexican workers are paid fifty-five cents per

hour, no benefits; they get no training in handling dangerous chemicals, no protective clothing . . . The company management needs no expensive disposal equipment—they simply drain the toxic waste directly into the Santa Cruz River.''

"How do they get away with it?"

"The Mexican officials look the other way, because the company brings millions into the country.''

"That's horrible.''

"But Horace Coleman is so thrilled with the profit margin, he is planning to move all of our manufacturing divisions to Nogales.''

"Can he do that?"

"If you sign the papers, he can." Mrs. Sperber took a sip of coffee.

"Are you telling me I should refuse to sign?"

"My dear"—the wryness returned to her voice—"you own the company.''

Patricia bit her lip. With her head down, she said softly, "Mrs. Sperber, I don't want the company. Can you imagine me contradicting Uncle Horace on anything?''

"Yes, I can—I think underneath your insecurities you are stronger than you know.''

"I'd just as soon give all the money away. Tom was going to show me how. Now that's over.''

"Give some consideration to what I said—you have real power, you know.''

Patricia was at a loss for words. She could hear the babble of happy conversations all around them, but she felt close to tears.

Mrs. Sperber patted her hand, getting up. "We shall

talk about it more another time. Right now, let me take you shopping.''

''No thank you, Mrs. Sperber. There is nothing I want to buy.''

They left the restaurant but as the driver opened the car door, Patricia hesitated.

''What is it?'' asked Mrs. Sperber.

''Can't we just walk back to the hotel?''

''Of course, of course, splendid idea. Lovely shops along Mount Street.''

Patricia started walking rapidly, hoping they wouldn't have to go into any of the ''lovely'' shops. She hated shopping.

Suddenly, she stopped and held her breath.

In a gallery window in front of her was an oil painting of a beautiful gray stallion—except that he had the head and torso of a man—a man with her father's face!

''What is it, my dear?''

Patricia felt unsteady as she walked closer to the window.

She could barely hear Mrs. Sperber asking, ''Are you all right?''

''Yes, yes . . . ,'' she mumbled, staring into the eyes of her father. ''I want that painting.''

''Well, we will go inside and buy it.''

The interior of the gallery was lined with striking canvases. An imperious matron approached them. ''May I help you?'' she inquired solicitously.

''That painting in the window . . . ,'' Patricia started.

''Ah yes, the satyr.''

''I want to buy it.''

''I am sorry, it is not for sale.''

"It is in the window," interrupted Mrs. Sperber.

"Yes . . . but it belongs to Lady McFadden."

"Lady McFadden?"

"The owner of this gallery, and the artist."

"And she does not wish to sell her paintings?" Mrs. Sperber pressed on.

"Yes she does—all of these—" And the matron waved her arm at the canvases on the wall. "But not the one in the window."

"Perhaps," said Mrs. Sperber, "no one has made a suitable offer."

"Her Ladyship has turned down many offers."

"Then why is it in the window?"

The matron gave them a condescending look. "It seems to draw patrons into the gallery."

"Ma'am," said Patricia timidly. "Would it be possible—"

"What is the problem, Miss Tindly?" a voice said from the back.

They turned around to see a young woman in a black tailored suit and a feathered pillbox hat to match. Her age was hard to determine—she seemed girlish with round cheeks and pink skin, but the large, very dark eyes were adult, steady, slightly intimidating.

"No problem, Your Ladyship . . . just someone else wanting to buy *The Satyr*."

"I'm flattered, but why don't you show them some of my other work." She pronounced the r's with a harshness that suggested foreign origins.

"No, you don't understand," Patricia burst out. "That's my father."

Lady McFadden's eyes seemed to bore into her. "So you're Patricia Dennison."

"Yes . . . I am, but how . . ."

"I knew you'd come someday."

"You did?" Patricia stammered.

Lady McFadden extended her hand. "My name is Luba."

Lisbon

MIGUEL FLICKED HIS LONG WHIP along the ground so hard he spun clouds of dust behind the fat French girl bouncing in the saddle around him. At the other side of the ring, his father was riding side by side with one of the more advanced students. The tough old bastard had allowed him only Sundays to work Ultimato for the bullring. The horse had come along quickly with the mechanical bull, but now he needed to put him to the real test with Emilio's "sexy little heifer." God damn it, he felt like a prisoner here.

"Again!" he spat out at the blubbering girl. He knew he was being cruel, but he couldn't stop himself. He was seething with anger at everything and everybody. The salt in the wound was the note he received from Patricia this morning. How could he have been so wrong about her—she had seemed sweet, sensitive, compassionate. What a fool he had been—mooning over her. She dismissed him like an inept groom. Now she writes him a note and practically calls him a horse thief!

"Again!" he bellowed.

Suddenly, he heard an anguished cry behind him. The student riding with his father had dropped her reins and was covering her mouth with both hands and staring at Paulo, who was doubled over and slumped in the saddle.

Miguel ran over in time to catch his father's body sliding off the nervous horse.

"Filipe!" he yelled to the assistant. "Call Dr. Braga!"

He carried Paulo's inert form to a bench in the gallery. The old man was breathing in quick, shallow gasps.

"Miguel . . . ," he whispered, regaining consciousness.

"Lie still, relax," Miguel ordered.

With a wan smile, Paulo closed his eyes again. But by the time the doctor arrived, he was insisting that nothing was wrong. Protesting loudly, he finally allowed the doctor to take his pulse and listen to his heart.

"Well, *mestre*." The doctor put away his stethoscope, "The blood is flowing and the heart is humming."

"Then I want to get back to my classes."

"Not so fast, not so fast." The doctor held up his hand. "My prescription is that you go to bed and rest for the remainder of the day."

Miguel looked at Paulo's worn, drawn-out face. His father's bravado vanished as he quietly allowed his son to pull off his riding boots. He agreed to go to bed, on the promise that the Centro's routine would not be disrupted. Then he waved everyone away as he shuffled to his dressing room.

How vulnerable he seemed now, Miguel thought.

Was this the man who had whipped him? Was this the man who had wielded the scepter of disapproval over his entire life? The power to intimidate was suddenly gone.

Miguel hurried after the doctor. "Dr. Braga—what do you think?"

"He might have had a bout of indigestion . . . or it could be an ulcer . . . but I detect some complicating symptoms."

"Like what?"

"Before I can answer that, I need to conduct a more complete examination. Make sure he rests for a couple of days, and then we'll get him into the hospital for some tests."

London

"AH YES, MISS DENNISON—m'lady is expecting you." The chubby Irish maid ushered Patricia into the antiques-laden sitting room of Lord and Lady McFadden's elegant town house overlooking the gardens of Sloan Square.

The walls were covered with paintings, obviously done by Luba. Patricia looked around, studying them with interest. Then she blinked. She knew that silhouette over the fireplace. It was the same as the man hanging the star in her favorite painting. It was Daddy! She came closer. The man was embracing a woman on a moonlit beach. A brass plaque on the bottom of the frame read: LOVERS AT TRÓIA. Tróia? Daddy had wanted to take her there—he said it was a magical place . . .

Her thoughts were interrupted by Luba's voice. "I'm so glad you're here. Please sit down."

The maid placed a silver tea tray on the table and quietly left the room.

"You were in Tróia?" Patricia asked.

"Yes—a beautiful place."

"My father loved Portugal too . . . he made a film there."

"Yes, I know." Luba's voice had a slightly dreamy quality as she poured tea for both of them.

There was an awkward silence. Patricia glanced back to the painting. Of course, there she is with Daddy, her arms tightly wound around him. *Did he really want to take me to Portugal to visit the Cardiga riding school, or did he want to take me on a pilgrimage of his romantic haunts?*

"I loved your father." It was as if Luba were reading her thoughts.

Startled, Patricia didn't know what to say. In silence, they sipped tea from elegant Staffordshire cups, Patricia trying not to look at the painting.

"Your father was the most important man in my life. He spoke of you so often that I feel I know you very well."

"What did he say?"

"Well . . . ah . . . he talked about how much he missed you . . . your great love for horses . . . he was looking forward to being with you again . . ."

"Daddy wrote to you . . . from Trieste . . . before he got on the plane for Switzerland."

Luba's eyes widened. "How in the world would you know that?"

"I found out from the attendant who mailed the letter at the Trieste airport."

"Well"—Luba took a sip of tea—"how resourceful of you."

"You see, he called me from there. He sounded so tense—said he was anxious to tell me something important—I need to know what it was."

There was another long silence as Luba's dark eyes penetrated Patricia. Finally, she took a deep breath. "The letter was personal," she said.

"Are you two hens still at it?" A strong robust voice interrupted. It belonged to a tall pudgy Englishman with rosy cheeks and a receding hairline, not too successfully camouflaged by long strands of hair pulled across it.

"This is my husband," said Luba, as the man approached them. He took Patricia's hand and kissed it in a continental fashion, then sat by his wife.

Luba snuggled up to him. "He's also my mentor."

A loud laugh rumbled out of His Lordship. "I am?"

"You know you are, darling," said Luba. She pointed to *Lovers at Tróia*. "This is the first painting I sold—to him."

"I was desperate," said His Lordship. "I would have done anything to get her into bed." And his laughter got louder.

Playfully, Luba threw a pillow at him. "Go get dressed, we'll be late again."

"What am I wearing?"

With feigned exasperation she pushed him out of the room, saying over her shoulder, "Oh, he's such a child."

Patricia picked up her bag from the table. "I know you're busy, and I won't take any more of your time."

Luba walked her to the foyer. "Patricia—I want you to know that I've thought of you many times. And I'm glad I finally had the chance to meet you."

"Thank you." Patricia's hand lingered on the door handle.

"I'm sorry I wasn't very much help."

"I appreciate the time you've given me . . . but . . . I wonder . . . I know you said it was personal . . . but it was the last thing my father wrote . . . his last words . . . do you think I could see the letter?"

Luba hesitated. "Well . . . I'm not sure where I put it . . . when you marry you don't exactly keep old love letters in your bedside drawer . . ."

Patricia waited.

"Of course, I can't look for it now . . . I'm late and . . ."

"I see," Patricia said resignedly. "I better go."

"Patricia—you're very young and beautiful—you should have much happiness ahead of you. I wish you the best."

The door of the town house closed behind her. Tears were obscuring her vision. She stumbled over the curbside and almost fell as she blindly ran across the street to the park. There, hidden by a tall boxwood hedge, she sobbed bitterly.

It was over. The last possible avenue that connected to her father was a dead end. It broke her heart—she'd never know what he wanted to tell her.

Chapter 12

London

"IT WOULD BE BEST if management did not know your purpose in Nogales. Arrange for a Mexican guide." Mrs. Sperber stood at the steps of the Stoneham plane, delivering last-minute instructions in her staid, business-like voice.

"Mrs. Sperber, I can't tell you how much you've helped me." Impulsively, Patricia kissed her cheek.

Suddenly, Mrs. Sperber seemed at a loss for words. She fiddled with the strap of her handbag. "I feel like my daughter is shipping off to school for the first time."

"I am going off to school—I hope I learn something." Then she added softly, "And I do feel like you've become my second mother."

"Well . . . well . . . ," Mrs. Sperber stammered,

glancing at her watch, "you'd better be on your way . . . and . . . I am proud of you, Patricia."

Nogales

As THE PLANE TAXIED down the deserted airstrip on the U.S. side of the border, Patricia could see a lone battered cab waiting. A swarthy Mexican, displaying crooked teeth, stood holding open the cab's door with such pride you'd think it was a stretch limo.

"Buenos días, señora."

"Buenos días—do you speak English?"

"Oho—like a Yankee."

"Wonderful." Patricia smiled. "Please take me to the Stoneham factory on the Mexican side."

Looking out of the cab window, Patricia was impressed with the beauty of the Arizona countryside. The hills were verdant pastures dotted with leafy trees, puffs of white clouds floating overhead. They crossed the Santa Cruz River shimmering in the sunlight. Could those waters flowing north from Mexico be polluted with toxic wastes? Surely, Mrs. Sperber was exaggerating.

The border gates cut across Interstate 19, connecting Nogales, Arizona, with Nogales, Mexico. Immediately after the barrier was lifted, the ride got more bumpy as they traveled over a road pitted with potholes. But then the driver made an unexpected turn to the right and she found herself speeding through the wrought-iron gates of Colonia Kennedy, the Beverly Hills of Mexican Nogales. Beautiful homes behind high stone walls and well-manicured lawns exuded prosperity. "Are we on our way to the Stoneham factory?" she asked.

"*Oh sí*," said the driver, "but usually the *turistas* like to see this nice place. Big shots live here."

Finally, the cab turned onto a wide street leading through an industrial section with two- and three-story structures on each side. "*Maquiladores*," said the driver. "American factories."

They all seemed brand new, sturdily constructed of cement block and neatly painted in pastel colors. The cab pulled up to a group of large buildings painted blue, each prominently displaying the Stoneham logo—a globe of the world with the letter *S* girdling it like a snake. The entire complex sat on a plateau overlooking the green rolling hills in the distance, and was protected by a high brick wall. It was impressive.

Now that she was here, Patricia realized she had no plan of action. She couldn't very well go inside and start walking around without identifying herself.

"Do you think it would be possible to talk with some of the workers without going in?"

The driver looked at her curiously, thought for a moment and then said, "*No problema* . . . I take you Raphael . . . he arrange."

"Thank you."

"We walk—okay?"

She nodded.

They left the cab, and he led her around the complex, behind the brick wall. As they were circling the buildings, Patricia noticed a tiny white stuccoed structure tucked into a niche between two warehouses.

"What's that?"

"Chapel of Saint Ramon—a very holy man. He is . . . guardian of . . . how you say . . . *conciencia*."

"Conscience?"

"*Sí.*" He nodded. "Stoneham people try to tear down chapel, but the machine . . . the bulldozer . . . it overturn. Two workers die." He crossed himself. "So they leave it."

Once they were behind the factory, on the very edge of the plateau where the ground dropped off sharply, he pointed below. "This is Colonia Zapata. The workers live here."

Patricia looked down a hillside littered with debris. Then she realized that it wasn't debris at all. No—it was a congestion of hundreds of shanties. A maze of rutted dirt paths weaved among the shacks, old tires holding back the sliding mud.

She headed down toward them, slipping on loose stones, drawn as if by a magnet to this squalor. The cabdriver followed.

Now she could see the shacks better. They were made of cardboard! Pieces of cardboard attached to wooden stakes by nails pierced through bottlecaps. The roofs were bits of plywood or corrugated tin weighted down against the wind by old car batteries.

Squealing children were running up and down the steep dusty roads; mothers were hanging clothes on suspended bits of wire, while others were hoeing patches of dirt. For a garden? She couldn't fathom growing anything in this soil. She passed a young girl drinking water from a can she had dipped in a big steel drum. The drum had the Stoneham logo on it.

Patricia walked closer and read the label. WARNING: FOR INDUSTRIAL USE ONLY. DO NOT REUSE EMPTY DRUM UNDER ANY CIRCUMSTANCES. DO NOT ALLOW RESIDUE TO COME IN CONTACT WITH SKIN. INGESTING RESIDUE MAY BE FATAL.

Patricia was aghast. "Why is this here?"

"Factory give—cheap way to get rid of dirty drums."

"But look at the warning!"

"They no read English."

For a long time Patricia said nothing and kept walking. She stopped by a carboard shack covered with tar paper. Out in front, an old woman was zealously watering a small rosebush protected from careless feet by a circle of crooked twigs. Patricia closed her eyes to erase the vision that forced itself on her mind—her vast field of white roses.

"Here is the leader of the colony," the driver said, motioning in the direction of a group of men talking animatedly. "Raphael!" he called out.

A bald-headed stocky man with a dark beard waved, and moved quickly toward them. The cabdriver let out a long stream of Spanish, pointing to Patricia.

"Ahh—" Raphael chortled. "This is a little different from the Colonia Kennedy." His heavily accented English was amazingly good. "The rich name their place after an American, we name ours after Zapata." He pointed to his T-shirt on which were embroidered the words *Libertad y Tierra*. "You understand?"

"Yes," she said, "Land and Liberty."

His white teeth gleamed in his dark beard. "That's what we have plenty of. What we need is water, electricity, sewers . . . and a few bricks to build houses."

"Why are these people living like this?" Patricia asked.

"Good question." He pulled out a large red bandana from his pocket and wiped his sweaty brow. "American companies lure them from the farms . . . fifty-five cents an hour sounds like a lot in south Mexico. But they don't say food up north costs the same as across the border. Across the border, in the States, the minimum wage is *five dollars* an hour. Here, you can barely feed yourself—forget about rent—and building a house is a crazy dream. People work two jobs and what do they bring home at the end of the week? Forty-six dollars."

"How do they live?"

He smiled again as if the question amused him. "Let me show you." And he took her arm and led her to one of the shacks.

Inside, he said something in Spanish to a woman cooking beans on a Sterno hot plate. Patricia looked around—there was no furniture, just a couple of old mattresses leaning against the cardboard wall decorated with religious pictures. In the corner, a young man with doleful eyes was sitting on a cinder block, his left hand heavily bandaged.

"Eight people live here," Raphael said. "This young man lost two fingers yesterday in the factory."

Patricia was almost afraid to ask, "Which factory?"

"Stoneham—they're the worst."

She cringed. Quickly, she reached into her wallet and put its entire contents on the table. "Please make sure he gets proper medical attention," she said to Raphael. She had a lump in her throat when she walked out.

But Raphael was jovial again. "Anything more you want to see?"

She shook her head.

He graciously kissed her hand. "Thank you for coming. Most tourists go to Acapulco . . . Cancun . . . Cuernarvaca . . . but this—" His hand swept around him. "This is the real Mexico." He said it proudly, defiantly.

Shaken, Patricia made her way back up the hill and got into the cab. As the driver made a wide U-turn in front of the Stoneham complex, they passed the chapel again. She could see many candles burning in the darkness behind the iron grillwork; little beacons of hope for the people who placed them there, praying fervently that Saint Ramon would prick the conscience of factory owners.

Lisbon

THE DOOR OF THE OPERATING ROOM opened and Dr. Braga walked out. He pulled down his surgical mask, revealing a worried expression.

Miguel waited anxiously for the doctor to speak.

"The gastroscope shows us that we need to go in."

"What does that mean?"

"I'm sorry, but we have to do a biopsy."

"A biopsy?"

"To see if the tumor in his stomach is malignant."

Before Miguel could respond, Dr. Braga disappeared back into the operating room.

Stunned, Miguel didn't know what to do. Should he stay? Should he leave? How long would it be? He slumped in the chair and looked around. In one corner, a gray-haired woman was quietly sobbing; a young girl, probably her daughter, was holding her hand and whispering words of comfort. Was this the same room where his father waited the day they chopped off his leg? What do they do with the pieces of arms and legs they chop off in hospitals? He shook that macabre thought out of his mind. He had been cruel to Paulo back then, because he was so angry; now he wanted to make it up to him. Was it too late? Maybe everything that had happened with Patricia was God's way of punishing him. He smiled bitterly—it certainly had been a long time since he ever thought of God.

"Miguelinho—how bad is it?" He felt Emilio's arm around his shoulders.

"I don't know yet. They're cutting him open."

"Oh my God!"

"He has a tumor."

"Cancer?" Emilio whispered.

"I'm waiting to hear."

"I'll wait with you. Come on, let's have a cup of coffee."

But Miguel was staring at the operating room door as if he hadn't heard.

Emilio sat down next to him quietly.

New York City

PATRICIA WAS SURPRISED to find Horace Coleman alone at his desk when the secretary ushered her into his office. He made an effort to lift his bulk, succeeded halfway, then flopped back down in his seat. "Nice to see you, Patricia." He smiled benignly.

"Where are Mr. Rosemont and Mr. Ash?"

"Well—you called from the plane only a few hours ago. They have business to attend to. Ted is in Washington, and Bob is in Las Vegas"—and then he chuckled—"probably disappointed that you were using J. L.'s plane and he has to suffer on the company Lear jet." (They referred to it as "J. L.'s plane," as if he were still alive.) "I was on my way to Dallas," he continued, "but you seemed so anxious to have a meeting. What's so important?"

"I've just spent two days in Nogales."

Coleman's lower lip sagged down to meet his chin and his eyebrows rose like McDonald's arches. "Well, my dear girl," he said patronizingly, "and what did you learn about the manufacture of insecticides?"

"That it's a dirty business, which exploits poor people and contaminates the environment."

Coleman's eyebrows fell. "So you've become an instant expert?" His tone of voice was laced with cynicism and it unsettled Patricia.

"I didn't mean that. But Uncle Horace—you should see what's going on over there. And the Stoneham Group is responsible."

"You mean I am responsible, don't you?"

"No, Uncle Horace." She knew she was losing ground. She had meant to challenge the way the company conducted business in Nogales, but found herself on the defensive instead. "I mean that . . . that . . ."

Laboriously, Coleman rose out of the overstuffed

chair; the cushions seemed to let out a sigh of relief. He towered over her as his voice rose with indignation. "I helped your grandfather build this company and I've been running it on your behalf for the last three years. And now you make *one* trip to Mexico and tell me you find fault with my work?"

"No, no . . ." She pressed her lips together, resolved to carry through with her plan. "But I find fault with a company that abuses people, poisons the water they drink, forces them to live in cardboard boxes . . ." She was surprised by the determination in her voice.

With his chins quivering, the usual sign of agitation, Coleman sat back in his seat. Then the benign smile returned to his face. "I should have known. You're such a sensitive, impressionable girl, and you've been exposed to so little in life . . ." He paused. "What you saw is an underdeveloped country trying to catch up with industrialization. Overcrowding, as ugly as it may seem to someone used to luxurious surroundings, is one of the signs of expansion—of progress. In a few years, all that will be gone, replaced by high-rise apartments, you'll see."

"But we can't let people live like that now—it's inhuman."

"Patricia—the Stoneham Group follows the letter of Mexican law and we take pride in the millions we have poured into their economy. There is nothing inhuman in that. If we—and I might add, other American corporate giants—weren't there, these people would be worse off, believe me."

"But you always told me that this company had billions in assets—couldn't we just spend some of that money to make Nogales better?''

His exasperation with her was barely contained now. "Liquidate valuable assets to put in sewers for Mexicans?''

"I don't know what to liquidate . . . I just . . .'' She faltered. "If this is my company—I must do something.''

"My dear—I know you want to be a great humanitarian, and it's a noble goal. But if you really want to dedicate yourself to helping the disadvantaged, take a few courses in economics, inform yourself about international investments, then let's talk about it again.''

Patricia bit her lip. She wished Mrs. Sperber could be there to tell her what to say. She made one last attempt. "Uncle Horace—I don't have to take courses in economics to see that people are suffering.''

Coleman sighed. He leaned his forehead against his clasped hands so that she couldn't see his face. "Patricia, I've tried so hard to fulfill my corporate responsibilities and to please you.''

"I know you have . . . and I'm grateful.'' She was suddenly aware that it was very cold in the room.

He said nothing and Patricia waited, watching the little ribbon fluttering on the air-conditioning vent, listening to the air coming out like the hiss of a hidden serpent.

Finally, Coleman raised his head. She was startled by the tears in his eyes. "Patricia—I've known you since you were a baby—oh, how often I've listened to your grandfather talk about you—how pretty you were, how clever, the horse he picked out for you, the jewelry . . .'' He brushed his hand across his eyes and looked at her intently. ''I was on the plane flying back with him—after he visited you in Switzerland.'' His eyes didn't blink. ''He was upset, very upset—about the things you said to him.''

Patricia shivered—he knew—he knew that she had wished J. L. dead.

''We were over the Atlantic.'' Coleman looked off as if he was visualizing the scene. ''J. L. asked to see me. I went to his bedroom.'' He swallowed. ''I held his hand. His last words to me were 'Look after that troubled girl as if she were your own grandchild.' ''

Coleman shook his head slowly from side to side. ''I feel that I have failed him—and I have failed you.''

Patricia got up slowly. In a daze, she walked over to the window. ''I never wanted his money,'' she said, barely above a whisper.

''My dear girl.'' He followed her and put his arm around her. ''You have been burdened with a tremendous responsiblity.''

''I never wanted any part of his company . . . and after what I've seen in Nogales . . .''

''Patricia, please—you are confused. We have done nothing bad. We've given a boost to an underdeveloped country's economy, and our stockholders are delighted with the seventy-percent increase in profits. Have you any idea how much money this means to you?''

''I don't care about the money.'' She whirled away from him. ''I just don't want Nogales on my conscience.''

"But Nogales is an integral part of the Stoneham Group."

"I don't want to belong to that group!" Her voice had a desperate edge to it.

He studied her for a long time as if trying to digest what she had said. "Then there is only one solution to this." His tone was suddenly very businesslike. "Patricia—sit down and listen to me."

Chapter 13

Stone Ridge

HUDDLED IN THE BACKSEAT OF THE CAR, Patricia wrapped her arms around her knees, not caring that her loafers, still caked with the brown dirt of Nogales, were getting her slacks dirty. She had been quietly crying most of the way home. The driver glanced in the rear-view mirror several times, and once he asked, "Is there anything I can do, Miss D.?" But she only shook her head, blinking back her tears. Mrs. Sperber had told her she was strong, but she knew better—what she had just done meant she was totally weak, and she hated the weakness, hated herself.

Through her swollen, tear-filled eyes, the farm came into view. The trees were thick with young buds ready to burst open. The first delicate growth of grass made the pastures seem like an emerald sea. She could see the old horses greedily grazing. She sighed with relief. She was home.

Taxi was whirling in a mad circle, jumping up and down, when the car finally pulled into the farmyard. She rushed out of the car and he jumped into her arms, knocking her down and licking her face. She got up laughing and raced him to the house, while the driver unloaded her bags.

She opened the kitchen door, calling "Laura!" and stopped in astonishment. Dirty dishes were piled in the sink; empty liquor bottles and ashtrays overflowing with cigarette butts were strewn across the counters. A half-eaten sandwich swarming with flies was on the table. Oh my God, Laura was drinking again.

Eager to make her rounds of the farm, she ran upstairs to change her clothes, scooping up a sleeping Phoebe from an armchair and showering her with kisses. On the landing she stopped before the picture of *The Starhanger*—she now knew it had been painted by Daddy's lover. She was a little jealous—but why? Everyone wants to be loved. It must have been hard for you, Daddy—with Mommy dead and me completely in J. L.'s grasp. I wish we could have been closer. She smiled sadly at the painting. But here you will always be, never looking back, always looking upward as you hang a star for me.

She heard someone stumbling around in the study. The door was flung open and a disheveled Laura, still in her nightgown, appeared.

"Oh Laura!" Patricia embraced her friend. "I'm so glad to see you."

"I missed you too, kiddo," said Laura, her breath reeking of alcohol.

Patricia pulled away and looked at her. "You promised me you'd stop drinking."

"But it's been so lonely here without you." Laura clutched her head, "Oh it hurts . . . I need some coffee."

Leaning on Patricia, she staggered down the steps. "What are you doing here—I thought you'd be in New York."

"I was—I talked with Horace Coleman. It was horrible."

"What happened?"

"Oh God—" Patricia's voice cracked at the thought. "I went in to talk about helping the people in Nogales but I just fell apart."

"Kiddo—that's you, always trying to be the do-gooder. I thought that disaster with the doctor would knock some sense into you."

"Laura . . . please don't . . . I feel bad enough about it. I wanted so much to do something right. I wanted to be strong, but I couldn't do it."

"Get a hold of yourself, kiddo . . . it'll be all right. Let the trustees run the show—you stay out of it."

"Uncle Horace thinks that the best thing for me to do is sell the company—get rid of the burden once and for all . . . I guess he's right—he knows so much more about these things than I ever could. It's all above my head."

"Well, then you should take his advice."

"I know, but still . . . Laura—why couldn't I stand

up for what I know is right? I just made a mess of it. Oh God—I make a mess of everything I start.''

"That's not true." Laura put her arm around Patricia. "You do a great job with this farm. You take great care of my Misty. You saved my life, taking him in. Don't beat yourself up."

Patricia hugged her in gratitude. "You always make me feel better. Laura—if I didn't have this farm . . . I don't know . . . I think I'd go crazy." She smiled wanly.

"Well, you're back home now. This is where you belong. Why don't you saddle up Sport—go for a ride—it'll do you good, and meantime," Laura laughed, "I'll try to make myself come to." She moved over to the sink, rinsed out a coffee cup, and filled it with a thick brew that had obviously been sitting on the hot plate for some time. She took a big gulp. "Ahh, I needed that." Then, catching Patricia looking around the kitchen, she added, "Yeah, it *is* a mess, but it's difficult without Concha."

"I know, I know. Any word from her?"

"Yeah—she called, said she had to walk five miles to the nearest phone. Her sister's no better."

"That's too bad," said Patricia, picking up some dirty dishes.

"No, no—don't you dare do that. I made this mess, and I'll clean it up. You go say hello to your babies."

Gratefully, Patricia kissed Laura on the cheek. "You're the best." She grabbed a few carrots from the vegetable bin and raced to the stable. Harpalo nibbled on them indifferently; he looked lonely next to the empty stall that used to house Ultimato. She fed a few to Sport, and in a burst of affection hugged him tightly around the neck. "Sportie—let's go for a ride."

She put on his bridle and jumped on his bare back—she didn't care that she was still wearing her traveling clothes. Taxi yapped happily—things were back to normal again.

She raced through the fields, filling her lungs with the scent of spring. It was so good to be home. She circled the cemetery, and was guiding Sport along the ridge overlooking the farm, when she saw the mailman's Jeep coming up the country road. She felt a twisting sensation in her stomach. How often had she waited for him to arrive—with a letter from Tom. Now she hated the thought of emptying the mailbox, but the mailman spotted her and waved, a handful of letters in his hand. He expected her to race down as usual and was waiting for her. Slowly, she made her way toward him.

"Glad you're back, Miss D.!" he called out.

"How are you doing, Mr. Koloski?"

"Fine, fine—but we missed you, especially my little Jimmy. He loved collecting them strange Lebanese stamps."

"Well—maybe we'll get some other stamps for him."

"Can he have these?"

He held out an envelope.

Patricia hesitated. She didn't want to hear from Tom. She glanced down—the Portuguese stamps were unmistakable.

She peeled off the stamps, her heart beating rapidly.

"Oh thank you, Miss D. Jimmy's gonna get a real kick out of these."

She sat on Sport's back with the envelope in her hand, watching the mailman's Jeep disappearing down the road. Then, tentatively, she unfolded the letter.

The words screamed out at her:

I am not a horse thief! You dismissed me—and you didn't even have the courtesy of doing it yourself—you had Miss Simpson do it for you. Since the terms of our contract were not fulfilled, I had the right to take both horses back. I left you Harpalo.

His signature was almost illegible—obviously written in great anger.

Patricia spurred Sport up the driveway and came to a slide stop where a tidied-up Laura was feeding Misty carrots.

"You're in a hurry, kiddo."

"Laura—did you fire Miguel?"

"Yes."

"You did? Why?!"

"You asked me to."

"What are you talking about?"

"Don't you remember? You *told* me to tell him his services were no longer required."

"I did?"

"Yes, just before you boarded the plane for Switzerland."

"You must have misunderstood. I don't remember saying that at all."

"Well you certainly did."

Patricia looked at her blankly.

"Kiddo, you sure you didn't leave that sanitorium too quickly?"

"No, no, I'm fine," Patricia said absentmindedly as she urged Sport on toward the house.

Lisbon

WALKING TOWARD THE RIDING RING with heavy steps, Miguel thought how much his life had changed in the last couple of weeks. Paulo was still in the hospital, but tomorrow the doctors were to send him home, where his last months would be more comfortable. His stomach cancer was too far advanced—no point in even trying chemotherapy. He still had spurts of energy, and was stubbornly insisting from his hospital bed that he could carry on with his classes. But the doctors told Miguel that he shouldn't let his father near a horse.

This great man, who had taught him everything he knew about horses, would never ride again. In comparison, the loss of a leg seemed like such a minor inconvenience.

How many people had been introduced to the magic of dancing horses by the great Paulo Cardiga. He had made his mark—his name was known in every corner of Portugal and revered by horse lovers throughout the world. He had fulfilled his dream—would Miguel ever fulfill his own?

But there was no more time for ruminating—the beginners' group was waiting for him. Miguel mounted

Ultimato and flicked his long whip. *"Sentido!"* he yelled so loudly that the little French girl almost fell off her horse. He grimaced—this child was hopeless; none of the other instructors would teach her, even patient Filipe who proved a lifesaver in every other way.

Miguel was resigned to the responsibility of running the riding school—he felt guilty about his earlier resentment. He tried not to think about how much it limited his training of Ultimato for the bullring; and yet the horse was making rapid progress.

Last Sunday, with a van hitched to Emilio's Ferrari, they had trucked to the country to finally play with that little heifer.

The adrenaline had flowed through Miguel's body as Ultimato, responding to the excitement, pranced around the pugnacious heifer with scorn, easily evading her prickly horns.

Replaying the day in his mind, Miguel stopped paying attention to his students and was jolted when one of the assistants tugged on his arm. "Telephone, Senhor Cardiga."

"Not now," Miguel snapped.

"The lady said it is very important."

Isabel again. She'd been calling incessantly since she found out about Paulo's condition, offering to comfort him. He tried to make it plain that he wanted to be left alone, but she continued to hound him, using any pretext.

"I told you never to interrupt my lessons!" Miguel shouted at the assistant.

"Sorry senhor, but she said she was calling from America."

"Who?"

"Senhora Dennison."

Miguel pushed Ultimato into a canter and reached the wall phone in the arena in four strides.

"Hallo!"

Patricia was immediately intimidated. "Miguel?"

"Yes!" His voice sounded harsh over the humming of the international cable.

"Did I get you at a bad time?"

"I'm in the middle of my lessons."

"Oh, I'm sorry . . . I'll call later."

"You can talk."

Patricia was grateful that he could not see the color flooding her face. "I just got your note—"

"Good."

"We . . . ah . . . obviously, we had a misunderstanding."

He said nothing.

"I . . . ah . . . just wanted to apologize for the garbled message you received from Laura Simpson."

"Garbled? What does that mean?"

"Oh my—I'm not explaining it very well. I . . . I . . . just wanted to say that I didn't want you to leave the farm."

"But you dismissed me."

"No, no—I did not. That was garbled. Miss Simpson misunderstood. I guess I didn't make myself clear to her . . . ah . . ."

"You garbled it to Miss Simpson?"

Patricia had to laugh. "Yes, I garbled it to Miss Simpson. You see, I was very upset, because I broke off my engagement that night."

"Oh, oh—well, I extend my condolences—I'm sorry for you," said Miguel, his voice warming up.

"I hope you have better luck with your engagement."

"It must be contagious—is that the word?"

"What do you mean?"

"I broke mine too."

"Oh my," Patricia said with as much sympathy as she could muster. She was glad that he didn't seem sad. "Now—you still owe me two months of riding lessons."

"That is correct, and you will be reimbursed."

"No, no . . . I *want* my lessons."

"But I cannot return to the United States, my father is ill, and I must take care of the school."

"Perhaps I can come there."

"Yes—come to Lisbon and take your lessons here." Patricia hoped he didn't hear her sigh of relief. "Well," she hesitated, "I can only come for a short time."

"When shall I expect you?"

"The day after tomorrow?"

"Perfect."

Miguel hung up the phone, whirled Ultimato around, and the amazed students watched their somber teacher on his stallion skipping across the ring, changing leads at every stride.

New York City

ASH AND ROSEMONT barely had a chance to sit down, when a smug-faced Horace Coleman announced: "You know, fellas, Patricia is a nice girl—we may not have to go through the proceedings of declaring her incompetent.''

Ash threw him a look that said "I don't believe my ears.''

Rosemont was equally incredulous. "But Horace— we agreed that's the only way we can keep control! How can we drop it?''

"Ted, I didn't say drop it, I said we may not have to use it. There is another way.''

"What's that?''

"Plan B.'' Coleman looked like a contented Buddha as his eyes went from one to the other. "Buy out the controlling interest in this corporation.''

They both stared in disbelief.

"Are you nuts too, Horace?'' Ash asked.

"I think the girl is ready to sell her holdings.''

"You mean all her stock?'' Rosemont's voice lowered an octave. "Fifty-two percent of everything?''

Coleman nodded.

"She'd hand us the company on a silver platter?''

"Exactly.''

Ash chuckled, "You're right, she is a nice kid.''

Rosemont started doodling—dollar signs. "How do we come up with the cash? That's some hunk of change you're talking about, Horace.''

"Gentlemen—it will be simple to raise the money against the assets. The deal should be signed, sealed, and delivered in less than six months.''

"Holy shit!'' exclaimed Ash.

"What would you offer her for the stock, Horace?'' Rosemont asked.

"The going price—sixty-three dollars a share."

"Geez, it's worth a lot more than that," Ash said in awe.

"She'd sell it for less," Coleman announced.

"Well then, let's buy it for less."

Coleman gave Ash a dirty look. "*You* explain that to the SEC—a transaction of this size will be very closely scrutinized."

"Why would she do it?" Ash piped up again.

Coleman made a circle with his index finger and tapped his cranium. "Because she wants to be a great philanthropist—and I say, let her. Let her build all the hospitals she wants, buy caskets for dead horses . . . whatever."

"You're right, Horace." Ash's voice was full of glee. "Make the girl happy."

Coleman leaned back in his chair. "At this time in my life, I don't need the whims of a crazy heiress keeping me awake at night."

"You're brilliant, Horace," Rosemont said, getting up and pulling out a bottle of champagne from the wet bar. "I think we should toast your genius." He filled three glasses, but before they could drink the toast, the secretary's buzzer interrupted the celebration: "Mr. Coleman—Miss Simpson is here."

Rosemont grimaced. "Well, now we can get rid of that drunken bitch."

"Come on, Horace," Ash chimed in cheerily. "I want to see you kick her out on her ass."

"Hold it, hold it. Not so fast," Coleman said. "We need her for insurance. I'm not going to abort any part of plan A until the stock certificates are in my back pocket.'' He pushed the intercom button. ''Send her in.''

Laura walked in and made a beeline for the wet bar. ''How inconsiderate of you boys to drink without me.'' And she poured herself a hefty shot of scotch. Horace Coleman eyed her with distaste. ''What do you have for us, Miss Simpson?''

''Just wanted to tell you that Ladybug has flown the coop,'' she said after taking a gulp.

''Are you drunk? What the hell are you saying?'' Coleman snapped.

''As we speak, the company plane is winging her to Lisbon.''

''Oh shit!'' Ash exclaimed. ''I wanted to fly to Palm Springs tomorrow for a golf tournament!''

Coleman gave him a dirty look. ''Lisbon—why?''

''To that riding academy.''

''Just what she needs—another horse,'' Ash snorted.

''She's not going there to get a horse, she's going there to get a man.'' Laura guffawed, sending a spray of scotch over the sparkling glass tabletop.

Ted Rosemont winced and looked up from his doodling. ''A man? Who?''

''That foreigner . . .'' Laura hiccupped. ''The one-legged fella.''

''What?!'' Rosemont and Ash asked in unison.

''Yeah. She's determined to get herself hitched and get rid of you boys.''

''All right, that's enough of your sarcasm.'' Coleman stood up and took the glass from her hand. ''The stock sale will change everything.''

''Well, I don't know about that.''

"You don't know about what?"

"The stock sale—you made her feel pretty bad, Horace. The poor girl came home crying. She might just get married and change her mind."

"It's your job to make sure it doesn't happen."

"How am I gonna prevent it—jump in bed with 'em?"

"You figure it out."

Chapter 14

Lisbon

TAXI SNUGGLED AGAINST PATRICIA on the seat of the cab whizzing along the highway. Phoebe the cat purred on her lap as the car headed into the hills beyond which lay the Valley of the Almond Tree.

"How far is it to the Centro Equestre da Cardiga?" She hoped her voice didn't show her anxiety.

"Oh—about fourteen kilometers—eight miles," the driver answered.

The countryside, which she had considered bleak when she was last here, now seemed very romantic— the Moorish influence in the architecture gave it a fairy-tale, Arabian Nights feeling.

She could feel her heart pulsating under her thin silk blouse as they drove up the tree-lined driveway. Taxi started barking at the two young riders who, dressed in colorful Renaissance costumes and mounted on beautiful Lusitano horses, formed the welcoming committee. In a slow canter, they led the car past the ivy-covered manor house to a building Patricia knew to be the indoor riding arena. A groom looked after the cat and dog as Patricia was guided through a side door to a gallery filled with empty benches. She quietly sat in the back row and looked down into the ring. She kept her hands tightly clasped together, forcing herself not to chew on her nails.

Miguel, dressed in his usual tight-fitting black outfit and flat-crowned hat, was standing in the middle of the arena instructing a group of students cantering in a circle. All the riders held a glass in each hand from which a red liquid was slopping down their white britches. Patricia brought her hand to her mouth to suppress a laugh, and yet she felt sorry for these miserable creatures—especially the girls—who were trying so hard to hold back their tears. When it seemed as if the glasses were empty, Miguel called out, *"Termo!"* And the bedraggled students, heads hanging down, were led out of the arena by the assistants.

Miguel stood motionless for a few moments; then, as if he felt her presence, he turned around and walked toward her with a faint smile. Patricia broke the silence. "You must use up an awful lot of wine."

"Cheap wine," he said. "With you it was always the best of the Fonseca cellars."

She laughed. "I'm ready for my first lesson."

"Not today—school is over."

He touched her hand resting on the balustrade. "I'm glad you are here, Patrizia. Where is your baggage?"

"One of your grooms took it."

"Good, let me show you to the guest apartment."

Without a word, he led her over a stone bridge, its walls adorned with exquisite delft-blue tile murals, through the wrought-iron gate that opened into the cob-blestoned courtyard of the manor house. It was peaceful here—two large trees gave plenty of shade, and water splashed from the fountain at the center. The house was a gray stucco building arranged in a quadrangle with numerous French doors opening onto the courtyard.

"Here are your quarters," Miguel said, taking her to the west wing of the building.

Inside, on an antique four-poster, Taxi and Phoebe were already snoozing away. "Shh." Patricia put her finger to her lips as she unzipped one of her bags and handed him a small gift-wrapped package. "It's just a little book—to remind you of our nature talks on the farm."

"How could I forget," he said with a smile. Then he pointed to a slim volume on the bedside table. "I also have some reading for you."

She picked it up. "*Méthode d'Équitation?* Hm . . . my French is a bit rusty, but I'll do my best."

"The author lost the use of both legs and had to reinvent riding. My father made me read it when I was in the hospital."

"Oh, how is your father feeling?"

"As well as can be expected. He is confined to his bed now, but he is eager to see you. Would you like to say hello?"

She followed him through the house, down a narrow

hallway to a low stone portal which framed a massive door, partly ajar.

Paulo was not in bed. He sat behind a large, ornately carved table, wearing a white Moorish caftan, belted with a red sash.

"Father—you remember Miss Dennison?"

Paulo rose with a glint in his eyes. "Ah yes—indeed, I do." He leaned over and admonished her with his finger: "You charmed me out of my two best horses. My son was very angry with me."

She threw a questioning glance at the smiling Miguel. "Why?"

Miguel winked. "I hated to see our two best horses go to some fat American heiress."

Patricia laughed. "Well, now you have Ultimato back." She felt at ease with both of these men.

"Sit down, sit down," said Paulo, motioning with both hands to the chairs in front of him. "I trust Miguel has seen to your comfort."

"He has—to all of us."

"All of you?"

"My dog and cat as well."

"Ahh—a dog and cat. It will give you balance. A dog to adore you—a cat to ignore you."

"I'm afraid I'm off balance. My cat adores me too."

Paulo's laugh turned into a cough.

"Father, you should be in bed."

Paulo cleared his throat. "I never receive a young lady lying in bed."

"Unless she's ready to join you," Miguel teased.

Paulo turned a twinkling eye to Patricia. "They won't

let me sit on a horse, they won't let me sit in a chair—
they always want me lying down, practicing for my
tomb.''

Patricia caught Miguel watching his father with concern.

"You will live a long time," Miguel said.

"I hope so, because I have much to do," Paulo chuckled. "While I am lying prone, Count von Steinbrecht
hoodwinks everyone into thinking that his military drills
are the true art of dressage." And then he added contemptuously, "The Viennese Riding Academy is a
fraud!"

Patricia raised her eyebrows in surprise. "Isn't it the
most admired dressage establishment in the world?"

"Patrizia," he said softly, pronouncing her name just
like Miguel, "classical dressage is training horses to
dance—with lightness, grace, and beauty." His voice
hardened. "All the Prussians care about is force, obedi-
ence, and precision—*eins, zwei, drei*. That is a sport,
not art. I hope Miguelinho has taught you the difference."

"Oh yes, it cost me many pairs of white britches."

Paulo laughed heartily. He seemed virile and
strong—not sick at all, thought Patricia.

"My father doesn't make his money on the horses or
riding lessons," said Miguel in mock seriousness. "He
makes it on the laundry."

"Don't make fun, Miguel—my quest is to preserve
a tradition that you chose to abandon for the bullring."

Patricia noticed that Miguel's smile disappeared.

"Do you disapprove of bullfighting, Mr. Cardiga?"
she asked.

"Yes and no. It has kept the art of horsemanship pure in Portugal, but it is still a blood sport."

"Father—please—not again."

Paulo ignored Miguel and looked directly at Patricia. "What do you think of it?"

"I have never seen a bullfight and I'd rather not see one."

"So! You disapprove too! Tell that to my son!"

"Stop it!" Miguel's anger was obvious.

Paulo continued undeterred. "You see how he talks to me, Patrizia, he has no respect for his father . . . I am sure you treat your father better."

"My father is dead," Patricia said simply.

"Ah, I'm sorry to hear that. You must miss him."

"Yes, I do—very much."

"You loved him." It was a statement, not a question. She nodded.

Paulo paused and his eyes went to the wall behind her. "It is sad to lose the one you love," he said dreamily.

Patricia turned, expecting to see a portrait of his wife, and was shocked to find that he was staring at the stuffed head of a horse mounted on the wall. "Oh my God," she muttered involuntarily.

"This is Amante," said Miguel. "My father's one true love."

"Yes," Paulo sighed, "I loved that horse." A beatific expression lit up his face. "And she loved me. I could not bear to be separated from her. Her legs hold up this table—"

Patricia was stunned to see him stroking one of the horse's legs upon which the tabletop was mounted. Then he pointed to a tanned hide spread out by the bed.

"When I wake up in the morning my bare feet touch her skin."

Patricia was totally at a loss for words.

"Of course," Paulo continued, "there are many beautiful females in the world. But why is it that only one touches your heart?" He was looking at Miguel. "Amante was a white cloud . . ." His voice rose again. "Riding her made me feel like a god."

Patricia thought it all so bizarre, yet she had never heard a man speak of a horse with such reverence.

Paulo's face was suddenly drained of all color; the gnarled hand on the desk started shaking. "Father," Miguel said sternly, "you should rest now and dream of Amante while Patrizia freshens up after her journey."

"Yes, yes," mumbled Paulo as Miguel helped him out of his chair and led him to the bed.

The last vision Patricia had walking out of the room was the great man sitting on the bed, his bare feet gently moving over the hide of his beloved Amante.

Stone Ridge

"FUCK HORACE COLEMAN," Laura muttered, and re-filled her glass. She was already pretty plastered. "What am I—a fucking magician?"

She banged the glass down on the table, the liquid sloshing all around, and buried her head in her hands. In frustration she scratched her head vigorously, willing some brilliant idea to come to mind.

"Shit! I am!"

She grabbed her handbag and rummaged through it.

Growing impatient, she dumped the contents on the floor. Out poured crushed packs of cigarettes, lipsticks, compacts, a dirty comb, a wallet, a half-eaten bag of potato chips. She sifted through the debris until she found it—a crumpled piece of paper. She smoothed it out with a smug smile on her face.

She walked over to the phone. "International operator? Connect me with Lisbon, Portugal—telephone number four-one-eight-oh-five-five-two, person to person, Miss Isabel Veloso."

Lisbon

PATRICIA DRESSED CAREFULLY, putting on one of her mother's gowns she had brought along—a delicate white moiré silk that flattered her slim figure. Taxi and Phoebe watched her intently from the bed.

"What do you guys think—will he like it?"

Taxi wagged his tail.

"Thank you," she said.

Through the window she caught sight of Miguel crossing the courtyard. Yes, she was sure she was right. He no longer limped, and there was a bounce in his step as he passed the fountain. What had happened?

She opened the door just as he raised his fist to knock. "Please don't hit me," she giggled.

"Never—and certainly not the way you look tonight." His fingers uncurled and tentatively touched her cheek. It was a gentle caress, affectionate.

"Where are we going to eat?" she stammered, not knowing what else to say.

"Well—I hope you don't mind, but I thought we'd eat in the kitchen."

"Oh, of course I don't mind—at home I eat in the kitchen all the time . . ." Then she smiled sheepishly, nervously tugging at the straps of her gown, "but I might be a touch overdressed."

"Not at all," he said, taking her arm and leading her through the main gate to Emilio's Ferrari.

"My friend sent me his snazzy car to impress you," he said, opening the door for her. "I don't have the heart to tell him you have your own private plane waiting at the airport."

"Do we need a car to drive to the kitchen?"

"Trust me," he said.

As he pulled out of the driveway to make the turn onto the road, Miguel noticed a white car idling across the street. It looked like Isabel's car, but he couldn't see the driver clearly enough.

He peeled out, watching his rearview mirror. The white car was following. Could it be Isabel, or was he just getting paranoid? Damn—the last thing he needed was a confrontation in front of Patricia.

He accelerated, speeding through the countryside into town, then whipped around a corner and turned down a side street.

"You sure drive fast!"

"Can't help it—this car has so much power." He glanced again into the mirror—the white car was gone.

"Where are we?" Patricia asked.

"Queluz. It means 'almond tree' in Arabic. And here's the kitchen." He pointed to an enormous pink palace, a stunning rococo imitation of Versailles, stretching out before them.

Patricia tried to figure out the joke, but his lips only curled in a smug smile. He parked the car at the far end of the building and guided her through a glass door.

"This is the old palace kitchen, now a fine restaurant, Conzinha Velha. Romantic, don't you think?"

She didn't get a chance to answer before the maître d' descended upon them. "Senhor Cardiga! So nice to see you here again," the man gushed, leading them into the interior of the restaurant, which was dimly lit by coach lanterns. They passed a fifteen-foot marble work-table, where the king's cooks once labored, and a giant open chimney elevated on marble columns, underneath which an iron spit stood ready for the wild boar roast.

"Right here, senhor." The maître d' pulled the chairs away from a corner table next to a stone gutter burbling with water.

"Oh, how unusual—any fish?" Patricia joked.

"As a matter of fact, the local stream was diverted through here so the cook could catch the king's dinner and wash the dishes," Miguel answered.

"That's practical."

With a flourish, the steward handed him the wine list. "What would you like to drink?" Miguel asked.

"Do I dare order Periquita?" she said with a twinkle in her eyes.

He laughed. "Perhaps not—you might be getting too much of that tomorrow."

"Is that a threat?"

"Patrizia," he said softly, leaning on his elbows and

looking into her eyes. "Do I look like a man who would threaten a woman?"

The wine steward cleared his throat.

"We'll have a bottle of Branco Seco," Miguel said, pushing the wine list away. "A white wine—also from Emilio's vineyards."

"I'd like to meet Emilio."

"He'll be here in a couple of days. We've been best friends ever since his father kicked him out for seducing one of the maids, and my father kicked me out for not cooling down a horse after a workout."

"He threw you out for that?"

"He would never have done it if I seduced one of the maids."

They both laughed.

Patricia sipped the wine; she didn't drink often, and it made her tingle.

Miguel ordered them gaspacho and a cheese called *Azeitão*. "I wouldn't dare order meat, knowing how you feel—this is sheep cheese from the Arrábida Peninsula. You remember my shepherd story?"

"Oh, yes I do." She took a bite. "It's delicious."

"It's supposed to have curative properties—" He fell silent, then added softly, "—if it could only cure cancer."

"Is there nothing the doctors can do for your father?"

"They tell me he has six months at most."

"Oh, how terribly, terribly sad . . . and yet he seems so vigorous. I really enjoyed talking with him—his love for that horse seems extraordinary."

"Yes. Amante was one in a million." Miguel brightened. The dark cloud passed as quickly as it came.

"*Amante*. What a romantic-sounding name."

"It means mistress," Miguel said with a twinkle. "Only my father would dare give a horse that name."

She laughed. "He really is someone very special."

"Yes, he's been called an artist, a genius, and a madman—you can see why."

"You have a great deal of your father in you—you're a little mad too."

"But I would never mount the head of my mistress on the wall, nor put her skin under my feet."

She grimaced.

"My awkward sense of humor I also inherit from my father. You see, my mother died when I was born, and he had to deal with me from the very beginning. Oh, we had our quarrels—I could never measure up to his expectations. We still irritate each other, but I do love the old *mestre*."

"Yes, I understand that. I loved my father too." Patricia felt an overpowering urge to continue. "You know, he died in the most horrible way."

Miguel sipped his wine, studying her.

"He was on his way to meet me . . . but . . . his plane was hijacked by Palestinian terrorists. They killed the Jews on board, and my father—he was mistaken for a Jew."

"That is tragic . . ." He shook his head. "I can never figure out why Jews are hated by so many people."

"I can't either . . . but my grandfather used to call them a sleazy lot—said they couldn't be trusted with money."

"How do you feel about it?"

"I know only one Jew—Dr. Solomon—and I love him."

"Well—now you know another."

She looked at him wide-eyed.

"My ancestors were Marranos."

"Marranos?"

"Yes, Jews forced by the Inquisition to become Catholics. Tomorrow, I'll show you the Rossio where thousands of Jews were burned at the stake."

"How terrible."

"How *stupid*. Most of the people in the world are part Jewish. I think the pope forgets that Christ was a Jew."

She listened attentively—he was constantly amazing her.

Miguel was working himself up. "I detest religion. It makes people hate each other, kill each other. Patrizia—the world would be better off if people paid more attention to God and less attention to religion."

"You make it sound so simple."

Miguel drained his glass. "Most things in life are simple—if you know what you really want." Then he took her hand in both of his. "Do you know what you want?"

"I'm not sure sometimes."

His eyes locked on hers. "I *do* know—I want you."

Unable to hold his gaze, Patricia looked down at his two strong hands enfolding her delicate fingers. Not daring to breathe, she slowly raised her eyes to his.

The bathroom door closed behind Patricia. Miguel turned out the lamp, struck a match, and lit the thick candle on the bedside table. He took his clothes off, sat down on the bed, and removed the single strap above his knee—so much easier than unbuckling that old harness, which used to lace his thigh with welts. The prosthesis dropped to the floor.

He watched the sliver of light coming from under the bathroom door, obscured from time to time by her movements. Then the light turned black, and his heartbeat quickened. The door opened.

Patricia wanted to run across the room and bury herself in his arms, but suddenly she felt shy. He was sitting on the bed, completely naked. His body was a honed sculpture of smooth muscle, his olive skin the color of raw honey in the candlelight. She couldn't quite make out the expression on his face. She took a deep breath and let her robe slip off her shoulders.

He leaned back on his arms, his eyes absorbing every part of her. "You are beautiful," he said.

"So are you," she whispered.

"Look at me," he commanded in a soft voice.

"I am."

"All of me."

Slowly, she walked over and knelt in front of him. Gently, she touched the thigh of his injured leg. He didn't move. "I want you, Miguel." Then her hand touched his erection.

He buried his fingers in her hair, then pulled her toward him and fiercely kissed her open mouth. An electrical current was racing through her body. It was the same sensation as when he had first kissed her in the stable. Then she was frightened; now she was not. "Oh Miguel," she whispered, "I'm sorry I pushed you away that night."

His laughter had a deep guttural sound. "Don't push me away again." And he rolled her over his body onto the bed.

"Never . . . never."

He stroked her neck, her breasts. Tenderly, he pinched her nipples and felt them harden. His hand grazed across her flat stomach and followed the outlines of her hips. Then his fingers went to that moist spot between her legs.

Patricia moaned softly as he crushed her beneath him and entered her.

Chapter 15

Lisbon

THE BELL CLANGED AT THE MAIN GATE. Miguel, worried that the noise would disturb his father, who had just drifted off to sleep after a difficult day, quickly crossed the courtyard. What a time for a visitor when he was looking forward to a quiet evening alone with Patricia.

He flung open the portals. Staring at him were the dark eyes of Isabel.

"Isabel? I . . . I'm just on my way out."

"But I'm not here to see you—I'm here to see your father." She held out a large bouquet of lilies, and moved forward to come in, but Miguel stood firmly in the doorway blocking her.

"I will give them to him," he said, taking the bouquet. "He can't have any visitors—he is very ill."

"Oh . . . I'm sorry to hear that."

"Thank you for your solicitude." He tried to close the gate but her hand reached out and held it back. "Miguel—don't shut me out." Her face was inches away from his. "I am ill too."

"Then go see a doctor."

"I'm serious—I'm sick, sick to death from not seeing you."

"Isabel, please . . . I don't want to discuss it. I have other problems right now—I'm concerned about my father."

Her lips curled into a twisted smile. "Really? I think you're more concerned about that deranged heiress."

Miguel was stunned.

"Yes," she continued. "Didn't she tell you that they just let her out of a nuthouse?"

Miguel's hand whipped across her face.

Slowly, she raised her gloved fingers to her cheek. Before she could say anything, Patricia's voice came calling from the darkness of the courtyard. "Miguel—where are you?"

"I'm coming," he answered quickly.

Isabel's eyes hardened into black pieces of coal. "Hurry, Miguel!" she snapped. "Don't keep her waiting."

She whipped around, and Miguel, shaking with anger, slammed the door behind her.

"A visitor?" Patricia asked as he hurried toward her.

"No—just a flower delivery for my father." He

raised the bouquet. "I'll have the maid put these in water." He needed a few moments to compose himself. Of course Patricia had told him of her stay at the Lausanne sanitorium, but how did Isabel know?

"Mr. Cardiga . . ." He heard Patricia's voice behind him. "You are tense, Mr. Cardiga. You are tense." Her arms encircled his neck, and the smile on her face dissolved all thoughts of Isabel.

All day at the riding school, Patricia felt like teacher's pet. A harsh command or a sharp rebuke to anyone else turned into a gentle suggestion or a smiling compliment to her. The whispers of the students made her wonder if they knew. But when he put her on Ultimato—a horse no one else was ever permitted to ride—the whispers turned to knowing grins.

In a few days, she was more than teacher's pet, she was teacher's assistant. Miguel asked her to work with the weepy French girl, who had alienated everyone else and was considered hopeless, nothing but a rich, spoiled brat.

Patricia felt sorry for the youngster, who seemed so pathetic, pulling along her reluctant Palomino, her britches saturated with wine, tears coursing down her chubby cheeks.

"*Quel est ton nom?*" Patricia asked, putting her arm around the sniffling student and guiding her to the far corner of the arena.

"My name is Lise," said the girl.

"Oh, you speak English?"

"*Oui*, I speek Engleesh. But I have trouble with the *cheval*."

Patricia smiled. "It's difficult at the beginning, Lise, but you must be patient."

"But Monsieur Miguel ees no patient. He's a monster . . . I deetest heem," she blurted out.

Patricia pressed her lips together to muffle her laughter.

"Well, yes. Monsieur Miguel can be a little harsh at times. But your horse is your friend."

"*Non*. He's a dragon. He want to throw me off hees back and stomp me with hees hoofs."

"Oh my, that can't be true. Come here—look—look into his eyes."

The girl timidly raised her head.

"You see—he's just scared. He thinks *you* are going to hurt *him* . . ."

The little girl stared into the Palomino's gentle eyes. "You thinks so? . . . He's scared too?"

"Yes. Just be nice to him and everything will go better. I promise."

"You promise?"

"Yes. First, go and change your britches," Patricia said, taking the reins, "and when you come back, I will help you."

"*Merci, merci*, you are very kind," said the girl, and hurried off.

Behind Patricia, a male voice commanded her attention. "Senhora, I would like riding lessons from you." Patricia turned around to see a tall, lean young man approaching her.

"I suggest you speak with Senhor Cardiga," she answered, motioning toward Miguel, who was occupied with a student at the end of the ring.

"No. No. NO!" he shouted. "I will never take lessons from him!"

Patricia tried to pacify the man, whose voice was getting louder: "Please, there is no need to—"

"He is a monster! You heard the little girl—everybody knows it!"

Patricia turned to Miguel for help and saw him approaching with a broad smile on his face.

"Emilio," Miguel said, "must I throw you out of here again?"

The man grinned.

"Patrizia, this *used* to be my very best friend," Miguel said.

Emilio kissed her hand with mock elegance. "Ahh— you don't know how happy I am to finally meet you. I have heard so much about you, but Miguel lies so often,"—and then he winked—"I'm glad to see this time he tells the truth."

Late that afternoon, Emilio insisted that he be the guide on Patricia's tour of Lisbon. As the three huddled in his sports car, he bragged, "With Miguel you will see a lot of stables and horseshit . . . but with me you will see the voluptuous luxuriance of Lisbon."

Patricia could see what made them friends. Everything Emilio said made Miguel laugh.

He drove them to Alfama, the old Moorish quarter, where they parked the car and made their way on foot up narrow, cobblestoned alleys strung with laundry drying in the spring breeze. The tall, colorfully stuccoed buildings on either side of them seemed to lean toward each other as if trying to meet at the top. Some of the streets were crowded with tables and chairs, men, women, and children eating and drinking, music playing, the smell of barbecued fish in the air. It was fiesta time.

"Did Miguel ever tell you, Patrizia, about the time our fathers kicked us out?" Emilio asked, taking her by the arm.

"He did mention it."

"We lived right near here for a little while. Those were the wild days. Remember, Miguelinho?"

"How can I forget it? We were going to run away to Paris and start a horse circus." Miguel laughed. "We had some crazy ideas in those days."

"Not so crazy. Zingaro did it, and he's a huge hit— people can't get enough of his horse magic."

"Zingaro was my father's most promising and difficult student," Miguel explained. "Now he is in Paris, pretending to be a gypsy and mesmerizing people with his horse show. I'll take you to see his act sometime."

"I'd love that."

"Be sure to go early," interjected Emilio. "Before the show, waiters standing on horseback deliver wine to the audience—a very fine vintage, I might add."

"Fonseca?" Patricia giggled.

Suddenly Emilio stopped. "There it is!" and he pointed in the air.

"What?" asked Patricia.

"Up there was our apartment. Ahh," he sighed, obviously relishing the memory. "It was an evening like this—fiesta time—I was down here, in the street, trying to get a head start on picking up an attractive companion

for the night, while he's getting dressed *up there* . . .''
Emilio pointed again.

Miguel cut him off. "Patrizia doesn't want to hear
that story."

"Oh, yes she does," Emilio went on without pausing
for breath. "He comes out of the shower—"

Miguel grabbed his friend. "I'm going to knock you
on your ass if you say more."

"That's unfair, Miguel," Patricia teased. "Emilio
started a story and I want to hear it."

Miguel moved away with feigned disgust. "Well, *I*
don't want to hear it."

"Then don't listen!" Emilio shouted after him. And
in a soft voice, almost in Patricia's ear, he continued.
"He's drying himself off with a towel, when in the
window across the alley, he sees the bartender's daughter—a real beauty—stark naked, looking at him."

"Enough!" Miguel called out.

"You coward!" Emilio answered.

"So what happened?" Patricia prompted.

"I'm down here, four floors below, trying to find a
girl who'd let me hold her hand, and I can't believe my
eyes. He climbs out the window, right over my head,
and crosses the alley on the *clothesline*!''

Patricia started to laugh.

"It's not funny. He was naked. Everyone might have
seen him up there, but Miguel didn't care." Emilio
looked at his friend, who was still scowling at him.
"Okay, okay—I don't know what happened above, but
down below I got a big black eye. Her father started to
go upstairs, and the only way I could stop him was to

get into an argument. Finally, after fifteen minutes, out of my one good eye, I see Miguel going back across the clothesline.''

"Oh, I'm sure nothing happened in such a short time.'' Patricia winked at Miguel.

"You may be right.'' Emilio raised his arms in surrender. "All I can tell you is when he finally came down here he wasn't interested in holding anybody's hand.''

Miguel gave him a playful punch in the arm. Emilio feigned agony. "This is how you treat the man who saved your life? If that bartender caught you with his daughter he would have killed you.'' They all laughed.

That night as they lay in bed, side by side, Patricia's giggle broke through the dark quiet of the room.

"What's so funny?'' Miguel asked.

"Is that what turns you on—naked girls across an alley?''

"No—clotheslines.''

She giggled again. "But when you got there did she try to stop you?''

"Of course not. She pretended to be helpless. Whatever happened wasn't her fault.''

"Yes, I can understand that,'' Patricia murmured. Then she added softly, "I'd like to be helpless.''

"What?''

"So you can do with me what you will.'' She snuggled up closer to him.

For several minutes no one spoke. The heady scent of spring flowers, of lilacs and wisteria, filtered in from the courtyard.

"So you would like to feel helpless?''

Her answer was a gentle kiss on the lips.

"Walk over to the window," he said gruffly.

"Why?"

"Trust me."

She did as he asked. "Now what?"

Miguel looked at her silhouette illuminated by the slits of moonlight coming through the partially closed curtain.

"Take off the window sash."

She removed the satin cord and looked at him.

"The other one too," he said very distinctly.

Patricia walked over to him, and held out her arms, a cord in each hand.

His eyes locked on hers as he took the sashes. Without a word, she lay down on the bed before him. She was breathing heavily, the very anticipation arousing her.

He took hold of her wrist, wrapped the cord around it, and tied it to the bedpost. He crawled over her, extended her other arm, and did the same.

Then he sat back, taking in her naked form—outstretched, waiting. And his mouth began a descent down her body. He licked her like an animal licks its young, his lips lingering on her nipples.

She was writhing under him—the bonds confining her excitement, and making the pleasure all the more exquisite. Now, his fingers moved between her legs, opening her slowly, gently.

"I love being helpless," she moaned as his mouth sought her wetness.

A distant sound woke her, but she kept her face buried deep in the pillow. She could hear Miguel's rhythmic breathing next to her, Phoebe purring in her hair, Taxi snoring gently at her feet.

Quietly, she got up and moved away from the bed. With a smile, she picked up the two satin sashes lying on the floor and walked over to the window. She opened the curtains and tied them back with the cords.

From a distance came the sound that had awakened her—bells tolling loud and sweet. *Golden molten bells.* She remembered Daddy reading the poem: "*. . . what a world of happiness their harmony foretells . . .*"

With a sigh, she turned toward the bed. He was staring up at the ceiling. "Miguel—listen."

"Those goddamn church bells," he muttered.

She started to laugh.

"What's so funny?" he asked.

"You!" And she raced over to the bed, fell on top of him, and kissed him fiercely on the mouth.

When she released him, he gasped, "You do that again, and Sunday is shot. Poor Ultimato will never see me today."

"I wish you wouldn't go."

"Come with me."

"No, I'd rather not . . . it would make me too nervous."

"I know—you would be more worried about the bull than about me."

"Well . . . it gets bloody, doesn't it?"

"Patrizia—when we practice, the bull always wears a protective vest, and even in the real bullring, we don't kill it. Portugal is not like Spain. I wish you'd come out and see me just once."

"I will, but not today."

"All right—but I still have work to do." He threw back the covers with a flourish of determination, and the dog and cat scampered off. He sat on the edge of the bed, picked up his prosthesis, and strapped it on.

"I owe a lot to your ex-fiancé," he said over his shoulder.

"You do?"

"Yes—for this," and he patted his artificial limb.

"Oh, I remember—he gave you that brochure."

"You know, I hated his guts when I met him. I thought he was a phoney Mother Teresa. But I was just jealous because he had you." Miguel leaned over and kissed her cheek. "Now I think he's a great doctor. Do you know that he called Seattle and arranged everything? Someday, I have to thank him for that . . ." He walked into the bathroom and then stuck his head out. "And for breaking his engagement with you."

Patricia stretched out on the bed, feeling deliciously content. She was here in Lisbon with the man she loved. And Miguel was right about Tom. She would never forget what he said about "the mere act of caring."

She got up, wrapped a robe around herself, and leaned against the bathroom door, watching Miguel shave. "You know, Tom really hurt me, but it doesn't matter now. I'll even thank him for you."

"You will?"

"Yes. I'll give an endowment to his foundation. I'll have the money when I sell the company."

"What?" Miguel put down his razor.

"I'm selling all my shares in the Stoneham Group."

"Why would you do that?"

"Oh Miguel, we have a division in Nogales—I'm ashamed of it." And she described what she had seen.

Miguel listened to her intently.

"I can't be part of it," she finished the story.

"But will selling the company solve the problem?"

"I don't have the power to solve the problem, and I have no other choice."

Patricia couldn't see the expression on Miguel's face as he dried himself with a towel. He walked back into the room and started getting dressed. "You can find a way—I know it. I know you, Patrizia."

"There is nothing else I can do," she insisted.

"Nothing else? Well—maybe you're right." He went on dressing.

Patricia bit her lip. He didn't understand at all, but she couldn't find the words to explain it to him. She watched him heading for the door. He opened it and then turned around with a sly smile. "Hey, Patrizia—people are almost as important as animals."

The sound of the closing door echoed his rebuke.

She could not shake off the feeling of shame that was beginning to creep over her as she put on her riding clothes. Miguel had shined a spotlight on her dark side—where she hid her weakness, the part of her she hated the most.

She picked up her jacket and practically ran out of the room, eager to seek solace where she had always found it—in the stable. The stiff soles of her riding boots clattered on the floor tiles.

"Who goes there?!"

Oh God, she had awakened Paulo.

"I'm sorry to disturb you," she called out. "I didn't mean to make so much noise."

"Come here!" It was an order.

She opened the door to his room, and found him sitting up in bed.

"Going riding?"

"Yes . . . I am so sorry to wake you."

"You didn't wake me—the damn bells did that. But why are you in such a great hurry?"

"Oh no, I'm not . . . not really."

The stern expression on the angular face softened. "Good—come sit here." And he patted the bed beside him.

She obeyed.

"You do not go to watch the great bullfighter?"

"No, I decided to stay home."

"Ahh, it makes you uncomfortable. Well, I can understand that. I don't approve either. I think my son is wasting his great talent with something so crude."

She didn't know what to say.

"Bullfighting has kept me and my son apart—we have exchanged many angry words about it. Don't let it get between the two of you. Learn to accept what you can't approve of, Patrizia."

"I hope Miguel can learn to accept what he can't approve about me," she said softly.

"He will—that's part of falling in love."

She was grateful to Paulo, so grateful for these words of reassurance, she almost kissed him.

Sensing her warmth, he took hold of her hand and stroked it gently. "You know, Patrizia—my son is a remarkable man."

"Yes, I know he is."

"Do you know that he actually considers his handicap a gift."

"A gift? He told you that?"

"Oh no, he never tells me anything. Most of what I know comes from Emilio, and Emilio doesn't tell me all. He only tells me what he thinks I should know"—he smiled—"and what he thinks I would like to hear. He is not my son, so we can talk easily. Do fathers and sons ever really communicate?"

The touch of his gnarled, bony hand was strangely comforting, and she listened to him, not interrupting.

"Emilio said that Miguel thinks his injury changed him—made him a better person. And it led to so many other things—because of it he trained Ultimato . . . because of it he met you . . ."

Patricia was strangely moved by this aristocratic, hardened man who spoke of his son with reverence.

He looked at her with soft blue eyes. "You mean the world to him, Patrizia."

"Thank you for telling me that—I needed to hear it just now."

"Well, what is an old man good for if not a little meddling." He started to laugh. Then suddenly, his laugh turned to a cough. She grabbed a glass of water from the nightstand and, putting her arm around his neck for support, brought it to his lips.

Exhausted by the spell, he lay back on the pillow and smiled wanly. "Too bad I did not have a daughter . . . but maybe someday I will."

Patricia kissed him on the cheek. "You better rest now. I'll check on you later."

As she moved toward the door he called out, "What horse are you riding?"

"Corsario."

"Ah yes, a wonderful horse, Miguel trained him, but like Miguel he can be stubborn sometimes. Take care, Patrizia." He winked at her.

It was difficult to concentrate on riding. She kept thinking of Miguel's enigmatic smile and his words: "People are almost as important as animals." And the feeling of shame clung to her.

As if wanting to wash it away, she came back to her room and lay soaking in the tub.

She had come back from Nogales determined to help those abused people. She had walked into Coleman's office filled with resolve, and then he touched the button that released a torrent of guilt. She felt responsible for J. L.'s death, and Coleman knew it. He reminded her of the cruel words she spoke to her grandfather, and her resolve crumbled. She had pushed what she had seen in Nogales out of her mind, willing to give up everything—sell out.

But Miguel drove home the point. And then Paulo. Miguel had overcome his handicap—and wasn't her grandfather's wealth *her* handicap? Miguel found the power in himself to accept it, conquer its limitations, think of it as a gift. Couldn't she do the same? Miguel seemed so certain she could. He believed in her. In his arms she felt strong, invincible—she felt she could do anything, even take on Horace Coleman.

She got out of the tub and rubbed herself roughly with a towel. She wouldn't betray what she believed in.

Chapter 16

Lisbon

WITH GREAT CARE, Miguel was grooming Ultimato after their workout, Emilio observing with an amused expression. "That heifer is no match for your horse."

Miguel patted Ultimato's rump with affection.

"Goddamn!" Emilio continued. "The way he went around that ring shoving his tail between her horns . . ."

"That's what he's supposed to do."

"I think Ultimato is ready for the *corrida*."

"I don't know," said Miguel, leading the horse up the ramp into the van. "I don't want to rush him."

"Rush him? Come on, Miguel—that horse is dying to mix it up with a big bull. He's bored with that heifer."

"No—he needs more conditioning, and I can't give it to him on a schedule of once a week."

"Can't you break away more often?"

"Not now. I worry about Paulo. He gets over to the school once in a while, but he can't teach anymore. I try to make him feel a part of it—give him a report every evening."

"What a sad situation—for Paulo . . . you . . . for Ultimato . . . This horse deserves an audience. Too bad Patricia couldn't have been here to see him."

"She doesn't like bullfighting. She hates to see an animal get hurt."

"She'll get over that."

"I'm not sure."

"Is everything all right between the two of you?"

Miguel raised the ramp of the van, latched it, and then stood there looking off. "I think I'm in love."

"Santa Engrasia!" Emilio struck his forehead with both hands, and raised his arms in mock supplication to the heavens. "Love—a fatal disease."

Miguel laughed. "Haven't you ever been in love?"

"Yeah—in the eleventh grade—with a redheaded girl who sat in front of me. I even gave her my silver belt buckle."

"I guess it didn't last because you still have that buckle."

"Well, she gave it to the guy who sat in front of her, and I had to beat him up to get it back."

"Someday, Emilio, you too will fall in love."

"Not me. I want my romance short and sweet. A dance at the disco, a bottle of wine, a few hours in bed, and in the morning I want to wake up alone."

"I used to think that—but the right woman changes your mind."

Emilio grunted as he revved up the motor of his Ferrari and slowly pulled the van out onto the road.

Stone Ridge

WITH A DRINK IN HER HAND, Laura watched the farmhands raucously depart down the driveway on the back of a pickup truck. It was Friday evening and Edgar was treating them all to some beers at the local pub.

A brilliant sun hung low in the sky. She stumbled out of the kitchen door, found a wheelbarrow leaning against the barn, and pushed it in the direction of the insectary. As she entered the greenhouse, she shuddered. But there were no swarms of buzzing insects. All was quiet. On the brick floor before her stretched long rows of flowerpots, each sprouting a tuft of alfafa. This is what the bad bugs fed on, Patricia had told her. And then she saw them—encrustations of black dots covering the stems of the plants. Quickly, she picked up pot after pot and shook them till the insects fell like rain into the wheelbarrow, muttering obscenities all the while. "I don't get paid enough for this."

Huffing and puffing, she propelled the wheelbarrow to where the field of white roses just beginning to bud looked like a sparkling white carpet in the setting sun.

Lisbon

"EMILIO AND I HAVE something special for you to-night," Miguel announced as he and Patricia were putting the horses in their stalls after the lessons.

"Oh God—what happens now?"

"He is picking us up at eight o'clock this evening."

"Just the three of us?"

"Of course."

"Doesn't he have a girlfriend?"

A deep laugh rumbled out of Miguel. "He will find one or two before the evening is over."

She absentmindedly stroked Ultimato's head. "Were you like that?"

"Like what?"

"Like Emilio."

He hung up the bridle and walked over to her. He put his arms around her and moved to kiss her, but she pulled back. "Or did you always need a clothes-line—"

His mouth covered hers before she could say more.

Crammed in the Ferrari—Emilio always insisted they travel "in style"—they sped along to the Bairro Alto, the hottest disco of Lisbon.

"We have plenty of discos in America. When will we go to a fado club and hear some torch songs?" Patricia asked.

"When you go without me," Emilio snickered. "Since Miguel's stopped drinking he's become old-fashioned. Let him sing some of those old songs to you." And he bellowed out: *"I am mad with despair because you are so fair . . ."*

"Miguel sang that song to me yesterday," Patricia joked, and they all laughed.

When they entered the disco—an old mill house decorated with an odd, but intriguing, mix of faux Roman ruins and high-tech—Patricia felt she was back in the States: a loudspeaker was pulsating with the beat of Janet Jackson's "Rhythm Nation." The dance floors and tables were set up on two levels, which were connected by an open mesh iron staircase, both levels packed with girls in flimsy dresses and their partners in baggy pants writhing to the music. The sound level was deafening.

"Miguelinho! What a special honor to have you with us tonight!" Jorge, the club's owner, shouted over the music as he guided them around the statue of Venus into a dimly lit niche on the first level.

"Patrizia—I come here two or three times a week," Emilio complained. "Miguel never comes here and see the fuss they make."

"But you're so timid and shy they hardly notice you," Patricia teased.

Emilio didn't sit down. "I pay the tab, I get the first dance." He pulled Patricia onto the dance floor. "With you—they'll notice me."

Patricia blushed, but she knew she looked good and that other men on the dance floor were turning their heads. Tall and slender, with her curly blond hair cut short, she presented the picture of a tomboy-gone-sexy in a short tight-fitting black dress that exposed her bare shoulders.

Emilio's dance style was a cross between the Charleston and the lambada. She was pulled wildly in all directions and swirled dizzily around.

As the tempo of the music slowed down, Patricia saw Miguel talking with an attractive dark-haired woman in a purple dress slit up the side. Her body blocked the view of Miguel's face. She was gesticulating rapidly with one hand while holding a glass of wine in the other. Suddenly, she flung the wine at Miguel, who ducked just in time.

"What's going on?" Patricia exclaimed.

But Emilio only swirled her around faster. "Must be some student who got too much wine on her britches and wants to return the favor."

When they got back, the agitated woman was gone and Miguel offered no explanation. Patricia saw her walk up the mesh staircase and sit at a table near the edge of the second-floor platform.

Emilio loudly summoned the waiter. "A bottle of Garrafeira 1955." He winked at Patricia. "From my own vineyard."

"I'm well acquainted with your Periquita."

Emilio started to respond but Miguel broke in, "Am I allowed to dance?" and he took Patricia's arm.

The mood of the music had switched, and now the sultry voice of Billy Joel filled the room. Patricia was amazed at Miguel's deftness as he moved her gracefully around the floor.

"You dance very well," she said.

"Why not—dancing is like riding. You must be easy with the reins—feel your partner with your hips." He pulled her closer. "After a while you don't know who's leading, but both are willing to follow." He kissed the nape of her neck, and she melted against him.

Wrapped in his arms, she caught a glimpse of the dark-haired woman glaring at them from above, but forgot about her quickly as the music filled her mind. "Oh I love that song," she whispered. Softly, she sang: "*I know that everybody has a dream/And this is my dream, my own/Just to be at home/And to be all alone . . . with you . . .*"

They looked at each other.

"Let's leave," he said. "Emilio will understand."

"What took you so long?"

He hugged her tightly.

At the table, Miguel winked at Emilio. "Something important has come up and we have to leave. *Comprende-me?*"

"Oh sure, sure, I can't tell you how happy I am to be left alone"—and he pointed to the cooler—"with a fifty-dollar bottle of wine from my own vineyard." He made a face.

"Ahh, you won't be alone for long," Miguel said. He turned to go, but his path was blocked by the dark-haired woman. She let out a torrent of Portuguese words, darting angry looks at Patricia.

He tried to answer calmly, as heads turned in their direction. Her voice rose higher.

"Isabel!" Emilio bellowed, getting up and embracing her to stifle her outburst. "You have taken pity on me!"

She tried to pull away but he continued to yell over her protestations. "Come share the wine! Come dance!" He whirled her around and threw his car keys to Miguel.

Patricia was violently yanked along as Miguel twisted

through the crowded dance floor heading for the exit.
Another Billy Joel record was playing:

> *Well, we all fall in love but we disregard the danger*
> *Though we share so many secrets there are some we never tell*
> *Why were you so surprised that you never saw the stranger*
> *Did you ever let your lover see the stranger in yourself?*

Chapter 17

Lisbon

IT WAS BEGINNING TO RAIN when they hurried out of the disco. Without a word, Miguel packed Patricia into the car, got behind the wheel, and drove off.

She watched his tense face, waiting for him to say something, but he just stared at the road. Big drops of rain were splattering against the windshield, and he turned on the wipers, still saying nothing. Finally, she asked, "What was that all about?"

"Oh, some woman I knew years ago."

"Isabel?"

"Yes."

"I remember—she called the farm."

"That is true."

"You were engaged to her."

"That is not true. But she did want to marry me after her husband died suddenly . . ." And then he added softly, "He was killed by a bull."

"Oh, he was a bullfighter?"

"No—he was a bull breeder." Miguel shifted into a high gear, and the car sliced through the rain. "He was showing off his prize bull when . . . he was gored."

Patricia couldn't take her eyes off Miguel—he seemed haunted by the accident.

"I was there when it happened," he said.

"It must have been an awful thing to see."

"It was." He hesitated, then the words rushed out of him: "I killed him."

Patricia stopped breathing for a moment. The only sound was the steady swish of the wipers on the windshield. "You killed him?" she echoed almost inaudibly.

"Yes."

She hugged her bare arms to keep from shivering. "Why?"

"He tried to kill me. Twice." Miguel seemed calmer now, driving more slowly, but his jaw muscles were pulsating. He said softly, "You see, Patrizia, his wife was very beautiful—" He stopped.

"And you were having an affair?" she prompted.

"It didn't mean anything. But—"

"He found out."

"Yes."

"And what happened?"

"My last fight—he gave me a bad bull."

"Bad bull?"

"You see, after one fight, the bull learns how to

outmaneuver the horse and rider. That's why he is never used twice—he becomes a killer.''

''That's why you had the accident?''

Miguel nodded. ''I was bitter at first, but I understood. The worst thing that can happen to a man is to be cuckolded. But one leg was not enough for Veloso.''

''What did he do?''

''When I returned to Lisbon, he invited me to their home for dinner. Like an idiot, I went.''

''Why?''

''Patrizia—I've asked myself that question many times.'' His voice grew raspy, and he cleared his throat. He stared ahead through the downpour as if he were seeing it again. ''Just the three of us at the dining room table. When I looked at her I felt nothing. I kept thinking—what a price I paid.''

The car pulled up in front of the Centro Equestre da Cardiga and Miguel shut off the engine. Neither one of them moved.

In a monotone, still not looking at her, he continued. ''There was no one around the house, the men had all been sent out into the fields. After dinner, he insisted on showing me his prize bull. He taunted me into trying a pass. I had been drinking—I took the bait. Then I saw the scars on the bull's neck. That sobered me. This was another bad bull.'' Miguel's voice hardened. ''He had crippled me, and now he wanted to finish me off . . . I had to kill him.''

Patricia swallowed.

''I've never told this to anyone before—even Emilio.''

''Why did you tell me?'' she whispered.

For the first time since he began the story he looked at her. "I had to tell you all this before I could say I love you."

Abruptly, he shoved the car door open and got out, oblivious to the rain. Patricia followed him across the courtyard without a word. He killed a man. She was astonished that she felt no shock, no dread. But then, hadn't she done the same to J. L.—with words?

By the time they reached her room, they were soaked to the skin.

"I'm sorry, Patrizia . . . try to sleep well."

She reached out for his arm and gently pulled him inside. She looked up at him. "I love you, Miguel. Nothing can change that."

He cupped her wet face in his hands and covered it with kisses. Then he pulled her body close to him, almost roughly, his kisses growing more passionate, more demanding.

As they moved toward the bed, they both stopped. Taxi was stretched out across the blanket with his tail thumping contentedly, and Phoebe was nestled between the two pillows.

That night they made love on the floor.

Miguel was relieved—at last, he had confessed his crime. It had weighed on him heavily. He was grateful that Patricia never mentioned it again, never plied him with questions. She knew the worst and she loved him.

Now he felt lighthearted and his spirits soared. As he was cantering around the ring, Emilio drove up. Even from a distance, Miguel could see that his friend's face was badly scratched up.

"What happened?" Miguel called out. "You get caught in a wine press?"

Emilio approached him with a doleful expression. "Try dancing with Isabel when she doesn't want to dance."

Miguel couldn't hold back his laughter as he dismounted.

"Miguelinho, it's not funny. Isabel is crazy."

"Come on—she was just drunk."

"Hey, I know women when they're drunk. *She is crazy.* Keep away from her—"

"I intend to."

"Because I won't always be there to dance her away."

For Patricia, time had stopped. The horrible secret he had revealed to her only brought them closer together. All that mattered was that he loved her and that she loved him.

The farm seemed so far off. Each time she called, Laura urged her to come home, Edgar complained about the quality of hay, and she felt guilty about Sport and Harpalo, but she couldn't tear herself away from Miguel. That Sunday morning, with the church bells ringing, he had jolted her—he was right about Nogales and the stock sale, but she wasn't sure how to reverse the course of action she had initiated. She had tried to reach Mrs. Sperber for advice but the barrister was on vacation. She knew she had plenty of time—stock sales of this magnitude didn't happen overnight. She would talk with Mrs. Sperber when she returned to London. In a way, Patricia was relieved; it was so much easier, for now, to postpone facing Coleman and just enjoy the sheer bliss of being with Miguel.

He kept opening doors to rooms of secret pleasures—

some dark, some brightly lit—whole worlds of sexual experiences new to her. With him, she could be anything she wanted to be—dominant or subservient, a woman or a child. But best of all was lying spent, cradled in his arms, his hand gently stroking her hair, making her feel safe and secure.

She never wanted to leave this blissful haven, but the moment of decision was forced on her.

She was in her room diligently rubbing her riding boots with a chammy, her white britches laid out on the bed, when there was a knock on the door. She knew that knock.

"Come in, Miguel," she called out cheerily.

He came in dressed in his usual black riding outfit. My God, he was handsome.

"This arrived by Federal Express." He plopped a large envelope down in front of her. *"FROM: Horace Coleman . . . CONFIDENTIAL . . ."* She took a deep breath and ripped it open. Coleman wasn't wasting any time. She had thought it would take at least six months or more. But here they were—the documents to start the stock sale moving.

"The point of no return," she said softly.

"What?"

"I'm not going to sign these—I'm not going to sell the company."

His face wore a wide grin. "I knew you would rise to the challenge." He came over and kissed her gently on the forehead. "And, you should expect no less from me."

She looked at him quizzically.

"I must rise to the challenge too—I will try to teach the French girl."

"You're going to take her on again?"

"Yes, I'm beginning to like her; she's showing remarkable improvement."

Patricia watched him saunter out the door. Then she looked down at the package. Her hands were trembling as she leafed through the papers. Why was she so nervous—she had made her decision. She couldn't let this go through. But when she looked down at the voluminous stack of paper with x's for her signature and paper clips marking the precise pages, she felt intimidated.

Then the thought hit her—maybe it was too late—maybe all the arrangements had been made—maybe she was locked into the sale. What had she done?!

She grabbed the phone and, in broken Portuguese, her voice quavering, asked for the international operator. After a half a dozen calls, she tracked Mrs. Sperber to North Cornwall.

"Sperber here."

Patricia sighed with gratitude at the sound of the clipped speech. "Oh, Mrs. Sperber, I'm so glad to hear your voice."

"Likewise—are you still in Portugal?"

"Yes . . . and I'm in a mess."

"The riding lessons are not going well?"

"Oh no, no—it's not that at all. It's Horace Coleman."

"You'd best tell me everything."

When Patricia was through, Mrs. Sperber said, "First, let me assure you that it is not too late. It does not matter how many legal papers Horace sends you. No sale can go forward without your signature."

"But what should I do?"

"Actually, it is very simple—notify Horace Coleman that you do not wish to proceed."

"You mean, just call him up?"

"It would be preferable to do so in person. Simply say you have changed your mind—you are exercising a woman's prerogative." Mrs. Sperber made a peculiar noise—it sounded like a snicker— but Mrs. Sperber was always so proper, it couldn't be.

Paris

PATRICIA KNEW that she ought to say good-bye to Miguel like a mature adult and be on her way to take care of business in New York; after all, she would be returning to Lisbon as soon as she settled things with the trustees. *So, I'm not a mature adult*, she told herself, refusing to feel guilty about stalling to spend a few extra hours with him.

The idea for the side trip to Paris came up when she heard Miguel telling Filipe to get a young colt ready for shipment to Bartabas Zingaro; she volunteered to make the delivery on her way home.

"But Patrizia." Miguel had looked at her incredulously. "We're not talking about a dog and cat. This is a *horse*. Have you seen the size of the shipping container we have to put them in?"

"Have you seen the size of my plane?" she had replied.

"A horse won't fit into the cargo space of a private plane."

"Yes, it will—if it's a 727."

She convinced him, of course, and Miguel agreed to make the trip with her. They would see Zingaro's magic horse act and then finally say good-bye.

Zingaro was a surprise. A soft-spoken man who was uncommonly gentle with horses, he became a diabolic sorcerer on stage. In a candlelit arena, a black cape swirling around him, he rode out bareback on a black Frisian stallion, the horse stepping onto a large wooden drum placed in the center. Then, the horse's hooves began hammering out an eerie, rhythmic beat.

"Do you think he rides better than I do?" Miguel whispered.

"Almost," Patricia whispered back.

The finale of the act was the *pièce de résistance*. "He stole the idea from my father, but he has improved on it," Miguel said in her ear as two horses galloped into the arena free of saddles or bridles. Patricia was stunned. The white horse was a mare, obviously in heat; the black horse was a stallion, his enormous cock hard and extended, in close pursuit. The audience gasped as the stallion mounted the mare, who spread her hind legs apart to admit him, absorbing his deep thrusts.

Although she had seen horses mating many times, this one act, in Zingaro's bizarre theater, left Patricia strangely disturbed. It was erotic, yet she was too depressed about saying good-bye to Miguel to let herself respond to the feeling.

As the car sped them back to the airport, she sat in silence staring out the window.

"Patrizia—what's the matter, didn't you enjoy the show?"

"Yes . . . very much."

"What did you think of the ending?"

"I thought that it's much easier to be a mare than a woman—at least you know where you stand with the stallion."

Miguel laughed. "But Patrizia—surely you know where you stand with me—and don't you want me to treat you as my equal?"

"Oh I do, but you know what they say about the modern woman—she's confused—she wants to be treated equally, but sometimes, she likes to be dominated sexually."

"Do I have to tie you up each time?"

"Well . . ." She had a sly smile on her face. "Not if I can get the same service as the mare."

He laughed as the car pulled up to the 727 waiting on the runway.

"Miguel," she started shyly. "Let me take you back to Lisbon . . ."

"But Patrizia, shouldn't you be on your way to America?"

"It would only be two hours extra . . ." She bit her lip, expecting him to say no.

"Two hours? I'll take everything I can get," he said, and followed her up the stairs.

As soon as the plane lifted into the air, she dismissed the stewards. She wanted to have as much private time with Miguel as possible, to cuddle in his arms, to hear him murmur reassuring words. But he clearly had other ideas.

He opened the door to the bedroom.

"No Miguel . . . not there . . ."

"Why not?" he asked, and he picked her up in his arms.

"I never go in there."

"But the bed looks very comfortable."

"You don't understand . . . this was my grandfather's room . . . he died on this bed."

"I don't see any ghosts." He chuckled as he put her gently down.

He opened a bottle of wine—one from the gift case sent by Emilio—and filled two glasses. But she couldn't relax. The wine seemed to have no effect in this room.

She let him undress her, wanting to please him, but she still felt tense. His kisses, his hands, which could make her tingle any other time, now were touching a different body, not her skin. Lying naked on J. L.'s bed, she could only focus on the large flask of J. L.'s cologne, visible through the half-opened bathroom door, standing untouched on the marble sink counter.

"Patrizia," Miguel murmured huskily. "What do you want?"

I just want you to come so I can leave this room, she answered in her head, but out loud she said nothing because she didn't know how to say it without hurting his feelings.

"I love you," she heard him whisper as his tongue traced tiny circles on her stomach, moving downward. And suddenly, she felt a familiar warmth beginning to wash all over her body. Sensing her response, Miguel's mouth moved lower still.

Then he deftly turned her on her stomach, his arms encircling her waist. He pushed her legs apart and pulled her up to her knees. "So you envy mares, hey?" In response, all he could hear was her uneven breathing.

She was vibrating with anticipation of this new feeling. And then he entered her slowly as his hands grasped her breasts to keep her immobile.

"Am I hurting you?"

"No," she answered.

"Do you like it?"

She only murmured, "More . . . more . . . please more . . ." And his thrusts became insistent, deeper, faster.

She came before he did, and he held her quivering body to himself, a helpless receptacle of his mounting passion, until, for him, it too was over.

They lay in exhausted silence for a few minutes. And then slowly, Patricia got up from the bed.

Purposefully, she walked into the bathroom and looked at the cologne bottle filled with yellow liquid. She pulled out the stopper—the smell that hit her was unpleasant and stale, but nothing more than that. She poured the contents down the toilet and flushed it. Then she threw the bottle in the trash basket; it made a loud noise as it hit bottom.

"What are you doing?" Miguel asked.

"Exorcising ghosts," she answered.

New York City

BOB ASH STRODE INTO THE OFFICE. "Geez Horace, I'm shooting my best round of golf—had them down by five shots—and you yank me—"

"Shut up Bob, and sit down."

Ash, still miffed, sat next to Rosemont.

"Fellas"—Coleman's eyes speared both of them—"we're in deep shit. She's on her way back."

"Who?" Ash asked.

"The boss," Coleman said sarcastically. "Miss Dennison."

"So—I thought you wanted her back." Ash's face wore a blank expression.

Coleman leaned forward as he pulled out a piece of paper. Through his thick horn-rimmed glasses, stressing each word for emphasis, he read the fax Patricia had sent from Lisbon requesting a meeting and ending with: "*. . . and so, Mr. Coleman, since I will not be selling my stock, I plan to take a more active role in the corporation—together we can develop a company with a conscience.*"

Ash let the rubber ball slip out of his hand and bounce softly across the carpet.

Rosemont lifted his head up from his obsessive doodling. "She's planning to run the company?"

"I'm glad you got the message," said Coleman as he plopped back in his chair.

"But she's crazy," Ash said.

"That's right," said Coleman grimly.

"What do we say? How do we handle her?" Rosemont practically stuttered.

"That's the point of this meeting—and we don't have much time."

Ash was slowly recovering from shock. "Look, I say we meet her head-on. She's just a kid—she'll collect her dolls and go crying to her shrink."

Rosemont nodded. "We should be able to intimidate her."

"I'm not so sure," Coleman said almost to himself. "She sounds different somehow—somebody's feeding her ideas."

Rosemont and Ash looked at each other. "Sperber?" Ash asked.

"I can't be sure, but until we find out, I say we humor her, pretend to go along with anything she says, until we get our guns loaded."

"But Horace, how—" Ash was interrupted by the buzz of the intercom.

"Mr. Coleman," the secretary's voice came over, "Miss Laura Simpson is here, sir."

"About time." Coleman glanced at his watch. "Late as usual."

Without any greeting, Laura came in, aiming straight for her usual spot by the wet bar, and poured herself a stiff shot.

"Take the wrong turn looking for a saloon?" barked Coleman.

"That's damn unfriendly of you, Horace"—Laura gulped down the liquor and refilled her glass—"after I dash down here on a moment's notice."

"What have you got to report?"

"Well, I set a lot of balls in motion. I'm just waiting for the payoff."

"That's all you're doing—waiting?"

"What else can I do—the girl's still in Lisbon."

"Wrong, Miss Simpson. She's on her way back and she wants a meeting with us. You're supposed to know what's behind it."

Laura looked around at their grim faces. "What am I supposed to be—a fucking clairvoyant? Maybe she's gónna marry the one-legged fellow and throw you guys out on your ass.''

Coleman heaved his body up with surprising speed and violently slapped the drink out of her hand. Laura looked dumbfounded at his purple face; the liquor was making a dark stain on the immaculate rug. Roughly he pushed her down in a chair. "Now you listen to me, you bitch—''

Rosemont and Ash looked agape.

"That crazy girl has taken it into her head to cancel the sale and run the company.''

"I didn't know that,'' Laura blubbered.

"And why not? Do you think we pay you just to take some walks with an old nag? Now earn your money or get the hell out.''

Laura shriveled up like a pricked balloon as she mumbled, "I'm doing the best I can.''

Coleman moved his fat face close to hers and hissed. "It's not good enough.''

"Well . . . what do you want?''

"Information! Specific incidents! Evidence to show how mentally incompetent that girl has become.''

"I already got her convinced she's losing her memory,'' Laura said timidly.

"Good,'' Coleman encouraged.

"And when she gets back to the farm she's gonna be real upset—all her roses are dead.''

"Now you got it.'' Coleman patted her on the back and moved toward the bar. He poured a fresh drink, and handed her the tumbler. "The better you do, the more money you get.''

Ash quietly retrieved his rubber ball.

* * *

Patricia hated the city—she wanted to go right back to the farm, but Mrs. Sperber was right. She had to personally confront the trustees, let them know she was serious this time. That couldn't be done with pieces of paper and fax machines, while she hid in the arms of Miguel, pretending the outside world didn't exist.

She stepped out of the car and glanced up at the glass tower with stainless steel lettering above the door—STONEHAM GROUP. How would the trustees receive her? She felt a tremor of anxiety. But didn't Miguel tell her—your worst enemy is your own fear? She took a deep breath.

"Patricia!"

Down the block she saw a woman under a towering mountain of hair, approaching her. "Joanna!"

Patricia was overwhelmed by the scent of Chanel No. 5, and the loud clanging of bracelets as Joanna embraced her.

"Joanna, you're the last person I expected to run into down here."

"Well, I just had a meeting with the lawyers reviewing my husband's estate." And then she bent over and whispered loudly into Patricia's ear. "One of them is so adorable, I think I will have to come back tomorrow and review my portfolio all over again."

"Oh Joanna, I see you haven't lost your touch."

"Neither have you, my dear—I hear the good Dr. Keegan has abandoned the darkies and is now in residence at Lenox Hill Hospital on Park Avenue."

"I didn't know that."

"You didn't? I was sure you seduced him into it."

"I haven't seen him for some time. It didn't work out between us," Patricia said softly.

"Ohhh." Joanna stretched out the word, studying Patricia's face. Then she brightened. "Trust me, you're better off, and I speak from experience. I've had them all, my dear, rich men, poor men, bankers, thieves—that was my last husband—but doctors are out, too many night calls."

Patricia had to laugh.

"So what have you been doing with yourself—shopping *en Paree*?"

"No, I've just come back from Lisbon."

"So, I *was* right when I saw the two of you in Le Cirque—horsemen are in vogue this year, eh?"

"Yes, Joanna, horsemen."

"I was never any good at sports—too bad. But I think I've finally found my type."

"And what's that?"

"Can't you guess? Lawyers. Men of *juris-prudence*—I just learned that word . . . did you know that nothing in the world moves without lawyers?"

Patricia laughed again. She was so happy she'd run into Joanna—her impish manner relaxed her completely.

As Patricia and Joanna babbled on, they didn't notice that a heavyset woman with stringy hair was slithering cautiously along the wall until she reached the protective cover of the news vendor's booth. Then she turned the corner and ran down the street.

Chapter 18

Stone Ridge

"TELL ME EVERYTHING!" Patricia jumped out of the car and shouted to Edgar, who was coming out of the barn to greet her. "How is Harpalo? How is Sport? And the rest of the horses?" She hardly paused for breath. "Where is Laura?"

Edgar scratched his head. "Now which question you want me to answer first, ma'am?"

She laughed.

"Miss Simpson's gone to town—horses are fine and dandy—but the roses ain't doing too well."

"They'll perk up now that I'm back. Maybe they need some fertilizer. I'll take a look at them—saddle up Sport for me." And she quickly ran into the house to change her clothes.

The house was empty. It had a lonely feeling. She had left Taxi and Phoebe with Miguel, because she didn't want to put them through the stress of traveling back and forth. She'd return to Lisbon soon anyway.

The kitchen, with dirty dishes stacked in the sink, seemed especially bleak without Concha. Her sister must be very ill for her to be gone so long. And not a word. Of course, Concha's family had no phone, but she could have written. Patricia leafed through the stack of mail piled on the kitchen counter—nothing.

The good feeling she had arrived with was beginning to leave her. She mustn't allow herself to get depressed now. She had had a very good meeting with the trustees; for the first time in years, they seemed actually receptive to what she had to to say. They listened to her attentively and promised to consider her plan carefully. She should be grateful for that.

She changed her clothes and, in jeans and T-shirt, ran toward the stable.

Sport nickered softly when she approached; Edgar had already saddled him. Riding out, she reached over and scratched the top of Harpalo's head sticking out of his stall. "You did a great job with them, Edgar!" she called out as she started off.

The farm looked well taken care of; she found no problems anywhere—the horses in the paddocks seemed to recognize her as she trotted by. She slowed down where Misty was leaning over the fence waiting for his carrot and fed him one.

Then she rounded the bend and gasped.

She was expecting a mass of white roses in bloom.

Instead, she saw a field of bushes covered with something that looked like black ashes.

She raced Sport over to the field and jumped off.

What once had been her beautiful rose garden was now a graveyard of shriveled blooms completely peppered by black aphids. How could this happen? She was so proud of the insectary. The good bugs had protected her—but why were they now so outnumbered? She loved these white roses. She loved their scent. To her they were a symbol of beauty and loveliness and gentleness—all the things she associated with her mother.

She walked to that spot in the garden where she had explained to Miguel how the good bugs ate the bad bugs. She looked down and saw a little white rose, so clearly defined among the gray-black bushes. She plucked it off its delicate stem and smelled it.

When she got back to the house, she put it in a glass of water on her nightstand. Then she threw herself on the bed.

More than anything, she wanted Miguel to be there, so she could bury herself in his arms and pretend the roses were in full bloom. But he wasn't there, and the feeling of loneliness was overwhelming—a hollow, aching spot inside her.

She didn't know how to cope with it. She had been a loner all her life—by choice. As a teenager, she enjoyed disappearing for long treks on horseback. Even after her parents died, as much as she missed them, she didn't mind being alone—they had been apart from her for most of her life. Here on the farm, she found comfort in solitude. Dr. Solomon once told her that her strength came from her ability to like her own company. But now that she was in love with Miguel, she felt lonely, incomplete.

Every day since they had been together, she discovered something new about herself, about him, about how they fit together. When she felt weak, he was strong. The times he showed vulnerability, she became the stalwart one. But best of all was the feeling of belonging to each other. Then, it was as if they had been two broken pieces that had miraculously found each other and been mended into a complete unflawed whole—never to be alone again.

But now they were apart, and she didn't even have Taxi or Phoebe to cuddle for comfort—all she had was one tiny rose.

Of course, Miguel would say she was feeling sorry for herself, instead of accepting what fate meted out and dealing with it. That's what he had said when he reproached her about Nogales.

Nogales! She thought of that old Mexican woman carefully watering a pathetic withered rose bush protected by a circle of twigs. She felt ashamed of herself. She could clean up the mess in the garden; the roses would grow back. There were worse problems than that to deal with.

The phone rang.

"Miguel! I was just thinking of you."

"Only now? I think of you all the time. After all, you've been away so long."

"Yes—almost twenty-four hours."

"Patrizia—I'd like to tell you something."

"Yes?"

"Do you have the time now?"

"For you—always."

"Listen—" And he paused.

She waited.

Then she heard him whisper, "I love you."

Lisbon

WHEN MIGUEL HUNG UP THE PHONE, he sighed. He wanted to cry out, "Come back, Patrizia—I miss you terribly. I need you." The longing for her was unbearable. But he consoled himself that she felt the same way about him.

He had kept busy with lessons during the day, and in the evening spent extra time with his father, talking about the school, about Patricia, until Paulo dozed off.

He looked at the clock—it was midnight. So often, now that his father was so frail, he felt the urge to check on him several times during the night, even though he had hired a private nurse. He threw on a robe and quietly walked down the hall.

In the dimly lit room, Paulo lay sleeping, a serene expression on his gaunt face, the skin stretched over the sharp cheekbones like parchment. As Miguel motioned to the nurse to leave, his eyes fluttered open. "Miguel . . . I'm glad you're here."

"I didn't mean to wake you."

"Sit down—I want to talk."

"You shouldn't tire yourself."

"Why not? What do I have to do tomorrow?" he said with a weak chuckle.

"Don't—"

"Listen to me . . . I have something to tell you . . ."
Miguel sat on the bed beside him.

"I have not been a good father," Paulo started. "I
had good intentions—I think all fathers do—but that's
not enough. I did many things wrong. I wanted to make
you into my image . . ." His parched lips curled
slightly. "That is God's domain. I was always gentle
with my horses, but I curbed you too much."

Miguel listened, not daring to interrupt.

"I want you to ride the way I taught you—with pride
and pleasure . . ." He took a deep breath and with
glazed eyes stared at his son. "Even if it's in the bullring."

Miguel's throat was so tight he could hardly talk.
"But *Pai* . . ." He caught himself—he had not called
his father that since he was a child. "*Pai*"—his voice
cracked—"I was angry with you often, forgive me. It
was only because I knew I wasn't as good as you. I
resented what people said about you—I wanted that
praise for myself. Now I know I have reached the top
when I hear them say he's almost as good as his father."

Paulo moved his head slightly from side to side, a
broad smile on his face. "You have surpassed your
father—and who knows better than the *mestre*?" He
closed his eyes and continued, barely above a whisper,
"But what is more important—you must do in life what
you want to do. And when you have a son, don't make
my mistake—guide him with a very loose rein."

Miguel looked down at the ashen face. Paulo was
dozing again—breathing rhythmically with a faint
smile.

Miguel let the repressed tears course down his cheeks. He leaned over and kissed his *pai* gently on the forehead.

Stone Ridge

PATRICIA WAS PROPPED UP IN BED, trying to write a letter to Miguel—a glass of bicarbonate fizzing on the night table beside her. Laura had insisted on cooking dinner that night—"My famous vegetarian chili," she called it. Patricia did her best to clean her plate—she didn't want to hurt her best friend's feelings.

Of course, Laura could be exasperating—she drank too much, smoked incessantly, even during meals. Patricia tried not to see the ugly nicotine stains on her fingers. But just when you had too much of her, Laura did something to make you love her.

Yesterday, Laura had come home hiding a rolled-up piece of paper behind her back.

"What are you up to now?" Patricia prompted, seeing the mischievous twinkle in her friend's eye.

"It's just a little present to make up for what I've done."

"What you've done?"

"Kiddo, I'm sorry—I wanted to tell you about the roses, but you were having such a good time."

"Now don't blame yourself for that."

"Well—they started getting sick so mysteriously."

"But it's not your fault."

"I should have done something—I just didn't know what. Anyway, please say you forgive me."

Patricia laughed. "Okay, okay, I forgive you."

And then Laura brought out the scroll from behind her back and handed it to Patricia. It was a print of van Gogh's *Vase of Roses*.

"Oh, it's beautiful." Patricia had tears in her eyes as she hugged Laura. "It even has one small rose lying on the table, like the flower I rescued from the garden yesterday. I'll hang it over my bed."

Now, she looked up at the print as she gulped down the salty liquid, trying to wash out the taste of the chili. She had wanted to tell Miguel about the roses, but it seemed such a silly little problem compared to what he was going through back in Lisbon with Paulo. She picked up the pen again and with a schoolgirl flourish scrawled *I love you* as many times as the page would hold. She put the letter in an envelope and licked it closed.

She yawned, stretched, and slid under the covers. She wrapped her arms tightly around the pillow. Good night my love, she thought; wish you were here.

She came to with a start. What had awakened her? She could hear far-off shouts. She jumped out of bed and pulled back the curtain.

Men were running, yelling. And then she saw it— flames were shooting up out of the roof of the hay barn.

When she got there, Edgar was frantically trying to move some of the bales of hay, while the men were passing buckets of water and Laura wielded a garden hose.

A fire engine was speeding up the driveway, siren

blasting. As Patricia watched the conflagration helplessly, she saw a flaming ember shoot through the night sky in the direction of the nearby stable building. The horses were neighing frantically.

"Oh God—let's get them out of there. Laura, help me!"

Together, they ran inside. "I'll get Harpalo!" Laura yelled, as Patricia threw open Sport's stall door and buckled on his halter.

The hysterical horse was spinning in fear; he almost knocked her down as she ran with him to the riding arena. Curls of smoke were drifting into the stable when she returned. Laura was still inside, pulling with all her might on the lead rope, but Harpalo, shivering, stood rooted to the spot.

"He won't budge!" Laura screamed. Patricia rushed into the tack room and pulled out a blanket. As she was running out, it caught on the door handle; she yanked on it until it ripped off. She threw the blanket over Harpalo's head to obscure his view of the flames. "There, there . . . easy, easy . . . it'll be all right." Reassured by Patricia's voice, the horse stepped out of the stall tentatively. She led him out to join Sport.

After all the horses in the stable were safely out, Patricia ran back to the burning hay barn, but the fire chief blocked her path. "Miss Dennison—the building is fully engaged. There is nothing we can do now until it burns itself out."

She looked over helplessly, and saw that Edgar was still trying to move bales of hay that were stacked too close to the fire. Suddenly, the roof of the barn collapsed, and he was completely obscured by a sheet of flames from the burning rafters.

"Get him out of there!" Patricia screamed.

Two young firemen dived into the flames and pulled out Edgar's inert form.

Chapter 19

New York City

HORACE COLEMAN STOOD at the head of a long table around which were assembled the CEOs of the various companies comprising the Stoneham Group. He made a point of making eye contact with each of the twenty-three men—Mrs. Sperber was the only woman present—as the roll call was read. Then he smiled benignly.

"I am happy to say that nearly all the entities within the Stoneham Group have shown a marked growth in the past year. The overall value of Stoneham stock has risen twelve points, but the top prize goes to Pete McCratchen, who heads up our Mexican operation—the only one here able to boast a seventy-percent increase in profits."

There was polite applause as McCratchen, a beefy man in a plaid suit, got up awkwardly and bowed.

When the room quieted down, Coleman took off his glasses; he now assumed the pose of a bereaved at a funeral. "With every bit of good news there is some bad," he continued. "Unfortunately, we've had a problem with our majority stockholder—Miss Patricia Dennison."

"The trustees"—he pointed to his left, where Bob Ash was squeezing his rubber ball, and Ted Rosemont was doodling as usual—"myself included, have a double duty—not only to set policies for the Stoneham Group, but to protect the personal position of Miss Dennison. This poses an inherent conflict of interest, although thus far we've had no problems. But now Miss Dennison has taken steps which could *destroy* this company." He paused for dramatic effect. "The future of us all is threatened."

Murmurs rippled through the group. Coleman waited until they were all listening attentively again.

"Miss Dennison is interfering with the operation of this great conglomerate. Bob, Ted, and I have been wrestling with this for some time. At first we thought the problem was eliminated by her desire to sell her stock."

Coleman turned again to Ash and Rosemont. "In fact, weren't her exact words—*get rid* of the company? Isn't that right, Bob?"

Ash, squeezing the ball nervously, nodded.

"But she suddenly switched to a course of action that is erratic to say the least. In the middle of the stock transfer, she changed her mind, and now insists on *personally* running the company." He looked around the room for emphasis. "Think of it—a disturbed, twenty-one-year-old girl running this corporation on a whim. Things have clearly gone beyond our ability to control." He cleared his throat.

Mrs. Sperber leaned foward in her chair as Coleman valiantly pushed on.

"Please appreciate the gravity of my dilemma. Believe me—" Coleman's voice was now filled with emotion. "I've gone through my Gethsemane. My very dear friend, J. L. Stoneham, asked me on his deathbed to look after this troubled girl. But I see no choice."

There was a hush over the group.

Coleman raised his head and his three chins receded into two. "We must start proceedings to set up a conservatorship. That is the only way we can negate her power to override our decisions in the future."

Coleman now stood very erect, his paunch bulging under his buttoned coat. "Are there any comments?"

They sat quietly, a few heads turning, and then Mrs. Sperber got up. "Mr. Coleman—"

"Yes, Mrs. Sperber."

"As a barrister, I would like to pose a question."

"Please do." Coleman stuffed both his chubby fists in his pockets.

"In order to institute such a conservatorship, do you not have to prove, before a court, that Miss Dennison is mentally incompetent?"

Heads jerked up.

"That is correct," Coleman said calmly.

Ash switched the rubber ball to his right hand and went on squeezing rapidly. Ted Rosemont kept his head low over his doodles.

"That is a very serious step," Mrs. Sperber said.

"We're fully aware of that," Coleman retorted, his annoyance showing.

Everyone around the table was looking at this tall thin woman confronting the power of the company.

"Do you have proof to proceed with such charges?"

"Beyond a shadow of a doubt."

Stone Ridge

PATRICIA AND LAURA had spent the rest of the night and most of the next day at the hospital, keeping vigil by Edgar's side. It was excruciating, watching this stalwart man trying to hide his agony. Fortunately, the doctors assured them of his full recovery. Poor Edgar. All he had wanted to do was save a load of hay.

By the time Patricia returned from the hospital with Laura, it was almost dusk. The farm looked peaceful in the hazy light as they drove up, but when they came closer, the workers, still clearing the charred debris, came into view. It gave Patricia a chill.

She stepped out of the car. Her clothes were smudged with soot, and she had a big bruise on her right cheek where panicky Harpalo had bumped her.

She had held up through it all, but suddenly seeing this scene of devastation, she crumbled. Hot tears trickled down her dirty cheeks. She slumped down on the car's bumper.

"How awful . . . ," Laura said, putting her arm around Patricia. "How unlucky . . . first the rose garden, now this . . . it's like there's a curse on you—" Laura stopped herself and started to stutter: "Oh no . . . I . . . I didn't mean that. I . . . I just meant there's been so much tragedy in your life."

Patricia kept her head down. "Too much," she said softly.

"More than one person can take."

Patricia just sat there motionless.

"Kiddo," Laura clucked, "you don't realize what you've been through—another trip to that there rest home of yours would do you good right now."

Lisbon

THE CLANGING OF SUNDAY MORNING CHURCH BELLS awakened Miguel. "Those goddamn bells," he moaned, rolling over. He used to get up early on Sundays to work with Ultimato, but now he couldn't leave Paulo alone even for a day. He pulled the pillow over his head. A sharp rapping on the door filtered through.

Annoyed, he raised himself up on his elbows and yelled, "Come in!"

The door opened. Standing there, fully dressed, was his father.

"*Pai!* What are you doing here? Why aren't you in bed?"

"Why aren't you *out* of bed? Isn't this your day to work with Ultimato?"

"No—not today."

"Why not?"

"I'm staying here with you."

"Oh, that's too bad. Because I'm spending the afternoon with Emilio."

"What?"

"He's my friend, too."

"Well, I know but . . ."

"I'd like to watch you and Ultimato in the bullring." Paulo had a warm smile on his face.

Miguel couldn't believe it—Paulo wanted to watch something he had always condemned. He looked at his father—his cheeks were rosy, his voice was stronger; maybe he was getting better. Miguel hadn't seen him in such good spirits in a long time.

"Okay, *Pai*." He jumped out of bed. "It won't take me long to get Ultimato ready."

Paulo winked. "I'll wait for you outside."

When Miguel stepped out, he saw Ultimato on the van, which was already attached to Emilio's Ferrari, his friend grinning his usual silly grin from behind the wheel, his father in the passenger seat.

"Oh—are you coming with us?" Emilio feigned surprise. "I thought you retired."

In the Castelo da Arrábida's bullring, Ultimato pranced up and down, suspiciously eyeing the young bull waiting to be released from the pen. Up above, in the loggia, Miguel could see his father seated in a lounge chair, a blanket protecting him from the cool afternoon breeze; Emilio, a glass of champagne in his hand, was animatedly talking at his side.

Miguel took a deep breath and guided Ultimato into

the arena. At the center, he brought the horse to a halt and cued him to bow on one knee. He doffed his cap to his father, who was smiling down at him.

Now the young bull—wearing a collar padded with cork to protect him from the steel darts of the *farpas*—thundered into the ring.

Miguel whirled Ultimato in a perfect pirouette and waved his little flag to attract the bull's attention. The bull charged immediately, but Ultimato swerved easily away.

Miguel's mind was completely on his horsemanship, his main concern that it meet Paulo's highest standards. The horse executed all the moves flawlessly and with an air of studied nonchalance.

"Bravo!" shouted Emilio, pretending to be a crowd of thousands.

When Miguel looked up, he saw that Paulo too was applauding and that his eyes were glistening.

Filled with confidence, Miguel dropped the reins and raised his arms above his head, holding a dart in each hand. He pushed Ultimato into a gallop on a collision course with the bull. As the horns came within inches, he planted the two darts simultaneously and danced away.

Finally, the exhausted bull was let out of the ring. Miguel approached the loggia in a Spanish walk, Ultimato throwing his legs in an exaggerated goose step of victory.

With a feeling of satisfaction, Miguel took a bow. He knew he had done his best. He knew his father approved. He raised his eyes.

Emilio was standing, leaning over the balustrade,

clapping enthusiastically. Miguel winked at his friend. Then he turned to see the reaction of the *mestre*.

But his father wasn't even looking up. His head sagged on his shoulder lifelessly.

"Pai!" Miguel screamed, jumping off the horse and racing for the loggia.

When he reached his father's side, Emilio was there frantically trying to revive the old man. Miguel grasped Paulo's hand, but there was no pulse to be felt. "He's dead, Emilio," he said softly.

He leaned over the inert figure and gently closed the vacantly staring eyes. There was a look of tranquillity on Paulo's face. The suffering was over. Miguel felt strangely serene, and then he heard strangled sobs behind him.

Emilio was hunched over the balustrade, holding on to a pillar, his body shaking. That clown who, no matter what the situation, always presented a picture of gaiety was falling apart. Miguel approached his friend and put his arm around his quivering shoulders.

"Emilio—it's all right. He's at peace now."

"But what about me?" Emilio blurted out between sobs. "You don't know what he meant to me."

"I do know," Miguel said soothingly.

"No you don't!" Emilio cried, jerking his arm away.

"Emilio, please—calm down—look at me."

Emilio raised his head, and Miguel saw his friend's face, tears coursing down his cheeks, his nose running. "When you ran away, cursing him, we talked together. He said, 'Take care of Miguelinho, until he comes back to me.' He loved you—" Gradually, Emilio's sobs subsided. "And once he said, 'You're like my second

son, Emilio.' You'll never know what that meant to me.
The only thing you had that I envied—a father who
loved you.''

Stone Ridge

PATRICIA WAS THROWING CLOTHES in a suitcase. Poor
Paulo! But she didn't ache for the *mestre*, she ached
for his son. Paulo's pain was over—Miguel's had just
begun. Yet in his moment of grief, he was more concerned about her reaction. When he telephoned, he
didn't seek sympathy; he tried to console her.

"Don't cry, Patricia. It's all right—Paulo died
happy.'' He told her everything—the talk he had with
his father, Paulo's insistence on seeing him in the bullring. "Before the end, he gave me everything that I
wanted—his approval and his praise.''

The tears flowed down her cheeks as she listened
silently.

"Patrizia, I need you here with me for the funeral—
the one thing I cannot face alone is this circus they are
planning at the cathedral. The president will be there,
the archbishop, the head rabbi, the head guru—every
religion that my father didn't believe in will be wailing
his passing. But all I want is for you to be there, next
to me, to help me through that day.''

"I'll come just as quickly as I can.''

"Hey, Patrizia,'' he said in a lighter tone, "you might
actually enjoy yourself—all the goddamn bells of Lisbon will be banging away—you'll love it.''

She had to laugh through her tears.

Now she couldn't pack fast enough. She diverted the 727 on its way to pick up Bob Ash in Palm Springs and ordered it at Stewart Airport in an hour.

She was zipping up her bag when she heard Laura's raspy voice echoing up the landing. "Somebody to see you!"

"I can't now—please take care of it."

"It's the police!"

"What?"

Making her way quickly down the stairs, Patricia saw Laura with a tall man dressed in a sheriff's uniform.

He spoke first. "Are you Patricia Dennison?"

"Yes I am."

He handed her a thick envelope.

"What's this all about?" she asked, bewildered.

"I'm sure the information is all inside. Would you sign here, please?" He gave her a pen and held a receipt in front of her.

As Laura let him out, Patricia looked at the envelope with a strange feeling of foreboding: SURROGATE COURT, BOROUGH OF MANHATTAN, COUNTY OF NEW YORK it said in the left-hand corner.

"What is it, kiddo?"

"I don't know," Patricia muttered as she scanned the contents. "Oh my God!" she exclaimed. "It's a subpoena."

"Subpoena?"

"They think I'm crazy."

"Who?"

"The trustees. They filed a petition, They say I'm mentally incompetent and can't run the company."

"Are you trying to run the company?"

"I'm trying to make some changes."

"And this is why they say you're crazy?"

Patricia nodded.

"Those bastards!" Laura put her arm around Patricia's shoulders and pulled her down on the sofa. "Listen, you don't have to put up with this crap. When you sell your stock, you'll be rid of them once and for all."

"No." Patricia shook her head. "That would give them control of the company."

"So what do you care? You want out, don't you?"

"No—not now."

"I don't understand you, kiddo. Don't you know what this subpoena means? They're gonna create one hell of a mess for you."

"I've done nothing wrong," Patricia said calmly.

"Then what are you going to do?" Laura asked.

Patricia got up slowly. "All I know is that right now I have to fly to Lisbon."

"You can't—you've just been served with a subpoena."

"I don't care—I have to go."

"Now, you listen to me!" Laura stopped her at the bottom of the staircase. "If you leave the country, you'll be a *fugitive*!"

"That can't be." Patricia started up the steps.

Laura grabbed her arm. "I mean it. This is a *court* order. Ask anybody."

"You sure?"

"Positive. You can't ignore it. You'll get yourself in more trouble."

"Oh my God." Choking back tears, Patricia slowly climbed the stairs.

At the landing she paused before *The Starhanger*. "Oh Daddy, what should I do?" she whispered, her hand gently touching the silhouette. But he just continued silently hanging his star with his back to her.

When the door to Patricia's bedroom closed, Laura quickly went into the kitchen and dialed the phone.

"Yes?" Horace Coleman's voice came on.

"Everything's on schedule."

"How is she reacting?"

"She's in a daze. And I stopped her from going to Lisbon."

"Good. What about the stock?"

"I urged her to sell."

"And?"

"She doesn't want to."

"Convince her."

"How?" Laura hissed.

But he had already hung up the phone.

Lisbon

THE LISBON *SÉ* CATHEDRAL, a massive Romanesque structure with grim towers protruding out against darkly billowing clouds, was a most fitting place for this somber occasion—the interment of a great man. The church was mobbed, the overflow crowd spilling down the ancient steps onto the street, where speakers were installed for everyone to hear the requiem for the famed Paulo Cardiga.

Miguel sat stiffly in the front pew, Emilio at his side. The eulogies droned on in endless waves. He felt anesthetized to the theatrics of an occasion his father would never have attended if he were alive. Suddenly, his thoughts were interrupted by the blaring sound of trumpets, and then the booming organ music reverberated against the stone walls.

Now the crowd started filing past the bier to pay their last respects. The archbishop waved the smoking censer, and the pungent aroma of incense filled the air.

For Miguel, it was becoming unbearable, and when one of the older *condêssas* fainted, he took advantage of the hubbub to slip out of his pew.

He walked down the side aisle where the great dead heroes of Portugal rested in walled niches, their bodies replicated in stone on the lids of their coffins. On one sarcophagus lay a famous warrior, his little dog carved wide-eyed and alert at his feet. He remembered that when he brought Patricia to see the cathedral, she gently rubbed the dog's head. "Oh look!" she said, "everyone loved this dog." And then he saw what she meant—the stone statue of the knight was pitted and dark gray in color, but the dog's head was shiny white and smooth. All the visitors—like Patricia—couldn't resist petting the dog.

He was glad he had returned Taxi and Phoebe to her yesterday. She had been so sure that she would be back in Lisbon soon, but now this terrible thing—subpoenas, lawsuits—crashing down on her head. His heart broke to hear her sobbing on the phone when she called to say she couldn't come to the funeral. She needed him. He would clear up affairs at the school and fly to the States in a few days.

Now he had come to the end of the cloister wall and

decided to return to his pew, when he saw, approaching him, a silhouette of a woman dressed in black, a veil covering her face.

"Miguelinho," she said softly. "I am so sorry for your loss."

She raised her veil—it was Isabel. Her dark eyes were hooded, her mouth a scarlet slash across her pale face.

"Thank you, Isabel."

He tried to move away, but she continued. "I wish to pay my respects . . . and I wish to apologize"—her face exuded compassion and sorrow—". . . for my behavior in the disco."

"I understand, Isabel—let's forget about it."

"Yes, let bygones be bygones."

He nodded and again attempted to pass her, but she clutched his arm. "Miguel—next week, I'm having a reception in honor of your father's memory. All his friends are invited. I hope you will attend."

"I appreciate that, Isabel, but I won't be here."

"Oh? Where will you be?"

"I have to go the States."

"I see." She studied him for a moment and then pulled the veil over her face. "We all must do what we must do. I wish you my best." She spun on her heel and almost knocked into Emilio, who bowed in an exaggerated manner as she passed.

"Sorry Miguelinho—I saw her headed your way, but I couldn't very well dance her down the aisle of the cathedral."

"Oh, she was fine actually—seemed in control of herself for a change—even wished me her best."

Emilio grimaced. "Her best what?"

Chapter 20

Stone Ridge

TAXI AND PHOEBE were snuggling close beside Patricia as if trying to tell her how much they'd missed her. How thoughtful of Miguel to send back the animals now that she couldn't return to Lisbon as she had planned. He had tied a note to Taxi's collar: *"I'll be with you in a week's time. Meanwhile, these two emissaries bring you my love."* He had also sent a cassette of the song they had danced to in the disco. It was playing now and her eyes misted over as she listened to the words:

I know that everybody has a dream
And this is my dream, my own
Just to be at home
And to be all alone . . . with you.

279

Laura, ever solicitous, came in with a cup of coffee. "This is for you, freshly made—" She looked at Patricia's red eyes. "What's the matter?"

"Oh nothing—I just got something in my eye."

"Want some drops?"

"Oh no, no—it'll be fine."

They sipped coffee while the tape played on:

So let me lie and let me go on sleeping
And I will lose myself in palaces of sand
And all the fantasies that I have been keeping
Will make the empty hours easier to stand.

"Why is Mrs. Sperber coming here?" Laura broke in over the music.

"What?" Patricia turned the stereo down.

"I said—why is Mrs. Sperber coming here?" Laura repeated.

"She's my friend."

Laura's lower lip turned over in a childish pout.

"Oh Laura—not as close as you . . . but she wants to help me with this awful mess."

Laura plopped down beside her. "Kiddo, I'll say it for the last time. Take the money and run. Sell those goddamn stocks."

Patricia sighed. "Well, maybe you're right."

Just then, they heard a car driving up the gravel roadway. Patricia hurried to greet Mrs. Sperber, immaculately dressed in a gray pinstriped business outfit, and was surprised to see, stepping out of the car behind her, a short man in a rumpled brown suit.

"Patricia—I wish to present Mr. Howard Binder."

"Just call me Howie."

Howie had a white pasty face that looked as though it had never been exposed to the sun. He peered at her through thick horn-rimmed glasses. A mat of black unkempt hair sprouted around his large ears. Standing next to tall, spindly Mrs. Sperber, he looked like an elf.

As they moved toward the house, Laura eyed them from the doorway.

"Oh, I'm sorry," Patricia said, "This is my best friend, Laura Simpson. Laura—this is Mrs. Sperber and Mr. Binder."

"Pleased to meet you—I'll make some more coffee."

After a few minutes of sipping coffee and polite conversation, Howie got up.

"You know, Patricia," he said with a smile, "they say you shouldn't talk about people behind their back. That's silly—don't you think?" Without waiting for an answer he continued. "It's the only way you can talk honestly. I'll take a little walk around your farm."

"Oh—oh—," Patricia stuttered. "Laura, would you mind showing Mr. Binder—"

"Howie."

"—showing Howie around the farm."

"Sure," Laura said, none too enthusiastically.

When they left, Mrs. Sperber started, "Do not allow Howie's appearance to deceive you—he is one of the smartest attorneys I have ever been privileged to meet. You need him."

"Oh Mrs. Sperber . . . lawyers . . . court fights . . . all I ever wanted was to make things better . . . Does that mean I'm crazy?"

"Of course not."

"Sometimes I don't know . . . maybe I should just sell the stock."

"Precisely what they would like."

Patricia walked over to the window. Outside, Laura was waddling with the little elf beside her toward the insectary. "And you think Mr. Binder can help me?"

"Howie is the best. He knows all about your situation, and he is most anxious to participate."

"But he looks so . . ."

"I know . . . I know." Mrs. Sperber nodded. "But believe me, he is a David who always slays his Goliath. And he is dying to take on the Stoneham Group again. Three years ago he won an antitrust suit that cost us fifteen million dollars."

Howie was evidently a fast walker—Laura was puffing when they returned.

"I like your insectary," he said, putting his jacket over a chair. Underneath, he wore red lumberjack suspenders, more than qualified to hold up his two skinny pant legs.

"Well, it's not very good—my roses all died this year."

"Your ratio is off. I peeked inside and your insectary is swarming with red beetles and the aphid population is way down. You sure your keeper isn't releasing the wrong insects?"

Mrs. Sperber smiled. "Howie—are you an expert in entomology as well?"

Indignant, Howie puffed out his caved-in chest and seemed to rise to a height of five feet five. "Last year I represented the citrus growers in Santa Clarita Valley in their fight to introduce the Cryptolaemus lady beetles to control the citrophilus mealybug. The insecticide people were against it. I needn't brag which side won.''

Everyone laughed—except Laura.

The groom had just finished brushing Harpalo, but Patricia picked up the currycomb and started all over again. He looked at her bewildered, shrugged his shoulders, and walked away. How could she explain that she wanted to impress Miguel with the care she gave this beautiful Lusitano?

Tomorrow he would be here. In some magical way, his presence would dissipate the black clouds that were hanging over her. She had already made her rounds of the farm on Sport, but she decided to do it again just to make sure everything was perfect.

As she reined in at the newly rebuilt hay barn, Edgar called out, "See that, Miss D.?"

The men were mounting fire extinguishers on the walls.

Patricia smiled. "Good thinking."

Edgar, who insisted on coming back to work with his left arm in a sling, yelled out some instructions to the men unloading a hay truck, and then turned to her and said in his gravelly voice, "I'll sure be glad to see Mr. Cardiga again—that man's a magician with a horse!"

"Yes, he is," she said proudly as she continued on her rounds. Passing the house, she saw the new housekeeper, whom Laura had found in a nearby village, washing the windows. The woman was nice enough, but she could never replace Concha; it still seemed that a part of the family was missing. Why hadn't she heard from her? Laura said that Concha was probably too busy caring for her sick sister to travel god-knows-how-far to the nearest post office. But it had been such a long time—her sister must be gravely ill. She should do something—yes, she'd send a care package tomorrow.

Patricia had just pulled up at the stable, when a groom handed her the phone. "Call for you, Miss D.—Lisbon."

She quickly jumped off Sport and took the portable phone into the tack room for privacy.

"Miguel!" she said breathlessly.

"No, Patricia—Emilio."

"Oh." She hoped her disappointment didn't show.

"Miguel is tied up right now and he asked me to call."

She blurted out her worst fear: "He's not coming."

"Yes he is—but not tomorrow."

"Why couldn't he call me himself?"

Emilio didn't answer.

"What's wrong?"

"Nothing, nothing—things take time."

"Emilio—you're hiding something. What's happened?"

"He will work it all out soon."

"Oh my God—he's hurt. He's in the hospital."

"No, no, no."

"Please, *please*—tell me the truth."

Emilio muttered something in Portuguese, then took a deep breath. "It's a good thing that I'm not religious. I swore on my mother's grave that I wouldn't tell you."

"Tell me what?"

He took another deep breath. "Miguel is in jail."

"In jail?"

"Isabel filed charges."

"What charges?" She asked the question even though she knew the answer.

"Murder."

Lisbon

IT WAS ALMOST MIDNIGHT when the Stoneham jet set down in Lisbon. A pale-faced Emilio was there to meet her and escort her to the Les Meridien Lisboa Hotel, an elegant modern glass structure within view of the medieval silhouette that was the *Estabelecimento Prisonal*.

"Can't I see him now?" she asked.

"Impossible. But I will take you to him first thing in the morning."

She sighed in resignation.

"Now get some sleep—it will be a difficult day for you tomorrow."

But Patricia couldn't sleep. She walked out onto the street and started across the Parque Eduardo VII, in the direction of the prison. He was so close, just behind that wall. She couldn't touch him, she couldn't talk to him, but, at least, she was here. Laura had confused her about the subpoena earlier—Howie joked that Laura suffered from too much television, and he reassured her that she was free to travel anywhere, as long as she was on time for her hearing Monday morning. But nothing would have stopped her—she would have come here even if it was against the law. She didn't care. She would gladly give the trustees everything, if that would help Miguel.

She reached the end of the park. Before her loomed the brightly lit yellow walls of the prison, its medieval turrets painted white, fronds of palm trees peeping out from behind. It looked bizarre—something from Disneyland—not ominous at all.

But inside, her lover was lying in a lonely cell. Perhaps he could hear her thoughts, perhaps her love could penetrate the walls and keep him safe and warm this night.

Patricia was dressed hours before Emilio came to pick her up the next morning. At the prison, more waiting. Even though Emilio had filed the necessary papers for a visitor's pass, they were still obliged to sit in the anteroom, where mothers, wives, and girlfriends all anxiously waited for the iron gates to swing open and their names to be called.

Finally, the guard led them down a tunnellike hall into the visiting room. Patricia had to bend down to enter through the low stone portal. Inside stretched a twenty-foot long table; on one side, shoulder to shoulder, sat the prisoners, on the other the visitors. Miguel wasn't there.

"Just wait here and keep quiet," Emilio told her and disappeared. A few minutes later, he came back with a different guard speaking rapidly in Portuguese. He motioned her to follow.

As the guard went on ahead, Emilio whispered in her ear. "A case of my finest wine did it—don't open your mouth—I told him you're Miguel's sister."

The guard led her up a wrought-iron spiral staircase, to the top of a tower. At the landing, he took out a large key and opened the door. She found herself in a small circular chapel furnished with some benches lined up against the wall. Stained-glass rosette windows refracted the rays of the early morning sun on the smooth surface of the altar.

She heard the key in the lock again and held her breath. And suddenly, there he was, walking slowly toward her, the door clanging shut behind him. She could see the words he wanted to utter in his moist eyes. She showered his face with kisses, trying to draw into herself all his suffering.

Miguel found he couldn't speak. He buried his fingers in her hair, cupping her fragile face. His hands caressed her tearstained cheeks, moving down her neck, enveloping her breasts. He crushed her to himself—he wanted to pull her inside and keep her there forever.

Out of breath, they crumpled to the floor. Their surroundings—the city, the country, the world—seemed to be racing away. They were alone, separated from everything, just the two of them, locked together, melding into one before the altar.

Emilio had waited to escort her out of the prison. Walking beside her, he chattered nonstop, trying to cheer her up, but she heard nothing he was saying. As he drove off, she didn't ask where they were going, nor did she care. She closed her eyes and thought of Miguel making love to her on the chapel floor.

Emilio chattered on. Finally, she interrupted him. "Take me to see Isabel."

"What?"

"I want to talk with her."

"You can't talk with her—she's mad."

"If she loved him once, I can persuade her to drop the charges."

"She won't listen to you."

Patricia clasped her hands in prayer. "Please, Emilio . . ."

"But Patricia, even if you succeeded—it's not that simple. There is a criminal investigation under way— they don't let anyone just *drop* a murder charge. Isabel would have to *recant* her entire story. She'll never do that!"

"I must try—I must see her."

He shrugged his shoulders. "Well, you'll find out." He reached for the car phone.

The conversation was in Portuguese and all that Patricia understood was "Isabel" and "Miss Dennison." When Emilio hung up, he muttered, "I can't believe it . . . we got a lunch date." And he spun the car around in a U-turn.

By the time they arrived at the Veloso ranch, it was noon, the bright sun exaggerating the vivid hues of the bougainvillea that engulfed the facade of the house. Framed in the blaze of color, Isabel stood in the doorway, wearing a tight purple jumpsuit and high-heeled sandals that revealed scarlet toenails matching her fingers and lips. "*Bem-vindos*," she welcomed them in Portuguese, her large dark eyes communicating only friendship.

She graciously invited them into the dining room, where a maid was placing huge silver platters laden with food on a table set for three. She sat down and, with both arms regally outstretched, motioned for them to join her at either side. Patricia's attention was drawn to a large portrait on the wall that seemed to mirror the hostess facing it.

"You like it?" Isabel addressed Patricia. "My husband had it done just before . . . he died."

Two butlers were circling the table with fish and vegetable platters, while another wheeled in a cart with a steaming carcass of beef.

Patricia hadn't known what to expect, she hadn't rehearsed what to say, but this was totally absurd—the huge quantity of food—the graciously overpowering manner . . .

"You're not eating, Miss Dennison." It sounded like an accusation.

"I'm not hungry," she stammered.

"But you came to lunch!"

"No, I came to talk to you."

"Oh? What about?"

"Miguel."

"Please don't bring up that subject," Isabel said, beginning to slice the meat. "It upsets me."

"It upsets me too, Mrs. Veloso. He's in prison—and you filed the charges against him."

"Well, what would you have done?" Her tone of voice was almost flippant. "He murdered my husband."

Patricia looked over at Emilio, but he was watching Isabel, mesmerized by the bizarre scene.

"Mrs. Veloso—whatever happened, happened almost a year ago. Why file charges now?"

Isabel slowly put down the knife and faced Patricia squarely. "There was no other way—he was planning to leave the country. Another woman was trying to steal him away."

"You mean me . . ."

"Yes, *you*!" Isabel's eyes burned with hatred. "He loved me before you came into his life—he would have done anything for me. Even kill for me. And I would have done the same for him. No woman could have loved him more."

"Then how could you do this to him?"

"I had to keep him in Portugal."

"Behind bars?"

Isabel's fist hit the table. "It doesn't matter as long as he stays here. No harm will come to him in prison. We do not believe in capital punishment. He will be well fed, well taken care of. I will see to that." She leaned toward Patricia. "We are a civilized country— conjugal visits are encouraged." A twisted smile crossed her face. "I will be there every week for him."

Patricia's hands were shaking. Her voice quavered, but she blurted out, "Do you think Miguel could ever make love to you again?"

Isabel sprang to her feet. "Yes, yes—he loved me once. Until you stole him from me."

Patricia felt the world caving in. How could she reason with a madwoman? "Mrs. Veloso—love can't be stolen," she pleaded. "It's a gift from one to another. Even if you won't admit it, deep down inside you know it." Patricia's voice was firm now. "I love Miguel and he loves me."

"*No!*" Isabel let out an anguished scream. She grabbed the carving knife and lunged at Patricia.

Emilio dived across the table to block Isabel's aim, spraying dishes and food in every direction. He knocked her down to the floor and twisted the knife out of her hand.

"You bitch!" he yelled. "Miguel never loved you. He told me. He was sick of you. He found you repulsive. He wouldn't touch you if you came every day for a thousand years!"

Horrified, Patricia stood watching, until Emilio grabbed her arm and pulled her out of the house.

Isabel was still on the floor, screaming like a wounded animal.

New York City

"YOUR HONOR, this proves our argument. She is an irresponsible child." Creighton Smith, attorney for the trustees, raised his lanky frame to its full six-feet-two height and leaned forward, spreading his palms across the plaintiff's table, the monogrammed cuffs of his white starched shirt peeking out from the sleeves of his immaculate gray suit.

"This argument is premature," popped up Howie. "My client has ten minutes to get here."

"Eight minutes," broke in Smith, checking his Rolex.

Howie rolled his eyes. "I appreciate your accuracy, Mr. Smith, but the proceedings were set for ten o'clock. Let's have a tiny bit of patience."

"My clients"—Smith motioned with his hand to the huddle of Coleman, Ash, and Rosemont next to him—"have been extremely patient with Miss Dennison for years, have been solicitous of her welfare, forgiving of her erratic behavior. They will sit patiently here not just for ten minutes but for an hour." With long strides, he approached the judge's bench. "However, Your Honor, Mr. Coleman has just spoken with the pilot of the Stoneham jet, which at this very moment sits at the Lisbon airport." He shot Howie a wry smile. "We have it from an unimpeachable source that she has a lover in that city. Even if she boards the plane this very minute, she can't be here in less than *eight* hours."

"Mr. Binder," said the judge, "what is your response?"

Howie was snapping his suspenders nervously. "Your Honor, I have no information concerning the matter brought up by the plaintiff."

"All right, Mr. Binder"—the judge eyed the wall clock over the door—"in three minutes we will commence with the disposition of this case."

Coleman, Ash, and Rosemont seemed to relax in their chairs, with an air of long-suffering patience.

Mrs. Sperber, seated next to Howie, patted his arm as if to reassure him.

"Hear ye, hear ye, hear ye," the court clerk took up his chant, "the Surrogate Court of New York County is now in session. The Honorable Judge Arthur Mason presiding."

The judge pounded his gavel. "I call the case of Stoneham Group versus Dennison." He looked to the back of the courtroom. "And as soon as Miss Dennison sits down we'll begin."

Horace Coleman whipped his huge bulk around so fast, he almost tipped over his chair.

Patricia was walking down the aisle.

"Call your first witness, Mr. Smith," the judge said.

Howie grinned at her from ear to ear and almost yanked her down beside him. "Your plane is in Europe and you flew here," he whispered. "You must be an angel."

"The Concorde is faster than an angel," she whispered back.

Patricia tried to switch her thoughts from Lisbon to what was happening in the courtroom.

"Your Honor, this is the most difficult thing I've had to do in my life." The falsely solicitous tone of Horace Coleman's voice projected from the witness stand and echoed in the high-ceilinged courtroom, dimly lit with crystal chandeliers; it was all so somber—the dark mahogany paneling, the brown velvet curtains, the armchairs covered in matching leather. "I have known Patricia since she was a little girl. I knew her mother," and he added in a soft voice, "who committed suicide. I knew her father, who was killed in a hijacking. I've watched with pity the burdens and problems she has had to overcome. They caused her to have a series of nervous breakdowns, and . . ."—he hesitated and lowered his voice again—"and to attempt suicide herself. She is a fragile girl. Her grandfather, J. L. Stoneham, the founder of this corporation, was very aware of this. We talked about it many times. Before he died——'' Coleman cleared his throat and his voice became stronger. ''He exacted from me a promise to look after her, and to protect her. I am here today to fulfill that promise.''

Patricia shivered, even though it was a warm July day. Coleman droned on. She could not bear to watch this mass of nobility. Instead, she studied the numerous gilded carvings in the courtroom's paneling——all seemed to be depicting masculine maidens carrying shields and weapons, the symbols of war. Just above the judge's head two helmeted goddesses, one wielding a sword, the other a torch, pulled on the arms of a naked child caught between them. She felt like that child.

''Your witness, Mr. Binder.'' Smith was clearly satisfied with his client's performance.

What a sharp contrast between the two lawyers, Patricia thought: Smith, immaculately groomed in his double-breasted spotless gray suit; and Howie in the same rumpled brown suit as usual——or perhaps he had a closetful of identical rumpled brown suits.

''Mr. Coleman——'' Howie slowly meandered toward the witness stand. ''Do you have any children?''

''No, my wife and I have never been blessed with a child, I'm sorry to say.''

''I was very touched by your testimony. Your attitude toward my client''——and he pointed toward Patricia——''is like that of a father to a daughter.''

''Yes sir.''

''And of course you would want the best for your daughter?''

''That is correct, Mr. Binder.''

Howie nodded his head vigorously in agreement, his black matted hair bouncing up and down. "You advised your daughter"—again he motioned to Patricia—"to sell her stock."

"That is not correct."

"Oh?" Howie blinked. "Then correct me."

"Patricia made the overture of divesting herself of her interest in the corporation."

"And you agreed?"

"That is correct."

Howie moved closer. "Why, Mr. Coleman?"

"Her grandfather had left her with a terrible burden—the controlling interest in a megaconglomerate. This was too much for Patricia. She was obsessed with spending her money. She repeatedly proposed irrational schemes to that effect. The last one involved a homosexual doctor whom she planned to marry."

Patricia sat stiffly, her hands clenched in her lap and her eyes tightly closed.

"Are you referring to Dr. Thomas Keegan, the Medal of Freedom winner, under whose guidance she built a hospital for crippled children in Beirut?"

"Yes."

"Did you commend Patricia for these altruistic activities?"

"No sir."

"Why not?"

"The Stoneham Charitable Foundation has done more than its share for eleemosynary institutions."

The court stenographer raised her hand. "Elee—what?"

Howie shook his head in exasperation. "Mr. Coleman is making the court stenographer's job difficult—he means *charitable*."

There was a faint smile on the judge's face.

"As a trustee then," Howie continued, "you curtailed her charitable endeavors?"

"I did my best."

"And you were not concerned that once she sold all her stock her giveaways might escalate?"

"Yes—but I felt this would be the lesser of two evils—at least it would relieve her of a burden that was putting a strain on her delicate psyche."

Howie smiled, nodded his head again, and began pacing. "And who would buy this stock?"

"It would not be difficult, Mr. Binder, to find a suitable group."

"And would it be correct of me to assume that you and your cohorts—"

"Objection." Smith rose. "Derogatory to the witness."

"Sustained."

"You and your *colleagues* would head such a group?"

"That is correct."

Howie had stopped his pacing and was squinting at Coleman.

"But that would give you control of a ten-billion-dollar corporation."

"Nothing would change. We would continue to perform the same duties—to protect all stockholders of our company."

"But now *you* would own the controlling shares.

There would be nobody to interfere with your decisions—say, raising your salary, your use of the company aircraft—''

''Objection.'' Smith was up again. ''Speculative and unsupported.''

''Sustained.''

Without breaking stride, Howie whipped out a sheaf of papers from a file on his table. ''I have here a document labeled 'Tender Offer.' It appears to be signed by you, Mr. Ash, and Mr. Rosemont. Would you kindly authenticate these signatures?'' And he placed the papers in front of Coleman.

''Yes, that is the proposal we submitted to Miss Dennsion.''

''Offering to buy out her shares?''

''That is correct.''

''For a dime on the dollar?''

''I resent that, Mr. Binder. The offer was fair—the going market price of Stoneham stock.''

Howie whirled on his heels and produced a bulky leather-bound folder. ''I have here a Price and Waterhouse audit of the Stoneham Group stock, commissioned by you, Mr. Coleman. You are familiar with this document, are you not?''

''Well—yes—ah—''

''And this appraisal states that the going market price undervalues the true worth of Stoneham stock by a considerable sum.''

''That is *speculation*, Mr. Binder—speculation that someday the Stoneham stock will appreciate in value.''

''I see, Mr. Coleman. So what happened next in your quest to protect my client?''

"The sale did not go forward. She changed her mind. Instead, she insisted on injecting herself into the running of the corporation—something she knows nothing about."

"Did she say why?"

"She said she wanted to give the company a 'conscience.' "

"And you were opposed to conscience?"

"Conscience has its place. But conscience in business cannot mean philanthropy. Our company is built on profits."

Howie rose on his tiptoes. "But her idea of conscience was to treat your employees like human beings—particularly in your Nogales plant, isn't that correct?"

"She was ill advised. Our neighbors along the Mexican border are reputable giants—General Motors, ITT, Ford, IBM, United Technologies, Xerox, and many others. We all maintain the same standards."

"Standards below the required minimum of U.S. law?"

"Mr. Binder, in Nogales we obey Mexican law."

"And avoid the expense of protecting the workers and the environment from chemical hazards? Isn't this what Patricia objected to?"

"She wasn't qualified to make such judgments," Coleman snapped as his face reddened. "She wanted us to become a philanthropic entity—she wanted to ignore profits to the detriment of the stockholders. *She* is the principal stockholder—she was hurting *herself*."

"But Patricia didn't see it that way, did she?"

"No."

"And so you instituted incompetency proceedings against her?"

"Only because we were convinced, after careful and painful consideration, that we had no other method of protecting Patricia."

"Protecting Patricia? By dragging her through the courts? By exposing her 'delicate psyche'—to use your own words, Mr. Coleman—to these emotionally charged proceedings?"

Coleman puffed out his chest. His voice was shaking with indignation. "Mr. Binder—we had no other choice!"

Chapter 21

Stone Ridge

BRUISED AND BATTERED by the accusations that had been hurled against her all week long, Patricia was grateful for two days of respite before the ordeal resumed again on Monday. She was so tired. She ached in every bone of her body. She curled up in a ball and pulled the covers over her head, oblivious to Taxi and Phoebe, who were crowding the bed beside her. If only she could sleep—she'd had so little of it recently.

The roses . . . the fire . . . Edgar's injuries . . . Paulo's death . . . . Miguel's arrest. How much more could she take?

She had no way of anticipating the strain of sitting at a table with the judge peering down at her over his spectacles as she was incessantly pummeled from every side. They described nervous breakdowns, suicide attempts, irresponsible behavior . . . The pilot testified how erratic she was . . . go back to America . . . no, go to Lisbon . . . no, land anywhere. Then the worst of it—she was a witless romantic who almost married a homosexual.

By now the judge must believe she was crazy. She was beginning to believe it herself. She shuddered at the thought of sitting in that courtroom again. Why didn't she just sell the stock . . .

Miguel would be disappointed that she gave up, but right now he seemed so very far away. And she was so tired, she just wanted to go to sleep—peaceful sleep—and never wake up.

There was a soft knock on the door, and Laura entered with a glass of warm milk and a couple of pills.

"Here kiddo, you take this now." And she brought the pills up to Patricia's mouth and handed her the glass of milk. "You need some rest."

"Oh, Laura, you've been so good to me, I don't know what I'd do without your help."

"Well you know the song—that's what friends are for. You'd hate me to sing it though," Laura guffawed.

Patricia smiled weakly. "I don't think I can go through with it, Laura."

"You don't have to, kiddo. Tell them all to go to hell and sell the stock."

Drowsily, Patricia muttered, "I don't know . . . maybe you're right . . . I don't know."

And she fell asleep.

Laura tiptoed out of the room and quietly closed the door. She hurried down the steps to the kitchen and picked up the phone.

"What?" Horace Coleman answered.

"I think she's about to break."

"Hmm . . ." Coleman seemed to be weighing his words. "Laura—how would you like a bonus of a quarter of a million dollars?"

Laura gasped. "I'd like that."

"Make sure she does."

Lisbon

MIGUEL DID NOT DARE open his eyes. He wanted to continue to hold Patricia in his arms. He could feel the softness of her skin, he could taste her open mouth . . .

A church bell rang out and he flinched. He had been dreaming—he was still in prison, lying on the pallet in his cell. Would he ever see her again?

He asked permission to visit the chapel every day— he was considered the most religious of all the prisoners—but he only went there to relive his moments with Patricia. He usually went in the afternoon when the sunlight streamed through the windows the very same way it did when he walked in and found her standing there before the altar.

He stared up at the large yellow stain on the ceiling, outlined by a jagged dark-brown border, obliterating most of the stucco. Each morning, he tried to guess what might have caused the stain. Today, he decided that an enraged inmate on the tier above had smashed his toilet and flooded the cell.

He got up and walked over to the barred window. Out in the prison yard, a large pile of trash was smoldering,

sending up spirals of black smoke to deface the blue
Sunday sky.

When would the trial take place? Emilio said it would
be some time before the court could complete its investigation. The waiting was the worst part—it was unbearable.

But once the trial got under way—what could he say
in his defense? He had killed Luis Veloso. It was a
fact. Now Isabel was wreaking her revenge—a woman
scorned. He would never forget the day when she
brought the police to arrest him.

She staged it well. At the cemetery—beside Paulo's
grave.

He had been going there every day to sit quietly on a
stone near his father's final resting place. He imagined
they were talking, repeating words they had spoken to
each other in the days before Paulo's death.

That day, just as he was leaving the cemetery, he saw
the black-clad figure of Isabel approaching, escorted by
two policeman.

"You're under arrest."

"For what?"

"The murder of Luis Veloso."

He looked at Isabel, her face obscured by a black
veil.

"Isabel," he said softly. "Why?"

He could feel the hidden venom, but she gave no
answer.

That happened on Sunday, two weeks before. It
seemed so long ago.

As he watched the dark blue smoke coiling from the
trash pile, the annoying clamor of church bells grew

louder and louder and the city awakened on the other side of the prison walls. *Oh Patrizia, where are you? I swear I would do anything for a few more minutes with you—even learn to love church bells.*

The bells kept clanging. Was Ultimato standing in his stall waiting to be taken to Emilio's? He had done so well with the young bull—he must feel abandoned now. Miguel hoped Filipe would give him an extra carrot and let him run around the indoor arena and roll in the soft sand.

Out in the hall, the shuffling of feet could be heard; the other prisoners returning to their cells from breakfast. He had stayed behind; he wasn't hungry.

A key jingled in the lock, the door was thrust open, and a guard called out, "Hey peg leg! They want you in the front office."

He was led to the receiving room where he had first entered the prison. "These are your belongings," the guard said, throwing him a package wrapped in brown paper and tied with hemp rope.

Miguel looked blankly at the man.

"Cheer up," the guard guffawed. "There's lots of chapels on the outside."

"I'm getting out?"

"So it says here."

When they opened the steel reinforced gates, Emilio was standing there with a solemn look on his face. "Follow me," he said mysteriously.

"But what—"

"Don't say anything—just get in the car."

As they drove away from the prison, Miguel demanded, "Would you mind telling me what's going on?"

"You're out of prison, my friend—isn't that enough?"

"Yes, yes but—"

"But nothing. Be happy." Then Emilio chuckled. "Well, maybe you shouldn't be too happy—you might have a funeral to attend."

"Who died?"

Emilio crossed himself. "Isabel."

Miguel grabbed his arm so hard, the car swerved.

"Hey—watch out!" Emilio pulled up to the curb.

"No more jokes—I've had too many laughs in prison."

"It's no joke. You are free. No one to testify against you."

"What happened?"

"She committed suicide."

"Suicide?"

"Yeah—she stabbed herself. It happened after Patricia left her house."

"What are you talking about?"

"It's a long story. Patricia insisted on seeing Isabel. She tried to persuade her to recant. Isabel went nuts—tried to kill her."

"Oh my God." Miguel was frozen with fear.

"Hey—nothing happened to your precious girl. But I got my face scratched again, taking the knife away from Isabel."

Miguel didn't laugh.

"She used the same knife on herself."

"She really was sick . . . how pathetic."

"Save your sympathy for me—I was damn lucky the maid was there when she did it."

Miguel looked at him questioningly.

"My fingerprints were all over that knife. We might have been roommates."

For the first time, Miguel smiled. "You'd have to take the upper bunk."

"Oh no! I get vertigo."

Miguel had to laugh; then he grew serious. "Emilio— I need a favor."

"If it involves dancing—I'm out."

"No, no—I need a ticket for New York."

Emilio pulled out an envelope from his pocket, "Sorry it took so long."

Stone Ridge

OVER THE WEEKEND, Patricia tried to stick to her usual routine. But she could tell Sport sensed something was wrong—he would turn his head and stare at her with his wide brown eyes. And even Taxi was just dragging his long legs morosely. She purposely avoided the path leading to the wood—her favorite spot to daydream, the place she brought Miguel so often. It would be too lonely to go there without him.

She was now nearing the last paddock, heading for the stable, when she noticed one of the horses behaving peculiarly. He was walking around in a tight circle, biting his side. She looked at the others. Two more were doing the same thing. Colic? Horses lacked the ability to vomit, and a stomachache could make them act this way. She decided she'd better rush to the barn and start mixing up some hot bran mash. Her eyes searched the group.

Old Cricket, the oldest horse on the farm, stood, head hanging down, lathered with sweat. Suddenly, his legs gave way, and he toppled over. He writhed on the ground for a moment and then lay still.

She screamed, "Edgar! Edgar!"

He came out running, one of the grooms following.

"Over there! Hurry!"

In the space of time that it took Edgar to run over to the paddock, three horses had dropped to the ground and were lying there motionless.

"Mix up some bran mash! Quick!" Edgar ordered the groom. "And get the vet here on the double!"

By the time the vet arrived, ten horses were dead. The vet stared at the devastation in disbelief.

"What's wrong, Dr. Cronin?" Patricia was trembling uncontrollably. "What's happening? What's wrong?" she repeated.

"I don't know yet. Get these others into the stable— isolate them. Start pumping whiskey and mineral oil into them. I'll take blood samples right away."

With a lead rope in her hand, she walked over to Misty, who was standing quietly with his head hanging down. Then she saw that he too was covered with sweat and foaming at the mouth. His eyes seemed to be pathetically begging for her help.

"Oh no, Misty, not you too." She could not hold back her tears.

She reached to pat his neck, and Misty started to

quiver. His knees buckled under him, and he fell to the ground. Patricia stared at his stomach, which was heaving up and down with great effort. Then all movement stopped.

"Misty," she whispered, and blacked out.

She didn't want to wake up. In the cloud of her mind, she saw Miguel's face coming into focus. "Patrizia," he said, "Patrizia, I'm here . . . with you . . . everything will be all right."

She reached out to him and felt his body envelop hers. Oh, this was such a beautiful dream, she wanted it to last forever.

"Wake up, Patrizia." He shook her gently.

She jolted awake. It *was* Miguel! It was really Miguel. Not a dream at all. She was lying on the couch in the living room. And he was with her.

"Miguel," she said with a weak smile.

He kissed her tenderly. "I came to surprise you, but I didn't expect this."

"You're here—you really are here."

"Yes, Patrizia. But what has happened to the horses?"

"I don't know—I think I'm cursed. Poor Misty . . . My God, where is Laura?"

"I haven't seen her."

"Oh that's right—she went into the city today. She won't be back until tomorrow. How am I going to tell her about Misty? It will kill her."

He took her hand in his. "Yes—too bad about that old racehorse."

"No, no—Misty wasn't a racehorse. He was Laura's pet."

"I know—the chestnut that she used to walk around the farm. I'm sure he was a racehorse."

"He couldn't be. Laura raised him from a foal."

"Whatever you say, Patrizia. It doesn't matter, but I saw the Jockey Club tattoo on his lip."

"That's impossible . . ."

Honking of a car horn interrupted them. Miguel looked up. "The veterinarian's truck."

"I must talk with with him right away."

"No Patrizia—you should rest."

"Please, I can't rest now."

He sighed and put his arm around her for support. They walked together to the pasture where the vet was talking with Edgar. Off in the distance a backhoe was digging graves as the bulldozer scooped up another carcass.

"Do you know anything yet, Dr. Cronin?" Patricia asked.

"Yes—these horses were poisoned."

"Poisoned?" Patricia whispered.

"How were they poisoned?" Miguel asked calmly.

"With monensin."

"What?!" Edgar yelled, his face getting red with anger. "We've always kept the chicken feed separate."

"Dr. Cronin," Patricia said, "I don't understand."

"Monensin, Miss Dennison, is an antibiotic compound used in poultry and cattle feed. It's highly toxic to horses. Obviously, they were given this by mistake."

Edgar was fuming. "No, goddamn. No! It can't be!"

"But maybe," said Patricia, "after the fire, the feed got mixed up . . ."

"No way—I checked it myself," the foreman insisted.

"Edgar—please calm down—it's not your fault."

Edgar moved away abruptly to shout instructions in a raspy voice at the men burying the dead horses.

Patricia swallowed hard as she looked down at the body of Misty. "Miguel, do you think we should wait, maybe Laura would like to be here—"

"You're right, Patrizia . . . maybe she would."

And then Miguel reached down and pulled back Misty's upper lip.

Patricia's eyes widened. There it was. The Jockey Club tattoo. U65-82551.

Chapter 22

New York City

LAURA SIMPSON SAT ON THE WITNESS STAND, projecting an image far from her usual blowsy self: she wore a flowered dress with a busy design of lilacs and roses; her hair was washed and neatly combed; her hands demurely folded in her lap.

"Miss Simpson, I want to thank you for coming here today to testify on Miss Dennison's behalf," Howie opened.

Laura gave him an ingratiating smile. "I am happy to do it; Patricia is my best friend."

"Right now she could use a friend," Howie muttered under his breath. Then he cleared his throat, walked over to the table, and filled a glass with water. He looked at Patricia, sitting with her head down, Miguel just

311

behind her watching her intently. He took a sip and turned back to Laura.

"Miss Simpson—I want to ask you a few questions about your friend's behavior during some very trying times."

Laura smoothed her dress over her knees. "I am ready, Mr. Binder."

"When Patricia's rose garden was mysteriously destroyed, you were with her?"

"That's right."

"She loved that rose garden?"

"Yes," said Laura with a nod.

"By the way, most of those roses were sent to hospitals and nursing homes, weren't they?"

"That's right."

"When she found that the garden she had painstakingly cultivated was destroyed, how did she react?"

"She cried a lot."

"Normal reaction, wouldn't you say, Miss Simpson?"

"I suppose."

"Nothing more dramatic occurred?"

"What do you mean?"

"She didn't have a nervous breakdown—did she?"

"No, she didn't."

"When the hay barn burned down, you were with her?"

"Yes."

"It must have been a terrible disaster." Howie seemed to be talking to himself. "Edgar, the foreman, was seriously injured . . . How did my client react?"

"Patricia was very upset."

"And you suggested she go to a sanitorium?"

"Well, I felt she needed help. I was afraid that—"

"This awful thing would destroy her?"

Smith stood up. "Your Honor, Mr. Binder is leading the witness."

The judge looked over his glasses. "Rephrase the question, Mr. Binder."

"Did she fall apart?"

"She cried a lot, but I stayed by her side and gave her some tranquilizers . . ."

"But she didn't require psychiatric treatment?"

"No."

Miguel listened with growing discomfort. Patricia didn't tell him about the fire—she was too considerate; she knew his father was dying, she didn't want to add to his worries. He looked at Patricia's slender shoulders slightly bent forward, as if bearing a heavy weight. *Oh my love, you were wrong not to tell me—I want to share everything with you.*

"And then there was another disaster on the farm?"

Laura lowered her head and sighed. "Yes."

"The horses she loved and cared for were poisoned?"

"Yes."

Howie approached Laura and leaned both his hands on the witness stand and looked into her face. "Didn't it amaze you that there were so many disasters—one following the other?"

"I felt very sorry for Patricia."

"Of course. So many catastrophes would be difficult for any person to endure."

Laura said nothing.

"How did Miss Dennison react to the death of her horses?"

"I wasn't there—I was away for the weekend."

"Look at her." Howie turned and pointed at Patricia. "This woman has withstood tragedies that could have brought down a very strong person, and yet, she's here in full possession of her senses—ready to defend her rights."

"Your Honor—" Smith jumped up. "Is Mr. Binder going to make a speech or question the witness?"

"I'm here to win my case, Your Honor."

The judge frowned. "Please continue with the witness."

Howie played with his suspenders as he seemed to look at the heavens for inspiration. His head still tilted upward, he asked, "You do know, Miss Simpson, that the horses were poisoned by monensin?"

"Yes."

"Do you know what monensin is?"

"An antibiotic."

"Good for chicken feed, but toxic to horses?"

"That's what I've heard."

"Hmm—how did it get into the horse feed, do you suppose?"

"I wish to God I knew."

Howie shook his head and muttered, "One disaster after another—each one worse than the last—"

The stenographer raised her hand. "Speak up, Mr. Binder."

"And get to the point," the judge reprimanded.

"The point is," Howie said in a loud clear voice,

"it's as if someone was trying to drive Patricia crazy. Who would have such a motive?"

The courtroom was silent.

"Who were her enemies, Miss Simpson?"

"I don't know of any."

"Think, Miss Simpson—who would want to destroy the mental competency of my client?"

"I don't know."

"You don't know?"

"No."

"But surely you can guess."

Smith jumped up. "Objection. Your Honor, he's badgering the witness."

Howie wheeled around. "But she's *my* witness."

"I resent . . . ah . . . ," Smith stumbled, "any witness being mistreated."

The judge pounded the gavel. "Objection sustained."

Smith and the trustees were whispering among themselves. Patricia, alone at the defendant's table, looked over her shoulder at Miguel. His eyes met hers and he smiled at her encouragingly.

Howie again filled his glass with water. "I'm sorry, Miss Simpson . . ." He took a sip. "I realize that this was a great tragedy for you also. Your own horse Misty was poisoned, wasn't he?"

"Yes," said Laura.

"It must be a terrible thing to lose a horse that you love."

Laura nodded, her face registering pain.

"I understand you raised Misty?"

"Yes . . . got him as a foal for my son, Robert . . . ," she said in a low voice. "The two of them grew up together. And Bobby learned to ride him . . . and then my son died . . ." Tears were flowing down her cheeks.

The judge interjected. "Mr. Binder, this is very touching, but how does it bear on this case?"

"I am trying to demonstrate what a tragedy it is to lose a horse you love—Miss Dennison lost a dozen."

"All right, I'll allow it."

Howie took a large white handkerchief out of his pocket and handed it to Laura. "Go ahead, Miss Simpson, tell the court what Misty's loss meant to you."

"Misty was all I had left of my son." Laura dabbed her eyes with Howie's handkerchief and then loudly blew her nose. "My only pleasure was to walk him around the farm and think of Bobby." She broke into tears again.

Howie's face assumed the expression of great compassion. "Yes—I understand how you feel . . . A racehorse of his caliber deserved a better end than that."

Laura looked at him through her tears. "He wasn't a racehorse."

"He wasn't?"

"I just told you—he was a family pet."

"My mistake. But didn't Misty have numbers tattooed on his upper lip?"

"What are you talking about?"

Howie seemed a little bewildered. "Didn't he?"

"Of course not," she said as if answering a stupid child.

"I'm sorry," said Howie, moving away. And then he turned. "But if he *did* have numbers tattooed on the inside of his upper lip, would you know what those numbers meant?"

Smith shot up from his chair. "We have been listening with great patience to Mr. Binder jump from one non sequitur to another, taking us further away from the reason we are all here today."

The judge now glared at Howie. "You are trying the patience of this court."

"I beg the court's indulgence for one minute more."

"One minute is all you have," the judge said peremptorily.

"Your Honor, every horse before its first race has a number tattooed on the inside of his upper lip. It is the registration number assigned by the Jockey Club. The history of that horse, until the day it dies, is kept in the club's files under that number—"

"Your time is almost up," the judge interrupted.

Howie snatched a sheaf of papers from the defense table. "This affidavit, signed by the veterinarian of Orange County, attests that the number U65-82551 was tattooed on the upper lip of the horse called Misty." Laura looked at him bewildered as Howie went on, "Jockey Club files show that he was a pretty good runner, Your Honor, not a great one, but he did take third place in the Santa Anita Handicap in 1968—"

Smith's face was red with anger. "What do these irrelevant statements have to do with this case?!"

"I'll tell you, Mr. Smith!" Howie crossed the courtroom and waved the folder at the plaintiffs. "The owner of Misty was not Laura Simpson but"—and he pointed accusingly at the trustees—"Mr. Robert Ash!"

"I . . . I don't know what he's talking about," Ash bumbled.

Ignoring him, Howie continued. "Poor Misty, lying in his grave . . . has proven that Laura Simpson was employed by the board of trustees as a *spy*."

Bob Ash jumped out of his chair, "She was not a spy—she was there to protect Patricia."

The judge pounded his gavel. "You're out of order, Mr. Ash."

Coleman, chins vibrating, placed a restraining hand on Ash's arm. Rosemont sat with mouth agape.

Howie went on, his voice booming now. "Protect Patricia?! She was there to *undermine* Patricia—ply her with pills, create catastrophes."

"It's not true!" protested Laura.

Jabbing his finger at her, Howie roared, "*You* released the bugs that destroyed the rose garden!"

"I did not!"

"*You* set fire to the barn that almost ended a man's life!"

"No!"

His face very close to hers, he hissed, "And *you* poisoned all those horses, including Misty."

"No. *No!*"

"No, Miss Simpson?" Howie walked over to the table and reached into his briefcase. He pulled out a plastic bag filled with small brown pellets. "Your Honor, this is chicken feed. It's used to fatten chickens. But as we have learned, it contains monensin, which even in minute amounts is deadly to horses."

Howie walked toward Laura holding up the plastic bag with two fingers. "These bits of poison were found in your car, Miss Simpson."

"What are you talking about?" Laura was trembling.

"I have four witnesses who can attest that this came out of your station wagon."

"It . . . it . . . can't be true."

"It *is* true."

The judge pounded his gavel. "Are you saying that this witness poisoned the horses?"

"That's exactly what I'm saying. Furthermore, I submit that she did so for one reason only—to break down my client! But this frail young girl endured it all." He whirled around and glared at Laura. "Despite your best efforts to drive her mad, Miss Simpson."

Laura's eyes had a vacant stare. "I only did what I was paid to do," she said weakly.

"I rest my case, Your Honor."

The judge took off his glasses and looked over at Smith. "Your witness."

Smith was frantically whispering to Coleman. Finally, he raised his head. "No questions," he said in a low voice.

"Good decision," the judge said grimly. Then he turned to Laura, a disgusted look on his face. "Witness dismissed."

Laura rose like a zombie; her eyes didn't seem to focus as she left the courtroom.

The judge leaned over his bench and addressed the plaintiffs. "Serious felony charges have been raised here. If there is to be rebuttal, gentlemen—I must warn you that anything you say may be used against you in criminal proceedings."

"Nothing further," Smith said meekly.

The judge banged his gavel. "Court is adjourned." And he got up and left.

Howie turned to Patricia. "We won." He snapped his suspenders with glee.

"Thank you," said Patricia absentmindedly. She was watching the trustees slink out of the courtroom. Rosemont was ahead of the others, clearly eager to leave the scene of the crime. Ash followed behind, obviously unaware that he was still squeezing the rubber ball. Coleman waddled out last, looking like a partially deflated balloon rapidly losing air. He seemed so much smaller, shriveled up, desperately clinging to his dignity as he walked out the door.

Patricia felt an arm around her, and Miguel's warm eyes met hers. "It's over," he said softly.

She buried her face in his shoulder. "Oh Miguel, how can I tell you what it means to me that you are here."

"Shh, you can tell me at lunch—I'm taking you to the spot where I fell in love with you . . . and I didn't even know it." He hugged her tightly.

"Come on, you lovebirds." Howie swept all the papers from the table with a flourish and stuffed them in his briefcase. "Mrs. Sperber is waiting for us down at Wall Street; we got work to do."

Miguel shot Patricia a quizzical glance.

"It won't take long," she said apologetically.

"Let's go," Howie chortled. "We've got to lock those scumbags out of the Stoneham executive suite—Mrs. Sperber's got all the injunctions ready."

The private elevator zipped them up to the boardroom. Mrs. Sperber, wearing a wide smile, got up from a stack of papers. She came forward, arms outstretched, eyes glistening. "My dear," she began; then, at a loss for words, she embraced Patricia awkwardly. Embarrassed, she collected herself. "Congratulations," she said with more restraint.

"Mrs. Sperber, I want you to meet Miguel Cardiga."

They shook hands firmly, Mrs. Sperber smiling almost coyly. "Ah yes, Miguel, I know a great deal about you—and I am not going to tell you who told me."

"I am not sure if you are paying me a compliment— or insulting me." A sly grin appeared on his face, revealing his straight white teeth.

Patricia had never seen Mrs. Sperber so vivacious and talkative.

"Howie—I am so proud of you," the gray-haired barrister was saying. "You brought the proceedings to a close in time for lunch." She pointed to the side table where sandwiches and coffee had been set out.

"Well, frankly," said Howie, "I thought we'd make it here in time for breakfast."

"How can such a little man have such a big ego," Mrs. Sperber chided.

Patricia broke in over their laughter. "We're not staying for lunch. Miguel's taking me to—"

"But my dear!" Mrs. Sperber's voice registered astonishment. "The emergency executive committee is on its way—we must elect a new company president— appoint a new board of trustees . . ."

Patricia shot a glance at Miguel.

He squeezed her hand. "You do your job."

Howie was already devouring a sandwich. "One of my easiest cases . . . and all the credit goes to the bullfighter." He patted Miguel on the back. "When you found the tattoo it was all over."

Miguel grinned. "When you have another case that deals with horses—call on me."

"We do have another case," interjected Mrs. Sperber. "The criminal complaint."

Howie gulped the last of the sandwich and rubbed his bony hands together. "I can't wait to dash over to the prosecutor's office this afternoon—what fun I'm gonna have with those three yo-yos in criminal court."

"No, Howie," Patricia said firmly.

"Huh?" Howie peered at her.

"I don't want to file a criminal complaint."

"Are you serious?"

"Yes. Drop it—I don't want to go through all that again."

"But Patricia—," Mrs. Sperber started.

"Please. I want an end to it. I've known them all since I was a little child . . . now that we've won, I feel sorry for them. I want to forget it."

"I don't understand you." Howie reached for another sandwich. "After what they've done?"

"Mr. Binder," Miguel broke in. "You don't know Patrizia. She feels sorry for everyone."

Howie sighed with incredulity.

"I'd listen to her if I were you," Miguel added.

Patricia looked at him with gratitude. She didn't want to argue with her two allies—she was tired, so tired of it all.

Howie and Mrs. Sperber exchanged glances.

"I see I'm outnumbered." Howie munched on. "But you don't mind, Patricia, if I don't tell them the good news yet? With a threat of criminal complaint hanging over their heads, they'll sign all the resignations and releases I put in front of them.''

Patricia sighed.

''What are you thinking, my dear?'' Mrs. Sperber asked.

''There is only one thing I don't understand. Why? They made so much money, they had so much power. Why?''

Howie leaned over, and with his mouth full, whispered in Patricia's ear: ''Greed.''

Miguel sat quietly sipping a cup of coffee, and trying to follow their conversation, but without much success. Assets . . . liabilities . . . restructuring . . . dividends . . . capital gains . . . reinvestments . . . From time to time Patricia interjected ideas that seemed to impress Howie and Mrs. Sperber. He was proud of her, but it all sounded so strange to him. He had a good grasp of the English language, but with this group he felt like a complete foreigner.

Quietly, without being noticed, he slipped out of the boardroom into Patricia's office. He picked up the phone and put in a call to Lisbon.

''Emilio?''

''Miguel—you found time to call your friend? What's wrong?''

''What's the schedule before the Lisbon finale?''

''Well—you won't be able to make that *corrida*.''

''Why not? I still have six weeks—I can make the three qualifiers I need.''

''But you missed two bouts while Paulo was sick and

two more while you were in prison. There are only three left before the season finale—and you won't be here to make the one this weekend.''

"Yes I will."

"You will? But how can you—"

"Don't argue. Just set it up."

"Okay, okay. Your humble servant will take care of it.''

Miguel didn't know why he was so abrupt with Emilio. He was tempted to call him back, but he didn't.

He peeked through the partially opened door into the boardroom. A group of men, all in business suits, was filing into the room. This must be the executive committee. He didn't belong with these people. Maybe he should leave. Yes, that would be best—he would go back to Patricia's farm and wait for her there. He would feel better on Harpalo's back. Quickly, he penned a note and asked the secretary to give it to her. Patricia would understand.

Stone Ridge

BUT PATRICIA DIDN'T UNDERSTAND. She wedged herself in the corner of the car seat, completely drained. What a horrible two weeks it had been—it was over now, and she longed for the peace of Miguel's comforting arms. Why didn't he wait for her?

Well, of course, he was probably bored, and just wanted to get on a horse and ride. She should try to see things from his point of view. She shouldn't be so self-absorbed . . .

By the time the car turned into the farm's driveway, she managed to pull herself together.

Everything looked serene on the farm. Horses were grazing peacefully in the paddocks. The evening sun cast a mellow glow over the fields. The backhoe had been put away; the scene of carnage had been erased. In the beauty of the twilight, it was as if it had never happened.

Edgar was out by the new feed barn supervising the unloading of a hay truck. He waved to her.

"Where is Mr. Cardiga?" she called out from the car.

"In the woods—he just rode off," Edgar yelled back.

She smiled. It was a lovely summer evening for a trail ride, she thought; she would catch up to him. But, as the driver pulled around to the main door of the house, the smile disappeared from her face. Laura's station wagon was waiting out front, the engine running and tailgate open. Involuntarily, she trembled. She couldn't stand facing her now. She dismissed the driver and entered the house through the kitchen door to avoid a confrontation.

Inside, standing there, with a cup of coffee in her hand, was Concha.

"Concha! You're back!" Patricia rushed over and embraced her.

"Be careful, you burn yourself," Concha giggled, placing the cup down on the table.

"I'm so happy to see you."

"You send big package for sick sister."

"Oh, I'm glad you got it."

"But I no got sister. Eight brothers. I say—no good.

Miss Simpson tell me you in Switzerland—she say you tell me when come back. But when package come for sick sister, I say no good. I come back.''

Patricia hugged the housekeeper again. "I missed you so much, Concha."

"Edgar tell me all story." Concha tossed her head contemptuously in the direction of Laura's room upstairs. "*¡Mucha malicia!*" she spat out.

Patricia nodded silently. She sat down and quietly sipped her coffee. It was difficult to absorb all that had happened in the last twenty-four hours. The worst thing was Laura's treachery. For more than a year, she had confided all her innermost feelings to Laura, who pretended to be her best friend. How could she have been so easily taken in—how could she have been so stupid? But the thought of Laura feigning affection for poor Misty revolted her more than anything. Suddenly, she heard footsteps up above. In spite of herself, she felt compelled to once more look at this woman who had betrayed her.

When she walked into the living room, Laura was just coming down the stairs, carrying two suitcases. Her hair was tangled and matted, her eyes bleary. Obviously, she had been drinking. When she reached the entryway, she noticed Patricia standing there and snorted. She kicked the partially opened door. It flew ajar, slammed back, and knocked one of the suitcases out of her hand.

Patricia didn't move.

Laura, red-faced, struggled to pick up her suitcase. "What the fuck are you staring at?"

Patricia didn't answer.

"I'm glad to be out of here. You and your fucking problems—poor little rich girl doesn't know what to do with her money!"

Patricia felt oddly undisturbed by the venom.

Tears were now streaming down Laura's face. "Go ahead, put me in jail—you've got the money to do it. Prison can't be any worse than living here."

Patricia still said nothing. Impassively, she watched Laura storm out. She didn't move until she saw the red taillights of the station wagon disappearing down the driveway.

Chapter 23

Stone Ridge

THAT NIGHT PATRICIA SLEPT FITFULLY. She kept waking up to make sure Miguel was there with her. And he was—holding her, cuddling her like a child, stroking her hair, massaging her gently until she fell asleep again.

Oh, how grateful she was that he was with her—he had come when she had needed him most. Without him, she could never have withstood losing so many of the old horses. Without him, she would be back now in the barred room in Lausanne, mirror gone from the wall.

But when she woke up to find the strong sun streaming into the room, she was alone. Panic-stricken, she threw on some clothes and raced downstairs.

"Where is Mr. Cardiga?" she asked Concha, trying to keep the anxiety out of her voice.

"He with horse—but you eat first."

Over Concha's protestations, she dashed out of the kitchen.

In the stable, Miguel was chatting with Edgar; nearby, Sport and Harpalo stood saddled and waiting.

Ignoring Edgar, she threw her arms around Miguel's neck and showered him with kisses.

Edgar, muttering something about water lines, left them alone.

"Hey—control yourself," Miguel laughed.

She gave him one more tight squeeze and backed away giggling. "Do you realize that this is the same spot where one year ago I pushed you away?"

"Well then—let's tear down the stable and build a cathedral."

He picked her up and put her on Sport's back, then mounted Harpalo. "Ready?"

"Okay, mister boss. Where to?"

"The spot I visited yesterday evening," he said mysteriously. "Just follow me."

It didn't take her long to guess where he was leading her—the wood where they had talked together so often.

"Do you think those thousands of eyes remember when we were here last?" he asked.

"Yes," she whispered, dismounting, "let's talk quietly so they won't know that this is where we will build the American branch of the Centro Equestre da Cardiga."

He didn't react.

"Oh Miguel—let's start on it right away."

"But you can't."

"What do you mean?"

"I listened to your conversation yesterday . . . visits to the factories, overhauling management, auditing . . . you must do that first."

"Yes, but you'll help me."

"No Patrizia—I have things that *I* must do too."

"What are you saying, Miguel?" A feeling of apprehension was creeping over her.

"Time is against me. I have missed four bullfights, and in six weeks, I make my comeback appearance in Lisbon."

Patricia had a sickening feeling in the pit of her stomach. "You can't leave."

"I must."

"But I need you with me. How am I going to run the business without you at my side?"

"The same way I am going to fight those bulls without you at my side."

"You mean, you want to leave me to torture some animals?" she blurted out.

His face blanched. "I don't criticize what you do— don't criticize me."

She was stunned by the firmness in his voice. "I'm sorry."

Miguel watched her as she fought back tears. "Patrizia—you've got a job to do and you can do it. You have guts. You fought the trustees and you won."

"But I fought them because of you. You gave me strength to do it." There was a desperate edge to her voice. "And now I need you more than ever."

"I will be thinking of you all the time."

"That's not enough!"

Miguel looked at her steadily. "That is all I have to offer."

"Then why did you come here in the first place?"

"Do I have to answer that question?" he asked sharply.

"No, no—it's just that I can't help it—I want you."

"I understand—I want you too. But we both have responsibilities."

"The hell with responsibilities!"

"You don't mean that," he said soothingly. "I know you—the look in your eyes when you talk about the people in Nogales, the tone in your voice when you talk to the animals you love. I have learned much from you, Patrizia."

"Oh Miguel," she said softly, "stay just for a little while—a few days."

"I can't—I must leave on this afternoon's Concorde."

"Oh no, no—please—" She tried to keep the pleading out of her voice. "Just one more day."

He shook his head. "Tomorrow it will be more difficult to leave you."

They rode back to the stable in silence. At the house, Miguel quickly packed his bag. She did not object when he said he would go to the airport alone. Their goodbye was stiff. She concentrated on making the lump in her throat disappear. He tried to be soothing, promising to call often and painting a cheerful picture of their reunion in six weeks—the day of his comeback in the Lisbon bullring.

After he left, she sat in the bedroom window, watching the sunset. The contrails of an airplane passed over the farm. Was he inside, racing away from her?

The light grew dimmer, but there was not a star in the sky. *Oh Daddy—where are you?*

It had been months since she talked to her father. She didn't need to appeal to heaven when she was loved so much on earth. But now she felt unsure again, abandoned.

She wanted Daddy to take her in his arms and make the hurt disappear. No—not Daddy. She wanted Miguel to take her into his arms and be with her always. But he had just told her that tormenting bulls was more important to him than being with her. She couldn't cope with it—did he really love her?

Chapter 24

New York City

PATRICIA HAD NEVER WORKED SO HARD at the farm as she had for the last three weeks at Stoneham—it was the only way she could keep her mind off Miguel. She was exhausted, but she was too ashamed to complain about it to anyone. Mrs. Sperber and Howie were working just as hard, but they didn't seem to be the least bit tired.

Now, as she sat at the large conference table with the newly formed board of directors, she barely listened to Mrs. Sperber's report of their recent visit to the Ohio foundry. She looked at her watch—it had been a full day; how she hated meetings. Maybe she could make some excuse and leave . . .

Just then the door burst open and Howie walked in.

Patricia smothered a laugh—she couldn't believe the change that had come over him. Gone was the baggy brown suit, wrinkled shirt, and oversized suspenders. In their place, he wore a snappy striped shirt, a skinny tie with large eagles all over it, and—could it be? On Howie?—a designer suit in very stylish houndstooth. His Coke bottle glasses had been replaced by a hip aviator pair. Was being appointed the chief counsel to a megaconglomerate going to his head?

"Howie—how dapper you look," she said.

He blushed. "You like it? My new girlfriend has some very definite ideas."

He reached the head of the table and held up a copy of *Newsweek* magazine. On the cover was a photograph of Patricia. A murmur passed through the room.

Holding the magazine high above his head, he announced: "Ladies and gentlemen—this is the next edition of *Newsweek*, which will be in the hands of millions of readers tomorrow morning. I'm sure you recognize the picture of our heroine." He beamed.

Patricia glanced down at her clammy hands, not knowing what to say.

"Permit me to read some of the highlights of the story," Howie continued. He cleared his throat, and, in a stentorian voice usually reserved for the courtroom, he began: "The stock market has shown a surge of interest in the Stoneham Group, a company first formed forty years ago by the late J. L. Stoneham. Widely known and feared by many as a ruthless corporate raider, Stoneham had fashioned his empire to mirror his reputation. But now, his only heir, Patricia Dennison, is changing the direction of the company and causing a stir in the market with pronouncements such as this one last week: 'I want Stoneham to be a company with a conscience, a company that cares not only about its shareholders and customers, but its employees, its effect on the environment, and its impact on future generations.' ''

Patricia could feel her face redden. All eyes in the room were focused on her in admiration. Mrs. Sperber looked like a mother hen clucking over one of her chicks.

Howie went on, his voice rising for emphasis as he unconsciously strained his neck against the pressure of the new shirt.

''Although Wall Street skeptics predicted the demise of the Stoneham Group after Miss Dennison's takeover, the opposite has happened. News of what she was attempting caused a run on the company stock by those investors who applauded her objectives. As one entrepreneur working for the implementation of socially responsible values in business put it, 'Miss Dennison has shown that the mere act of caring about something other than profits brings its own reward—huge profits.' ''

Howie came to a rumbling conclusion. ''Let's hear it for the brilliant Miss D.!''

They all stood up applauding and cheering. Patricia, her head hanging down, mumbled something that sounded like ''Thank you,'' waved her hand in protest, and ran out.

In her office, she closed the door behind her. Why couldn't she enjoy her moment of triumph? This was exactly what she had been trying to achieve. She was reforming the company and setting an example for others to follow. So why did it feel so empty?

She knew why—Miguel wasn't here to share it with her.

It had been a week since she last spoke with him. She tried many times, but he was very hard to reach—moving about the provinces of Portugal for the qualifying bullfights—and the time difference didn't help, either.

She picked up the phone with trepidation. In their last conversation, he had seemed so cold, distant, preoccupied. Of course, he was involved in what he was doing. She couldn't blame him, she too was busy. But her work at Stoneham was nearly over—Mrs. Sperber and Howie would soon assume control of the company, and they would run it better than she ever could. What then? Could she find a place in Miguel's life? She wanted so much to help him, but what could she do—follow him from bullfight to bullfight? It depressed her to think about it.

She put the phone back on the hook.

Walking out of the Stoneham Plaza, she noticed a tall blond woman with hair like Joanna Benson's, piled so high she might tip over in a strong wind, standing at a large white limousine. My God—it *was* Joanna Benson! Patricia was about to approach her when Howie ran out the front door, panting. "Darling! I'm sorry to keep you waiting so long."

Joanna, towering over him by a good foot, bent down

and kissed his forehead, straightened his tie, and patted his curls into place.

Patricia hid behind a pillar and stared in amazement. Joanna and Howie! How incredible!

She watched them drive off and then got into her waiting sedan. Who would have thought those two would end up together? And they seemed so happy. She couldn't help feeling a little jealous. They had the kind of intimacy she once had with Miguel, a closeness she knew was slipping away.

Her car was zipping up First Avenue—toward that dreadful place, the Park Avenue mansion, where she had been staying because of her hectic schedule. At least, J. L. Stoneham's portrait no longer intimidated her. Somehow, over the past year, J. L.'s features had softened—his eyes no longer drilled through her and his granite countenance seemed to be made of flesh at last. Even if J. L. didn't approve of the direction his company was taking, he had to be pleased that it was showing profits.

The car slowed down by the United Nations—a protest group was holding up traffic. The driver turned around. "You wanna wait this out, Miss D.? Or you wanna try going up Third? It won't be a picnic cuttin' over."

"I think I'll walk."

"But Miss D.—it's another twenty blocks."

"I need the exercise."

As she got out, the heat rising from the pavement hit her with a blast. Suddenly she realized how much of her time was spent in the open farm air or in air-conditioned cars and boardrooms. This was the first time she could remember walking through the city, instead of stepping out of a car in front of an entrance.

She wended her way through the demonstrators who were protesting the treatment of Palestinians on the West Bank. Jostled by the crowd, she continued up First Avenue. She had been driven along this street many times, but she had never seen it—always preoccupied, reading some report or listening to music.

She walked slowly, looking at the people—all of them in a hurry, each wrapped up in his own world—boys and girls oblivious of each other, hurrying in opposite directions to the beat of music pulsating in their Walkmans. Ignoring all the bustle, a bag lady sat against the wall of a building, a bundle of belongings in her lap topped by a raggedy little dog. No one noticed her. As Patricia stooped to pet the little dog; she slipped the woman a ten-dollar bill.

Walking on, she came to a corner food stand emitting a pungent smell of hot dogs, falafel, hot knishes, pretzels. She didn't know what a knish was so she bought one and bit into the hot dough—it was good. She continued up the street munching with satisfaction.

Passing a news vendor's booth, she saw a bundle of magazines being hurled from a truck. The vendor slashed the string and copies of *Newsweek* spilled out. There it was, staring at her—her own face.

A phrase Howie had read jumped into her mind—"the mere act of caring . . . brings its own reward . . ." Those were Tom Keegan's words—he had started her thinking like this. And he had helped Miguel too. She had meant to send a contribution to his foundation, but with all the court proceedings, it had slipped her mind. I must do this right away, she thought, as the crowd carried her across the street.

Down the block she saw an ambulance fighting its way against traffic. The cars didn't budge. Nobody seemed to care that someone might be dying inside. What a mess, trying to reach a hospital in Manhattan. Finally, the screams of the siren subsided as the ambulance stopped in front of the Lenox Hill Hospital up the street.

Lenox Hill! Maybe Tom Keegan was there right at this moment, caring for someone near death.

Of course, it was late in the day, but at least she could stop in and leave a note for him. Was it almost a year ago that she saw him last? So much had happened. On an impulse, she crossed the street and walked into the hospital lobby.

She approached the reception desk. "I'd like to leave a message for Tom Keegan."

"Just a minute," the pretty candy-striper said, checking her computer. "You can go right up—room six-oh-two."

"Well, no . . . I . . . ," Patricia stammered, "I just wanted to leave a note for him."

"I'm sorry, but I'm not allowed to hold anything for patients."

"But he's a doctor here."

The girl looked at the computer screen again. "I show he's a patient in room six-oh-two."

Bewildered, Patricia took the elevator to the sixth floor. She walked down a long cavernous hallway checking the numbers. An emaciated figure of a young man was wheeled past her on a gurney, a nurse walking alongside holding up an intravenous bottle.

She hesitated in front of the door marked 602. She knocked. After a while, she heard a muffled, "Come in."

At first glance she thought she made a mistake. The face lying on the pillow was gaunt, the sunken eyes burning dark in hollow sockets. Purple sores covered the cheeks. Involuntarily, she shrank back, but the eyes held her rooted to the spot.

The silence was broken by a raspy voice coming through parched lips. "I never thought I'd see you again."

Patricia couldn't answer. Suddenly, she had a feeling that her legs wouldn't hold her up any longer. She sagged into a chair by the bed, rivulets of tears streaming down her face.

"Don't cry," he said, motioning as if he wanted to touch her. The veins on the back of his hand stood out like small cords against the blotchy skin. He caught her looking at it and hid his arm under the sheet.

"What's wrong?" she asked softly.

He didn't answer right away, but looked up at the ceiling. "The curse of the gods." His mouth twisted in an attempt to smile. "Acquired immunodeficiency syndrome."

She looked at him, not comprehending.

"AIDS."

"Oh no, Tom, not you."

His eyes gazed vacantly into space. "I'm the perfect candidate."

Speechless, Patricia stared at this emaciated figure covered with a dingy-colored white spread. And then her words poured out in a cascade. "You've done only good, you've tried to help others. You've gone to a godforsaken part of the world . . . to save people who were starving, afflicted, people that others abandoned. You've done nothing but good all your life."

"Bullshit."

She wasn't sure she heard him. "What?" she said, leaning toward the bed.

"I hated those fucking Arabs."

Patricia slowly recoiled. He must be delirious.

"The only one I tried to help was me," he continued in that sepulchral voice as his head slowly turned toward her. "That's right . . . I was only thinking of me."

"Tom, please, don't be so hard on yourself. You spent two years under such harsh conditions, nursing those helpless people."

"That's crap."

"How can you say that?"

His head lolled back on the pillow, and his eyes closed momentarily. "Patricia, I don't have much time left, and I'm trying to be honest. It's difficult, because I've never been honest before. But what would you expect from a closet queen?"

"Tom, your sex life has nothing to do with the extraordinary things you've accomplished as a human being."

"I wish I had been the person you saw in me," he said, smiling faintly. "But I was selfish."

"Selfish?"

"Yeah—I wanted to be the great white hope of Park

Avenue. And here I am—on Park Avenue." A strangled laugh came out of his throat, then turned into a cough. He took a deep breath and continued. "With the money that I siphoned off from all the charity benefits you set up, I took plenty of vacations."

"I don't believe it," she whispered.

"Well, you better believe it. There's no time for lies." He sank deeper into the pillow, exhausted by the speech.

Patricia didn't know how to respond to his confession. As she grappled with her thoughts, the door opened. A nurse entered the room with an intravenous bag; she attached the tube to the cathether on his chest and left without saying a word.

"Is there anything you need—anything I can bring you, Tom?" Patricia finally managed.

"Yeah," he said. "A couple of more years."

She bit her lip.

"I'm sorry." His eyes seemed softer.

In a wave of pity, Patricia leaned over to kiss him.

"Don't," he said sharply, and turned his face away from her.

"I'll be back again, Tom," she said, and quickly walked out, softly closing the door behind her. She couldn't take any more. By the elevator, she leaned against the wall, trying to absorb all that had happened.

She was about to push the button when a nurse came running after her with something in her hand. "Dr. Keegan wants you to have this." Patricia glanced down at the package wrapped in brown paper and tied with string. She took it without a word.

She held it limply in her hand as the elevator descended. In the lobby she had to sit down. She looked at the small packet in her lap. Slowly, trying not to tear the paper, she removed the wrapping, which covered a wooden box elaborately carved with hieroglyphics. She opened it and blinked. Glistening inside was a mound of diamonds. Carefully, she took out the necklace that she had donated to Tom's hospital at the fund-raising dinner. Underneath was a short note:

> *I am so sorry that I didn't trust you enough to tell you my secret. It seemed too dark to bring out into the light. I lacked the courage and I hurt you, the person who deserved it least. Forgive me, if you can.*
>
> *You gave this to me with your love—a priceless gift. Please take it back with mine. Tom.*

Cartaxo, Portugal

"WHAT THE HELL were you doing out there today?" Emilio shouted.

Miguel kept his back to his friend. Deep in thought, he kept pacing the dirt path encircling a crowded bull pen. Inside, the animals bellowed angrily.

"Did you hear me, Miguel?!" Emilio followed after him.

"The crowd seemed to like it."

"Oh shit! This is a little hick town, ecstatic to see the son of Paulo Cardiga, no matter what kind of an ass he makes of himself."

Miguel shot his friend a steely look over his shoulder.

But Emilio just carried on in a louder voice. "The brave fucking *toureiro* who does not even look at the bull when he sets up a pass! You could have gotten hurt."

Miguel stopped pacing and leaned over the cinder block enclosure—inside, the mass of undulating black flesh was moving restlessly. "But I didn't get hurt," he said matter-of-factly.

"Thanks to Ultimato! He was the only one paying attention."

Miguel clenched his teeth. "Knock it off—what the hell do you want from me?"

Emilio took a deep breath. "I want you to work the bull like you did at my place, when you brought that look of pride to your father's eyes—"

"He was watching me ride. I don't think he even saw the bull."

"Today, I don't think *you* saw the bull."

Miguel turned to face his friend. "Emilio—when I decided to fight again, I thought it'd be like the old days—but I can't get the same feeling back. It's . . . I don't know . . . *gone*."

"Oh fuck! Now I've heard everything. You'd get the feeling back if you'd only concentrate on what you're doing."

For a moment, a tense silence hung between them.

"Miguelinho—I beg you . . . for the next couple of weeks, try to concentrate on *them*—" And he pointed down at the bulls. "That's your enemy. Look at them—they're waiting to kill you. One of them took your leg. You want another to finish you off?"

Silently Miguel's gaze followed Emilio's hand. The bulls were swaying their powerful heads, impatiently pawing the ground with their hooves as if angry at being confined in such a small area. Until a few days ago, they had had little contact with human beings, roaming the fields freely—now they were prisoners, held captive to fight once before their death in a slaughterhouse.

A massive bull separated from the others and approached Miguel. He was drooling slightly, and from his black mouth a long pink tongue darted out, flicking up against one flaring nostril and then the other. Standing there, he looked like a magnificent statue, the afternoon sun casting a sheen over his black hide and amber horns. Then he raised his head toward Miguel and emitted a long deep bellow. What was he trying to say?

The eyes held no answer; almond shaped, like deep bottomless wells, they reflected points of light eerily.

Suddenly, Miguel remembered something he had read in the book Patricia had given him. The world was separated into killers and runners, the author had said, and you could tell them apart by the position of their eyes. The runners had eyes far apart so they could see all around them; the killers had eyes close together so they could focus on the prey they chased. Man, of all the animals, had his eyes most closely placed together.

For the first time, Miguel realized that the bull's eyes were very far apart indeed. He was the prey; man was the enemy.

The bull kept staring accusingly, never blinking. Miguel turned away.

Emilio put his arm around Miguel. "What's really eating you?"

Chapter 25

Nogales

HER EYES ON THE GROUND, Patricia stood embarrassed, as deafening cheers echoed across the factory floor. *"¡Gracias Patricia! ¡Gracias Patricia!"*

It had been a tumultuous meeting—Raphael and the workers' committee all talking at once, insisting on showing her the blueprints of sewer lines and electric lines, grinning so wide their smiles fairly lit up the room.

As Patricia started to leave, Raphael made a pathway for her through the crowd. "Tonight, we have a big fiesta—music, drinking, and food . . . tortillas, enchiladas, quesadillas . . ."—he smacked his lips together—"like you've never eaten before."

"I'm sorry, Raphael, I must go back this afternoon."

"But you cannot."

She didn't want to tell him how poorly she had been feeling for the past week and that the exhaustion was finally overwhelming her. Instead, she said, "They are waiting for me back in New York, I must be there."

"Oh, that's too bad—it will be such a wonderful party."

"Next time, Raphael."

The twinkle came back in his eyes. "Maybe it is best you go—I'd hate for you to see me drunk." And a deep belly laugh rumbled out of him.

"Raphael—before I leave, will you to do me a favor?"

"Anything."

"Take me to the *colonia*—there is something I want to find."

"What is that?"

"I'll know it when I see it."

They walked down the hill together to the settlement—empty at midday with all the workers still at the factory—Patricia carrying a large brown bag in her arms.

"Please let me," he said reaching out for the bag.

"No, no, it's not heavy."

They had to step aside when two big trucks full of cinder blocks rumbled by. "See, we waste no time. We start now," Raphael said.

Patricia smiled, and pointed to a narrow path. "Let's turn left here . . . if I remember right."

And then she saw it—the hut with the little rose bush out front still protected by a fence of crooked twigs. But no roses were blooming.

When they got nearer, the old woman came out.

"I want to talk with that lady," Patricia said to Raphael, "would you translate?"

"Of course."

"Señora Maria!" he called out. "You have a visitor."

The old woman waited as Patricia approached.

"I have something for you," Patricia said, while Raphael translated. And from the paper bag she pulled out a small rose bush in a pot. It had two white buds ready to bloom.

The woman reached for the pot with trembling hands. "Oh, oh—" No other words came out, but her eyes said she thought it was the most beautiful rose bush in the world. Then, with a broad, toothless smile, she pulled Patricia into the hut and motioned for her to sit down on a wooden crate. She said something in Spanish to Raphael.

"She wants to make you some herb tea," he translated.

"Oh no, no thank you." Patricia objected.

Raphael interpreted again. "She say you don't look well—you need this special potion."

Patricia waited patiently while the old woman busied herself over a tin pan on the Sterno stove, and then poured the brew into a chipped pottery bowl and handed it to her.

Patricia took it with both hands and sipped the spicy liquid, the woman watching her intently.

"*Sí . . . Sí . . . bueno*. Your baby be strong boy," she said.

"What?" Patricia was sure she misunderstood.

As Raphael repeated the translation, the woman touched Patricia's stomach gently and with gnarled trembling hands rubbed it in a circular motion.

"Oh, I wish it were true," Patricia said softly.

The woman smiled and nodded, her eyes full of wisdom of the ages. "Your baby will grow tall and beautiful like this rose bush."

In a daze, Patricia finished the liquid and stood up. "Thank you so much," she said.

Walking out of the hut, she suddenly felt no longer tired, but strangely invigorated, as if the woman's potion had given her new strength.

She climbed up the hill alone, leaving Raphael to talk with the truck drivers unloading the bricks. Her car was waiting in front of the factory gates. Pulling out, she saw the tiny chapel of Saint Ramon, alit with votive candles like before.

"Stop—wait just one more minute," she told the driver.

She went inside and knelt down, staring at the flickering flames.

She knew the old woman was right. Now she understood why she had missed her period—not because of the stress of recent events, but because she was pregnant. The baby had been conceived in the chapel of the Lisbon prison.

She wrapped her arms around her stomach. *I don't care what happens now. Even if Miguel doesn't want me, I have you to love, little one. Someday, you will hear the workers cheer you. And you will see a garden of white roses outside these factory walls.*

She got up and from a box in the corner picked up a fresh candle. She lit it and placed it among the others.

Lisbon

MIGUEL STARED at his image in the mirror. The midnight blue of his satin coat glittered with its gold filigree. "This looks familiar," he said to Emilio.

"It should—it's the one you wore three years ago. But I had the blood cleaned off." Emilio had an amused glint in his eye.

To Miguel, it seemed that it all happened yesterday. Here was his best friend in the dressing room with him just as he had been on that earthshaking day. He stroked the coat, thinking of the afternoon that had led to so many changes in his life. "Emilio, wearing it is a good omen."

He threw one last glance in the mirror. The reflection showed arrogance, defiance. He wished he felt as confident as he looked.

He had been afraid that Patricia would not come, but she was there, with the crowd, awaiting his entrance. He wanted so badly to impress her—to show her the best that bullfighting could be. He hoped he would succeed.

"Your horse is ready, Senhor Cardiga," came the voice of the groom from the doorway.

Miguel walked toward Ultimato, whose mane was braided with blue satin ribbons to match his coat. Ignoring the groom's clasped hand for a leg up, he lightly sprang into the saddle.

Emilio handed him his three-cornered plumed hat and Miguel placed it squarely on his head and winked at his friend. Soon, he would see Patricia's eyes anxiously gazing at him from the audience.

"Where did you seat her?" he asked Emilio.

"The VIP box, of course. She ought to have the best seat for her first bullfight."

"How did she look?"

"As beautiful as ever."

The horse was beginning to prance on the brick floor. "Patience, Ultimato"—Miguel patted his smooth arched neck—"we'll be there soon enough." And he turned toward the bright shafts of light filtering through the cracks of the massive arena gates.

The trumpets sounded, and the gates parted. Now, Miguel could see the waves of people reaching up to the rafters of the red brick bullring, kids standing in the Moorish arches. He felt a quiver of excitement course through Ultimato as they entered with slow measured steps, a deafening cry of *Miguelinho!* engulfing them.

Horse and rider appeared to ignore the crowd and walked, without changing pace or stride, to the center of the ring. There, they stood motionless until the cheering subsided, and all was quiet. Then, responding to an imperceptible cue from Miguel, Ultimato lifted himself off the ground and exploded in a *capriole*—all four legs flying three feet above the ground. The crowd roared. A true Cardiga touch.

With a flourish, Miguel removed his plumed hat and broke into a canter toward the VIP box. There she was, just as he had imagined her, nervously watching. As he threw the hat, her hands reached out and easily caught it. For a moment their eyes met. He was smiling triumphantly as if to say: Don't worry—Ultimato and I will do what has to be done this afternoon.

Patricia had never seen Miguel look better on a horse. The music, the arena, the costume—all showed off his horsemanship with new glamour. He and Ultimato were dancing fluidly, showing off the movements of haute école with a flair that took her breath away.

She wanted to shout *bravo!* along with everyone else, but the beauty of what she was seeing rendered her mute, able only to watch through misty eyes.

Then the trumpets blared again. Now, horse and rider moved over to the shady part of the arena, and stood quietly as a hush fell over the audience.

A sharp clang, like a shot, echoed in the silence and the doors of the bull pen sprang open to reveal a black tunnel. All was still. A few terrible seconds later a huge black beast roared out of the darkness.

For a moment, the tableau was obscured by the clouds of dust his powerful legs stirred up.

Then Patricia saw Miguel and Ultimato advance, Miguel waving a flag and yelling: *"Ehe! Ehe!"*

At first, the bull seemed not to notice them; then he lowered his horns and charged. Patricia's hands involuntarily grasped the scarf at her neck. She wanted to scream, but felt strangled.

Ultimato raced forward and when the bull, following the waving flag, came alongside, Miguel leaned out of the saddle and planted the sharp dart into his hump. The horse swerved easily out of harm's way as the crowd erupted in approval.

The bull stood confused, shaking his head as if trying

to dislodge the dart. Blood was spurting out and flowing down his neck. Involuntarily, Patricia closed her eyes.

When she opened them again, Miguel was taunting the bull for the second time. She willed the bull to keep still, stay rooted to his safe spot in the arena. But he did not obey her thoughts. He charged again.

Now she saw Ultimato galloping forward—on a collision course. The reins were draped over the horse's neck as Miguel arched in the saddle, both arms extended high above his head, a dart in each of them.

The bull gained momentum, barreling toward the horse. The two animals seemed to graze each other as Miguel leaned out of the saddle and planted both darts into the bull's heaving neck. The wounded bull dropped down on one knee, and she thought for a moment he was going to fall, but he didn't. He stood helpless, red blood flowing down his black legs into the yellow sand.

She felt nauseous. The screaming of the mob was unbearable. She was lost in this mad place. She couldn't watch any more.

She stumbled out into the hallway, holding on to her stomach. She wanted to protect her unborn child from this sight, this violence, this cruelty.

She didn't know how long she stood there, her face pressed against the cold plaster walls painted blood red. The yelling inside was incessant. What was she doing here? She had to leave this place—she had to leave Lisbon.

But her progress was arrested by the excited spectators streaming out. They flowed past, engulfing her like a river. She was afraid she would drown. All she could do was press her back against the wall, holding on to her stomach.

Suddenly, she felt a strong hand grasp her shoulder. She turned around to meet Emilio's laughing eyes. He winked. "Come with me, I've arranged a special private audience for you."

"No, no," she answered, a feeling of panic coming over her. "I'll wait for him with the others."

Emilio looked surprised. "But Miguel insisted that I bring you to his dressing room—he wants to see you alone."

He took her by the hand and elbowed his way through the boisterous crowd. Darting into a side door, he pulled her along narrow labyrinthine passageways. "Be careful here," he warned, as they climbed a scaffold and made their way along a rickety catwalk. Emilio pointed down at a black milling mass—the backs of penned-up bulls.

Finally, he opened another door, and they stepped into the blinding lights of television cameras and photographers' flashbulbs.

Patricia found herself in a large smoke-filled reception room among elegantly dressed women chatting animatedly with aristocratic gentlemen—obviously, the cream of Lisbon society. Champagne corks popped, glasses clinked, the raucously deep-throated laughter of the men mingling with the high-pitched gaiety of the women. Everybody was having an uproarious good time. She didn't belong here.

Several people slapped Emilio on the back, shouting words she didn't understand. Acknowledging the greetings, Emilio continued to pull her through the throng until they reached a door at the end of the room. He threw it open and practically shoved her in, shutting it quickly behind her.

Her eyes took a few seconds to adjust to the dimly lit interior. The first thing she saw was Miguel's coat draped across the chair. Mesmerized, she stared at the purple stains where the bull's blood had spattered it.

"Patrizia." He moved a step toward her, but she stood motionless, one hand leaning on the coat as if for support.

Miguel had rehearsed this scene in his mind a hundred times, but all was different now. She was looking at him, pale and frightened. She wasn't rushing into his arms.

He faced her awkwardly. He wanted to shower her with kisses, and yet he could not move. An invisible arm was pushing him away, warning him to keep his distance. Why?

He understood why.

"I should congratulate you," Patricia said softly, her eyes averted.

"You *should*?"

"Yes," she said. "You have accomplished what you've always wanted."

"Really?"

"Now you are the number-one bullfighter in Portugal."

He said nothing, his silence hanging heavy over the rumble of the excited voices outside.

"You mustn't keep them waiting, Miguel, they're anxious to see you." She turned toward the door.

Quickly, he crossed the room and blocked her path.

"You *should* congratulate me, but you can't—isn't that what you're saying?"

She looked up at his face, her eyes brimming with tears.

"Patrizia—I know you—I'm the man who loves you more than his life." He put his arms around her and continued to talk fervently, his face buried in her hair. "I came into that ring so anxious to show off for you, but as soon as they let the bull in, I knew what you were thinking. You were feeling sorry for him."

Silent sobs shook her body, and he hugged her more tightly.

"I knew what was in your mind all the time. And something happened to me—suddenly, I looked at that bull through your eyes and I saw what I had never seen before. I used to see rage in him as he charged. This time I saw fear—a frightened animal attacking desperately to defend himself. Ultimato finished that bullfight, not me."

"Oh Miguel, oh Miguel." Patricia couldn't find the words. "I love you so much."

There was a knock on the door and Emilio popped his head in. "All right you two—enough lovemaking. The mob is getting restless."

"Emilio—you have to handle it," Miguel said firmly. "They've seen the last of me."

"What?! There are a thousand people out there!"

"We're going out the back way."

"Television cameras! Photographers!"

"We're leaving."

"You're crazy!"

"Yes, Emilio. I am. But do as I say."

Emilio shook his head and sighed in resignation. "Never could argue with a Cardiga." He shut the door with a loud bang.

Miguel chuckled. "Poor Emilio. I hope they don't tear him apart."

Patricia smiled faintly.

"Oh Patrizia." He drank in her face. "Be patient with me, give me time. I've learned a lot from you—I will learn more."

She shivered in his arms. He picked up the coat, put it around her and crushed her to him.

She smoothed his curly hair with trembling hands, like a mother caressing a child. Both were oblivious to the cacophony of sound greeting Emilio's announcement outside.

They stood there—two people blended into one silhouette, wrapped in midnight blue that glittered with stars of gold.

SEVEN YEARS
LATER

Epilogue

Stone Ridge

"MOMMY, CAN I RIDE Ultimato after school?"

"No Paulo—you know the rules—only with your father."

"But when will he be back?" the seven-year-old boy whined.

"I've told you a hundred times," Patricia answered patiently, "next week."

"But Mommy, I—"

"You can ride the pony until he comes back. Now I don't want to hear any more. Go downstairs and finish your breakfast. Don't be late for the school bus again."

The towheaded boy ran down the steps still whining: "I can't wait till *Pai* gets back."

Patricia smiled—it always gave her a warm feeling when her son called his father *Pai*.

Once, when Miguel was explaining to little Paulo that he had been named after his very famous grandfather, the boy had asked, "Did you call your Daddy Paulo?"

"No, son—I called him *Pai*; that's Daddy in Portuguese."

From that day on, little Paulo called his father *Pai*.

She picked up a blue woolen shawl that Miguel had bought her on his last trip to Lisbon and walked out on the landing, Taxi and Phoebe at her heels. They both moved less quickly now, and Patricia had to push away the thought that they might not be with her long.

At the top of the steps, she looked at the large discolored spot on the wall where *The Starhanger* had hung until this morning. She missed it already, and almost regretted her decision to loan it to Lady McFadden's exhibit in New York.

At first, she had said no to the request. But Luba called and implored her "to borrow my very best work" for a few weeks.

Patricia was not sure why she had finally agreed, but after eight years she was curious to see her father's lover again. She decided to deliver the painting to the gallery herself.

Now, she picked up Phoebe, whose arthritic legs gave her difficulty with the steps, and hurried down to the kitchen.

Concha was there with a cup of coffee and a croissant.

"No, no Concha—I'm late."

But the housekeeper blocked her path, holding the cup.

"I promise—I'll pick something up . . ."

"I tell Mr. Miguel," Concha said menacingly.

Patricia sighed. "You two are a Mafia." She sat down at the table opposite little Paulo, who was wolfing down a muffin.

"Mommy," he said with his mouth full. "After school, can I ride in the woods?"

"No," Patricia said sternly.

"But I *like* riding in the snow."

"There is an icy surface under it, and you know that Daddy—"

Paulo started grumbling.

"Oh—poor little boy—has to ride in a nice big heated indoor arena. Well, you'll just have to suffer."

She gulped down the last of her coffee and kissed him. "I'll be back in time to ride with you." Heading for the door, she called out, "Concha—make sure he's not late for the bus."

Edgar was outside, the station wagon revved up and waiting. "The painting's in the back, Miss D." (She had corrected him many times, but somehow he could never get used to calling her Mrs. C.) "I wrapped it up real good."

"Thank you, Edgar. Sure you have the time to drive me to town? I *can* drive myself."

"And I get hell from the boss—no thank you, ma'am. There ain't that much that needs doin' this time of year."

As the car pulled out, Patricia's eyes scanned the pastures covered with snow, which was still falling. The horses, their thick winter coats dusted with snowflakes, were slowly moving around.

There was not much traffic, and the station wagon pulled up in front of the gallery about ten o'clock. Patricia wondered if she was too early.

"I'll take it," she said to Edgar, who unloaded the painting. She crossed the slushy sidewalk that was being scraped off by a young man. Mrs. Smith, the manager of the gallery, was standing at the open door. "I saw you drive up, Mrs. Cardiga," she said, taking hold of the cumbersome parcel. "How nice of you to bring it yourself!"

"Well, this painting is very special to me."

"But in such weather!"

"I like the snow," said Patricia, stomping the slush from her boots and shaking off the stray snowflakes from her shawl.

"We've got the right spot for it," Mrs. Smith gushed, pointing to the wall. "Lady McFadden knew the exact measurements."

"Yes, I did," said a voice behind them, and a smiling Luba approached. "I can't tell you how much I appreciate your allowing *The Starhanger* to be a part of my exhibition."

"It's really no trouble," Patricia replied.

Luba was eagerly removing the wrapping, "I haven't seen it in ten years."

"How long will you need it?"

Luba didn't reply. She was staring at the painting, which she had leaned against the wall. Patricia could see that her eyes were glistening. She must have loved him very much.

Abruptly, Luba motioned—"Come with me"—and walked to the back of the gallery.

Patricia followed, glancing at the colorful paintings on the wall. There was *The Satyr* from the Mount Street gallery window and *Lovers at Tróia* from above the fireplace in Luba's London town house.

They entered a sitting room furnished with large comfortable armchairs arranged around a gleaming mahogany table. Here, rich customers probably haggled over prices while sipping champagne.

"Would you like some coffee?" Luba asked.

"No thank you—I have to get back before the roads get any worse."

"Then I won't waste your time. I've thought of you often in the last eight years, and I've wrestled over the decision I made not to show you your father's letter."

Patricia studied Luba's face, still beautiful with full sensous lips, large dark eyes set wide apart, flawless skin, and a contagious smile. She was wearing a stylish jade suit with a matching ruffled blouse. "My father wrote to you, not me—and after all, I have no right to read his love letters."

Luba touched her hand, "But I understood your need to know the last words your father wrote on his way to see you." She hesitated, weighing her words. "I often saw a look of suffering in his eyes—a hidden torment. He never talked about it, and I never asked." She pulled out an envelope from her purse. "His letter tells it all."

A feeling of dread was creeping over Patricia.

"I think that he wrote to me," Luba continued, "as a rehearsal of what he was going to tell you. But fate decided you shouldn't know." Her voice was almost a whisper now. "I asked myself if I should be the one to reveal to you a secret buried long before you were born.

I was afraid . . . and so I avoided making the decision—until now.''

Patricia watched apprehensively as Luba placed the letter on the table. ''I'll be down the hall if you need me.''

Alone in the room, Patricia stared at the letter. On the other side of the door, she could hear a hammer pounding a nail into the wall. She turned her head toward the window—snow was still falling, and the cars made a slushy sound on Fifty-seventh Street.

She picked up the letter. It was bulky. The envelope had a slightly greasy feeling, as if it had been handled often.

So much had happened since her meeting with Luba in London. At that time, she was frightened of life. She wanted so badly to talk with her daddy, to have him reassure her, to hear what it was he had wanted to tell her. She couldn't accept—as Dr. Solomon advised her—that ''some doors are best kept closed.''

Again, she looked at the letter in her hand. It was addressed to *Miss Luba Johnson* in her father's elliptical handwriting.

Her mind drifted. She thought of little Paulo, not paying attention in class, too anxious to go riding. She thought about Miguel—he never liked going to Lisbon without her; usually they visited the Centro together. She hadn't gone with him this time, but he would be hurrying back soon. They had such exciting plans to enlarge their riding school at the farm, now more famous and bigger than the one in Lisbon.

She turned the letter over and over. Her thoughts

tumbled on. She was proud of the Stoneham Group. Mrs. Sperber, the stalwart head of the company, and Howie, now married to Joanna, were doing a wonderful job. Graciously, they gave her much of the credit for creating "the company with a conscience."

She put the letter down—then picked it up again. Poor Daddy. Yes, sometimes as a young girl she too had caught glimpses of torment in his eyes, but she preferred to remember the happy look when he read to her before she went to sleep. *"The lark's on the wing . . . the hill-side's dew-pearled . . ."* She looked up at the window—the snow was still falling gently, and individual snowflakes speckled the glass, each lingering for a brief moment before being transformed into a sparkling droplet of water. *"God's in his heaven . . . all's right with the world."*

That's the memory she wanted to keep alive; that's the door she wanted to keep open. She placed the bulky letter on the burnished mahogany table. This door would remain closed. She quickly left the room.

On her way out of the gallery, she stopped in front of *The Starhanger*, displayed on the wall now. Daddy, she thought, don't turn around. I don't want to see the torment in your eyes. Just keep hanging stars in the sky.

"Oh, Mrs. Cardiga," called out the gallery manager, "are you leaving so soon?"

"Yes, my son is waiting for me at the farm . . . Please thank Lady McFadden—for everything."

She got into the station wagon before Edgar could get around to open the door. "Let's go home, Edgar."

Feeling chilly, she wrapped the shawl around her.

Editor's Note: The secret that Patricia Dennison's father never told her is revealed in Kirk Douglas's first novel, *Dance with the Devil*, also published by Warner Books.